Praise for

The
SHELF

'I absolutely LOVED *The Shelf*. One of those
delicious books you just can't put down. So many
gorgeous **witty** one-liners. **Utter PERFECTION!**'
MARIAN KEYES

'I haven't been so immediately sucked in by a novel
IN YEARS. Not only is the idea **brilliant and original,**
but Helly's writing is also **compelling and hilarious.**
The Shelf is **a must-read** and I cannot recommend
it highly enough'
LUCY VINE

'I really loved it! **Subversive, feminist** and
a real breath of fresh air. I inhaled this!'
LAURA JANE WILLIAMS

'I absolutely loved it – such a clever concept,
so well executed and with a perfect ending!
Such a clever, brilliant book!'
KATIE FFORDE

The
SHELF

HELLY ACTON was born in Zimbabwe, and her family emigrated to the East Sussex coast when she was fifteen years old. Here, she finished school and spent her holidays in Saudi Arabia, where her father was working. She studied Law at King's College London before following a more creative path into advertising.

In her mid-twenties, Helly escaped the rat race and took a three-month career break to travel in Africa, India and Asia before landing in Australia. What was supposed to last one year ended up lasting six, and after a life-affirming break-up in Sydney she returned home to find herself the last of her single friends. Helly threw herself into the deep end of online dating in the city and uses her experience as a single woman in her early thirties, torn between settling down and savouring her independence, as a source of inspiration for her writing. Helly currently lives in London with her husband, Chris, and their dog child, Milo.

The
SHELF

Helly
Acton

ZAFFRE

First published in Great Britain in 2020 by
ZAFFRE
80–81 Wimpole St, London W1G 9RE

A CIP catalogue record for this book is
available from the British Library.

Hardback ISBN: 978-1-83877-087-7
Export ISBN: 978-1-83877-088-4

Also available as an ebook

1 3 5 7 9 10 8 6 4 2

Typeset by Palimpsest Book Production Limited, Falkirk, Stirlingshire
Printed and bound in Great Britain by Clays Ltd, Elcograf S.p.A.

Zaffre is an imprint of Bonnier Books UK
www.bonnierbooks.co.uk

To Mum and Dad,
who've made everything possible.

One

Amy Wright is lying in bed, staring at herself in the mirror on the wall and counting her chins. Her long dark hair is curled up on top of her head like the chocolate doughnut she ate in secret yesterday and, if she squints, she could be a sumo wrestler. But Amy isn't going to let a Fat Day spoil her mood. Not today. Instead, she blinks her blue eyes and takes a mental snapshot of the best day of her life.

What Amy doesn't realise is that the best day of her life will turn out to be the worst.

She takes her phone from the bedside table and opens Instagram to see who's got engaged, married or pregnant in the last eight hours. She breathes a small sigh of relief when there are no diamond rings or baby emojis in sight. She's been followed by some random called @shrinkitquick, and Jane's posted another close-up of the twins. This morning they're smeared in a rank blend of banana and

1

carrot, and she's commented about missing lie-ins. It says 'poor me', but it means 'praise me'.

Amy resists the urge to post a vomit emoji with *#pleasespareus*. She wonders what would happen to her social life if she was honest online. She'd be cast aside as a kid-hater, which would be unfair given she quite likes them. Some of them. What she doesn't love is being force-subscribed to a daily update of dribble, snot and tears. When she has kids, she'll limit her posts to real milestones, not mindless observations like *Henry did a poo! #growing-upsofast*, which is what Jane posted yesterday. For one grim second, Amy had thought she was seeing the evidence, but when the photo loaded it was just the prodigal son grinning with a bowl of chocolate ice cream. She flushes when she thinks about her *Don't eat it!* comment. The other mothers were full of congratulations, and Jane had liked everyone's comments but hers.

'Do you lose your sense of humour when you have kids?' Amy had mumbled rhetorically to Jamie, as he was chopping kale for his morning juice.

'Along with your figure,' he replied instantly, which made Amy hate him for a few minutes and then worry about him for a few hours. Jamie always jokes about not wanting kids. But why would he be with her if he didn't? It's just his sense of humour. And if she doesn't laugh, he'll accuse her of being 'so serious these days'.

Amy sighs at the banana smear post, double-taps and comments *#suchcuties* and *#lovethem*, as is the done thing.

She doesn't want Jane to think she doesn't like the twins. She does like them. From a distance, where they can't stare at her, scream so loudly that adult conversation is impossible or squirm when she tries to hug them.

#SOprecious.

Scrolling down her feed, she comes across a company trying to flog her a Neck Flab Fighter. She tuts at it, then saves it for later. One day she'll buy it, along with that weight loss thermal suit and the appetite-killer tongue patch.

Next up is Lottie Forrester, aka @lottietheexplorer, who's posted a selfie at a gong bath in Seminyak. Perma-tanned and all-round-perfect human specimen, Lottie started a travel blog after quitting PR two years ago. Her account has reached 280,000 followers and she posts daily from paradise with her *#lottieexplores* hashtag. It's more interesting than Jane's banana update, but it's just as nauseating.

Amy tosses her phone to the bottom of the bed.

Why should she feel jealous? Tonight she'll be living the dream, sipping champagne in business class, jetting off to her own paradise with Jamie, and posting *#jamy* (he hates that) to all 260 of her adoring followers.

It's been two years since Amy and Jamie matched on Soulmeets, and she has a sneaky feeling he might pop the question on this trip. Sure, they don't even live together yet, but he's been acting strangely around her recently. Quiet and nervous. Which isn't normal for someone who's so confident that when he first met her parents at her dad's retirement party, he gave an impromptu speech. He'd known them for an hour. His uneasy behaviour is a sign that something's on his mind. That he's preparing for something big, which could mean one of two things. He's going to dump her – or ask her to marry him. But he gave her a key to his flat a few months ago, and dumping her on holiday would be way too awkward. It has to be the second thing.

Rolling over, she buries her face in the pillow, hides a smile and stifles a long squeal. It pierces the silence and the sleeping beauty next to her stirs.

'Turn your bloody alarm off.'

Amy shuffles towards Jamie's ridiculously broad back. It looks like a cardboard cut-out and it makes her feel tiny, which is exactly what you want on a Fat Day. Photoshop-smooth, Instagram-filter tanned and cage-fighter firm. She stares at her fingers as she strokes her freshly gelled nude nails against his olive skin and imagines the diamond he's chosen. Flash Harry here will want it to make a statement. And while massive diamonds are more Jamie's style, she doesn't care about the ring.

What she cares about is that their relationship is making progress, at long last. She can finally prove to Jane and the other mothers that she isn't getting left behind. By this time next year, she'll be a married working supermum just like them. Goodbye espresso martinis in Soho, hello espresso mornings in suburbia.

God, that sounds tedious.

Amy loves this time of the day. When Jamie's lying right next to her, but she still feels alone. When it's quiet, and she can let her mind wander. It isn't the only time she feels alone in her relationship. She also feels alone when he's cooking, when he goes to bed earlier than her, when he looks at her in that way that suggests she should go back to her place for the night. But at least she doesn't *look* alone. With Jamie in her life, she manages to squeeze into their married couples social club. And she'll get full membership when there's a ring. The pressure to get married will ease, and then the pressure will be on to have kids. The next stage of the race she didn't sign up for.

Of course, there is another way. The way she doesn't like to think about for too long and the one she's always daydreamed of. The path she was about to take when she met Jamie, who convinced her to stay. It takes her straight to Heathrow with a one-way ticket on the next flight to Bangkok. Jamie would be fine. He has his start-up, his gadgets, his routine. Last month, Amy had teased him for talking to his Alexa more than he talks to her. He'd laughed and asked Alexa what she was wearing.

And last week, when Amy forgot to pack her toothbrush, she finally lost her patience and plucked up the courage to confront him about why they never stay at hers.

'Piggie, I would stay at yours, but you know how important my morning run is. If I don't run, my head gets foggy. I'm busting my balls with this start-up. You aren't being very supportive.'

'There's a park at the end of my road. Why can't you run there?'

'What, the cemetery?' he scoffed.

'It has grass.'

'Yeah, and like ten homeless people. No thanks. Don't you like it here?'

'I do like it here, Jamie.' She sighed, wondering how she was suddenly the bad guy. 'It's just a pain having to pack a bag every time I come . . .' She paused, hoping he'd take the hint and offer her a drawer. But he didn't. What he did do was wrap her in his arms, nibble her ear and ask her to whisper that last word again.

'Can I borrow your toothbrush?' she whispered instead.

'Don't be gross, Piglet.' He unravelled her and opened the fridge. 'Just go to the newsagent's, it's still open. Can you grab some almond milk while you're there?'

Typical Jamie. Typical her. While it might have been a last straw ten years ago, Amy has decided to roll with the relationship punches. She'll get her drawer eventually. Maybe more, if her predictions are right.

She shifts in his bed and returns to the moment. Yup. Jamie would be fine. She could go right now. There's nothing stopping her. Her suitcase is already packed, her freelance contract just ended and, as a copywriter, she can work anywhere in the world with Internet and her laptop. She could finally restart that blog she hasn't posted on for years. All she needs is a topic she's passionate about. Cheese. Doughnuts. A weight-loss journey. A journey. The Wright Way. A Wright of Passage. The Wright Turn. Amy could be like Lottie Forrester and all the other travel influencers she follows. If they can do it, why can't she?

Because you're thirty-two, Amy. It's too late to take chances.

Besides, there are plenty of things she can look forward to with Jamie, and despite his flaws, she does love him. He's familiar now. Comfortable. And she likes the idea of being married. A united team, ready to take on whatever the world throws at them. At least, that's how she imagines it will feel once their relationship is validated by a stranger, a rock and a signed form. She'll finally be an official member of the O'Connor team. Or the Wright team. No, Jamie would never take her name. Maybe she could pull off a Dawn Porter.

'Hi, I'm Amy O'Wright,' she whispers into the mirror. 'I'm Amy O'Wright. I'm Amy, oh right. All right. I'm Amy, all right?'

It sounds like she's picking a fight.

'Huh?' slurs Jamie in a doze.

'Nothing, go back to sleep, it's early.' She rubs his back. He moves further away. It always stings when he does that, but she knows he likes his own space in the bed. Lots of people do.

Last year, Jamie launched his own executive search agency, Headplace, which he says is going to be huge. It's one of the reasons they don't live together yet. She did float the idea a few months ago when he gave her the key – but he shut that conversation down quickly. He told her he was too busy, and that having her there the whole time would be a distraction. Amy wanted to take this as a compliment, but there was something about the way he said it that hinted it wasn't. Maybe it was the scowl. Then he sulked with her for the rest of the day, saying how ungrateful she was for his key gesture, how she always wanted more and how nothing he did was ever good enough.

She felt guilty going back to her place that night. Jamie grew up in a big Irish family, fighting over space with five older brothers, so she understands he finds it hard to share. And like he says, why would they bother moving in together when they see so much of each other anyway? She's often tempted to point out that if they already see so much of each other, it's just the same as living together. But Amy doesn't do confrontation. The key was a small step in the right direction. Jamie just needs time to get used to the idea.

The truth is, Amy doesn't mind living on her own. She likes her space, too. She loves having the freedom to scoff an entire pack of full-fat Babybels without judgement in her oldest, ugliest and comfiest knickers, washed down with a Diet Coke, watching *Say Yes to the Dress*. The freedom to narrate her make-up routine in the mirror every morning, pretending to be someone famous. Yesterday, she was Joanna Lumley, which ended abruptly in a hacking cough. When they move in together, she'll have to quit all sorts of guilty pleasures. No more going to the loo with the door open. No more Super Noodles for breakfast after a big night out. Jamie will never let her lick the flavouring off a crisp before putting it back in the bowl because she likes the taste but hates the texture. Maybe there won't be crisps at all. Maybe all there will be is a sad little bowl of celery sticks, waiting to give her a new complex about how loudly she chews.

No, Amy doesn't mind living alone. What she does mind is the ache in her stomach when she dwells on the fact that Jamie's never even hinted that he'd like to live with her. Ever. And worse, the boohoo face that Jane pulls at their biannual coffee catch-up, which is all she has time for nowadays with her promotion, the kitchen extension and the twins. Amy hates singing the same tune every time Jane asks when they're moving in together: Jamie's too busy with the business at the moment; we see enough of each other anyway; we'll probably do it next year; there's no rush. She's sung it so often, she's beginning to believe it herself.

'You're thirty-two, Amy, not twenty-two. If you think there's no rush, you're in denial. You're going to end up a sad old spinster, alone at Christmas. You're an only child. One day your parents will die and you will have no one to keep you company.'

Jane never actually says this.

But Amy knows it was what she was thinking the last time they met. Avoiding eye contact as she stirred her weak Earl Grey, pinging the side of her teacup with her spoon. After a long and awkward silence, she changed the subject to how incredible her new nanny was.

'Jane, Christ! We used to be so close! Why can't you admit your twins are feral, accountancy is fucking dull, you miss getting tanked at The White Horse and Pete has bad breath! Stop pretending that your life is perfect and be honest!'

Amy never actually says this.

Because she's not a social kamikaze pilot and Jane is one of the only school friends she sees anymore. Besides, Jane isn't all bad. She seems to genuinely care about Amy's future, even if it comes out as underhand compliments and semi-snide remarks, just like the jellyfisher in *Bridget Jones*. And she does invite them to the occasional dinner party. Nowadays Amy declines more often than she accepts, using Jamie's work commitments as an excuse. She has nothing in common with Jane's accountancy friends, who are gouge-your-eyes-out boring. All they talk about is money and all the expensive-but-useless appliances it buys.

Jane's pointed silence is fair. Amy is thirty-two years old. She is running out of time. But what is she supposed to do? She can't start again. Jamie is her best bet, her last chance to have a life like Jane's. The life that she's supposed to want at this age.

Amy knows that she has to take second place on Jamie's priority list for now, but she's playing the long game. Next month, the business will be up and running, and he'll have more time to focus on his personal life, their relationship and their future together. They don't need to live together to be close. They do see each other almost every night. She has a key. And she wouldn't care if they skipped the moving-in and went straight for the end goal.

'Headplace is going to be big, Piglet. I'll have a mansion and a Rangie by this time next year, just you wait and see.'

Amy had noticed the 'I' when he said this, but she let it go. Why would he buy a family-sized house and car if it was just him? She needs to stop overanalysing everything he says and does. He's whisking her away on a surprise holiday, so he must love her, even if he sometimes makes her feel like an unwelcome guest.

Two

Jamie sits up and strokes his hair back. It's the start of his daily pre-run ritual, in which Amy does not feature. Sometimes she wonders if he remembers she's there at all. The closest she ever gets to a morning greeting is a cough. Jamie stands up, pings on his Lycra and is out the door in five minutes, leaving Amy alone in bed and giving her the perfect opportunity to snoop in his suitcase. But she has standards, so she just reaches over and opens his drawer to look for a phone charger. If there happens to be a Tiffany three-stone diamond ring lying next to it, well, that isn't her fault. But there's no phone charger. Or ring. There's a wrist tripod for running selfies, a head torch for night jogging and a pair of ridiculous lime-green goggles that he hasn't worn since Amy told him he looked like Gareth from *The Office*. She rolls back to her side.

Last night, Amy shared her impending possible engagement news over a bottle of prosecco with Sarah, her best friend from uni, at Amuse Bouche. They've been going there since their first year in London and it was where they broke big news. At the same table, six months ago, Amy announced that Jamie had given her a key to his flat. Sarah announced she'd just bought her third.

Investment analyst Sarah was predictably sceptical of Amy's proposal theory.

'Go on, then. What's different this time?'

Amy made the same announcement before every trip, so Sarah was right to wonder. But now it really *was* different: Amy felt something big brewing.

'Last time you told me he was going to propose at his grandfather's funeral.'

'He was dropping major hints! Talking about how short life is, how we should be happy, how we shouldn't let chances pass us by.'

'He was talking about work again, wasn't he?'

'OK, fine, fine. There's more evidence. We've been together for two years . . .'

'Not evidence.'

'It's perfect timing! And Jamie likes things in twos – it's his lucky number.'

Sarah frowned at her.

'Two eggs in the morning. Double coffee shot. He's always telling me I'm his number two.'

'Who's his number one?'

'He is.'

'Wow.'

'He's joking! Plus, Mum cried on the phone for absolutely no reason the other day.'

'The *Strictly Come Dancing* final? Gin? Your dad's new socks and sandals retirement uniform? His constant presence, now that he's retired?'

'She's saying goodbye to her little girl! I'm an only child, remember? This is big for her.'

'You're thirty-two, Amy, not twelve.'

'Exactly. I'm sure Jamie realises it's now or never. He knows my clock is ticking.'

'Amy!' She choked. 'I can't believe you just said that.'

'What?'

'It's like you've accepted that Sword of Damocles with open arms. Your purpose isn't to reproduce – it's to be happy, whatever shape or form that takes.'

'I know, but maybe reproducing will make me happy. Maybe my happiness takes the shape of a melon under my jumper.'

'My happiness takes the shape of Daniel Craig feeding me mashed potato on a Mexican beach.' Sarah laughed and took a sip from her glass before squeezing Amy's hand across the table.

'Amy, just promise me you aren't doing the marriage-and-babies thing because of your age and because everyone else is doing it. You have to really want kids.'

Amy stared back at her. 'I know. I do.'

'You'll have to do things and go places,' Sarah continued. 'Like petting zoos and funfairs and kids' parties. No more being a slob on the sofa in your knickers on a Sunday, watching *Friends* back-to-back. Oh my God, Amy, you'll have to put pants on every day!' Her face turned to mock horror.

'Sarah, I do want kids! And not just because of my age or because everyone else is doing it. It's because I like them. I always have done – I just don't go on about it. I want to do more with my Sundays than watch Netflix marathons. And I can't ignore my age – it's science. Besides, why are we talking about kids when I'm not even engaged yet?'

'Why get married at all? Just have his baby. If you're sure Jamie's The One.'

'Well, he's the only one.'

Sarah stared at her.

'I'm kidding! I'm happy. Life is moving forward, just like it's supposed to.'

'You know, you don't have to be like everyone else, Amy.'

'I am me. And you are you. And Jamie is Jamie.' She hiccuped. 'And this empty glass is this empty glass.'

On the tube back to Jamie's, Amy wondered if Sarah's reaction was because she was feeling sad about losing her single sidekick. Or perhaps she was feeling upset that Amy was choosing to spend the rest of her life with a man she can't stand. The relationship between her best friend and her boyfriend was as awkward as a lone lift ride with a date you didn't text back. The first and last time she left them alone, she came back to find Jamie studying the ingredients on his low-carb beer label and Sarah pretending to send emails on a phone that had run out of battery. Alone, Amy probed them about their feelings towards each other.

'I'd like him if he stopped staring at my mouth,' Sarah had hissed.

'I'd like her if she waxed her moustache and stopped trying to be funny,' Jamie had muttered.

'You don't think any women are funny.' Amy had sighed. Why did he have to be such a dick, so often? Why couldn't he just make an effort with her friends?

'Well, maybe it's because they aren't,' he responded, before grabbing her by the waist and blowing a raspberry on her neck. 'Except you, of course. You funny little Piglet.'

And Amy had laughed and let it go.

Jamie's words can certainly bite, but his touch makes her feel adored. His go-to tactic for ending a heated discussion is a passionate Hollywood kiss, and while Amy has long suspected he does it to physically stop her from stating her case, she falls for it every time. Anyone would, with lips and a grip like his.

She rolls over and rubs her eyes. She has to stop thinking so negatively about the man she's hoping to spend the rest of her life with. Jamie isn't perfect, but he does do lots of things to show her that he cares. Last week he sent her a surprise supper delivery when he cancelled their Saturday-night plans because he had to meet a potential investor. The jackfruit salad went straight in the bin because the smell made her gag, but it was the thought that counted. And when he comes over after one too many, he is so affectionate it makes her heart explode. Squeezy hugs, sweet nothings, back rubs and head strokes. After a few vodka sodas, his true character comes out. Sometimes she wishes he drank every night. It's rare for Jamie to let himself go like that. He's too health-conscious, too focused, and his business comes before leisure. And that's OK right now. She wants him to do well, even if it means they see less of each other.

She could do far worse than Jamie. Before Jamie there was Beer Ben, who was only ever happy with his hands on a pint and his eyes on the sport. It didn't matter what sport it was, as long as there was a ball involved. She knew she had to call it quits when their fifth date was a bowling alley, and not the cool kind. Before him there was Dull Dan, who fancied himself as an amateur sommelier and bored Amy to tears droning on about the difference between Merlot and Shiraz, while picking at an overpriced char-cuterie board. She shudders when she thinks of his fingernails spearing the chorizo. They were always five millimetres too long.

Jamie's fingernails are short and clean. He doesn't smell of stale beer. He talks about the future, not goals or grape varieties. And although she's never been explicitly featured in this future, she must fit in somewhere. Otherwise why would he have said he'd buy her a brand-new wardrobe when he made his first million?

Amy hears the door go and Jamie bursts in, wheezing. He smiles at her and his crow's feet wrinkle up, making her heart beat a bit faster. And faster still when he bends over to remove his shorts, his six-pack tensing and his jet-black hair flopping in his green eyes. Climbing under the covers, he hugs her from the side and she tenses her stomach muscles to stop Tinky Winky, aka her Teletummy, from spoiling the mood. It's a nickname Jamie introduced the other day, and to be honest, she doesn't love it. She also doesn't love how he always hugs her stomach, especially after eating a huge meal.

'You're lucky I'm not sensitive,' she said last week, before patting him on the top of his head. 'And how's the switch to solar power going?'

Touching his crown gently, he had flown off the handle about her being nasty, gone running for two hours and given her the silent treatment for the rest of the day.

Amy knows she's slim but squidgy. But to change that, she'd have to go to the gym, and she'd rather step on a Christmas decoration than a cross-trainer. Jamie had bought her a gym membership for her birthday last year. Not for the one he went to.

Jamie squeezes his arms around her and addresses item one on their sexual order of business: kissing the back of her neck and giving her goosebumps as she nestles into his chest. Yes, Jamie can be a bit self-centred. Yes, this routine hasn't changed in six months. And yes, she is rarely the star of this show. But at least he still turns her on. At least he doesn't have bad breath, like Jane's Pete.

Just as Jamie moves on to item two, where she gets a bit

of action with a borderline-painful nipple pinch, his phone rings loudly and makes them both jump. When he takes the call, she stares at him in disbelief and he puts his finger on his lips and waves her away. Nice. She huffs, gets up and goes to the bathroom.

It's peaceful in there by herself.

Amy spends the next hour with her holiday essentials. She blew the whole of last week's salary on waxing, soaking, scrubbing, exfoliating, firming, fake-tanning and tinting. Two hundred quid literally down the drain. Probably the same price as a week-long stay in a beach hut in Phuket.

As she tries to master the impossible art of crying and looking pretty at the same time while perfecting her *Yes!* face in the mirror, she spots an eyebrow on the run. Her face falls. 'Thanks, Dad,' she sighs, yanking out the stray hair. She's blessed with her mum's lips and cursed with her dad's monobrow. Despite his insistence, the only character it adds bears a striking resemblance to Miffy, the family poodle. Miffy is not welcome on this holiday.

Jamie has given her one clue about their mystery destination. No coats required. Amy has translated this to mean an island in South East Asia, and so she's spent hours, days, truthfully weeks investing in her travel-beauty-fashion blogger look, complete with oversized floppy hat, rose-gold mirror sunglasses and a pair of toddler-sized ripped denim shorts, which she knows she'll be too embarrassed to wear anywhere. Her suitcase also includes five new bikinis, three of which fitted her when she was packing and two of which will definitely, absolutely, one hundred per cent fit her by the time she gets there. She's strategically saving those for the last few days, in case he hasn't asked her yet, and they show off more flesh than the cast of *Geordie Shore* combined. She's secretly hoping for a safe, but highly effective, tropical stomach bug.

Just as she grabs a triple-savings pack of Imodium, Jamie appears in the bathroom door in a crisp white shirt, pale blue chinos and trademark navy loafers. He gives Amy a long stare as she slowly puts the pills in her toiletry bag, hoping to God he can't see what they are.

'Is Miffy joining us?'

Amy darts back to the mirror.

'I'm joking.' He grins and opens his arms. 'Are you ready?'

'If we're off to Bali, yes. If we're off to Siberia, no.'

'You'll see soon enough, but you look fine to me. That call was important,' he says, by way of apology, giving her his wiggling come-here fingers.

'Did it go well?' she asks, as she steps towards him for a rare hug outside of the covers.

'Weller's on board. Another one bites the dust for those pricks at Simon Watts.' He whistles as he looks at himself in the mirror.

'Aren't those pricks your friends?'

'Not when it comes to money, little Piglet.'

If this was a film, Amy thinks, Jamie would be the caricature villain that everyone wants to see fall. Her guilt grabs her by the gut again. Jamie's ambition is an asset, not a flaw. It's business, and he has to be ruthless at times. It's a streak that could secure their future together.

She should feel proud. Lucky, even.

As she watches Jamie lock up the flat, Amy stares at the front door and lets out a sigh, wondering if she will ever see it in the same way again. She smiles as she imagines him sweeping her into his arms and swooping her over the threshold. Then she makes a mental note not to overindulge on waffles at the hotel breakfast buffet.

'I couldn't find my keys this morning. Do I need them?' she asks Jamie as they walk down the stairs.

'Nope.'

There's no doubt in her mind that she left them on the hall table, so this must be part of his big plan.

'Shall I get an Uber?'

'Nope, that's covered, too.' Jamie nods towards a shiny black stretch limo rolling up to the pavement.

'Oh my God.'

'After you, Piglet.'

Jamie is extravagant with his watch collection, whisky library and Egyptian cotton sheets, but he's never done anything like this before. Especially not for her. This can only mean good things. For the first time since forever, he is desperate to impress her. He wants this proposal to be perfect, from the first minute to the last.

Amy beams as she slides into the soft leather seats with their brand-new car smell, while Jamie reaches for a bottle of champagne resting in an ice bucket between them and pours them each a glass.

'Chin-chin, Piglet.' He smiles.

She tilts her head to one side. 'Very funny. How about *to us*, instead?'

Ever since Jamie had walked in on her doing neck-cercises in bed at the start of their relationship, he'd used 'chin-chin' to poke fun at her complex.

He looks at her as he sips his champagne slowly and reaches to tuck her hair behind one ear.

'I've been planning this for a while.'

It's a perfect moment for a kiss, but just as she moves towards him he turns his head to look out of the window. She takes out her phone to text Sarah.

I'm in a limo.

Is there champagne?

There is.

It's so on.

I think so. He just said he's been planning this for a while . . . 👰

Why does the bride emoji look scared? 😬

> She found a chin hair. 💀

> *Hope you waxed your left hand. Have an amazing time x*

> Thanks pooch x

The car is quiet as they cross the river at Hammersmith.

'The Apollo!' Amy puts her hand on Jamie's leg. 'Do you remember our first gig together?'

He shifts in his seat and catches the eye of the driver.

'Muse?'

'No, not Muse. Did we see Muse together? That Thai DJ, it was amazing.'

Jamie draws a blank but says, 'Yeah, he was cool.'

'She.'

'Right, she was great.'

Jamie keeps glancing in the rear-view mirror. Checking his own reflection isn't unusual, but what's different is that he isn't looking at himself. He's looking at the limo driver, and the limo driver is returning his gaze.

Out of the blue, the limo driver speaks. 'It's time, Mr O'Connor.'

Amy looks at Jamie, confused, as he takes her phone out of her hand. She panics inside, scared he might read her messages. Instead, he reaches forward and takes a long piece of black fabric out of the central compartment.

'What's all this?' Amy smiles tensely, like Chandler Bing in a photograph. There's a knot in her stomach.

Jamie smiles back, as he motions for her to turn around. He slowly places the blindfold over her eyes, and the outside world is shut off.

'How am I supposed to walk through the airport with this on?'

'Amy, we aren't going to an airport.'

'OK . . . Soho Farmhouse? Lime Wood?'

'Nope, not a spa either. Mate, can we turn the music on?'

The driver obliges and Classic FM fills the limo. As she leans back into the seat, Jamie places his hand on hers, squeezing it a little too hard, like he's trying to tell her something he can't bring himself to say. Not an airport, not a spa. She suddenly has a horrible thought and shoots up out of the seat.

'Jamie,' she whispers, 'are we . . . going to an orgy?'

'What? No. Just wait, we aren't far.'

'OK. Sorry, I'm just excited!' she whispers. She doesn't want him to call her ungrateful again.

Amy hears the car indicate as it moves to the side and slows to a halt.

'We're here.' Jamie sighs as he wriggles out of her grip and opens the door.

Amy hears a muffled conversation outside before the door opens and she feels Jamie take her hands. He guides her slowly out of the limo and walks her through what sounds like an electric gate.

'OK, Ames, there's a ramp coming up, we're going to be walking down it.'

His voice isn't as calm anymore. He sounds shaky. Amy wonders why he'd be taking her into a basement and not through a front door. Then she realises what's happening.

It's all so obvious now. He's organised a surprise party, and he's going to ask her in front of her friends and family. Hold on. She knows exactly what this is. It's a bloody flash mob. Jamie's obsessed. A few months ago, he interrupted her pouring her heart out about a problem at work to show her a flash mob proposal at Waterloo.

'God, I'd run for the hills if someone did that to me,' she replied, irritated that he'd changed the subject. 'Talk about a giant red flag. He doesn't want her having any of the attention.'

'So what? He's still asking her – isn't that enough for you lot? I don't think you'd complain if you got a million views at the same time.'

'Jamie, I'd rather you asked me on the loo than for the likes.'

'Steady on, Piglet.'

And that's how every conversation around marriage has ended.

'There's a door coming up, I'm going to hold it open for you,' he says, placing his hand on her lower back. She feels a draught in front of her as he guides her into what feels like a wide-open space. It's completely silent, and her laugh echoes through the air.

'Jamie, I feel like I'm in a prison – are you locking me up?' She laughs, in an attempt to disguise her growing unease.

The door slams shut behind her, echoing through the air.

'Jamie?'

'I'm here.'

She feels his breath on her cheek as he gently unties her blindfold. And, as he slowly removes it, he gives her a kiss on the forehead and takes both of her hands in his. The light comes flooding in and she sees his eyes staring deeply into hers.

Nervous, she looks up and sees a stark white ceiling with strip lights. She doesn't know where she is or why this place means anything. Turning her head, she sees a huge open-plan living area painted a thousand shades of pink, with a pink velvet sofa and a dining room table big enough for twelve. A surprise party, staycation and proposal all rolled into one isn't Jamie's style at all.

A mechanical whir sounds from a corner of the ceiling. She looks up and sees a small camera with a red light pointed in her direction.

'Jamie, where are we?' she says, still trying to smile. 'Why are you filming us? What is this place?'

He takes her face in his hands and leans in to whisper in her ear. 'Goodbye, Piglet. Good luck.'

With that, he turns and walks out of a large steel door at the end of a corridor. After it slams shut, Amy hears an ice-cold voice ring through the air.

'Hello, Amy. You've been left on The Shelf.*'*

WEEK ONE

WEEK ONE

Three

Amy spins around wide-eyed, but there's no one there. It's just the ceiling camera, which is still pointing at her. With her eyes locked on the lens, she takes a few steps to the left. It whirs as it follows her, its red light flashing.

'Jamie?' she says slowly through a locked smile. 'What's the shelf? Where are we?'

She walks over to the door Jamie left through and takes the handle. Trying her best to appear calm, she pushes and pulls, but it's locked tight. Next to the door are two large buttons, which read STAY and GO. She presses GO, gently at first, then harder and faster with each try until she breaks a nail. Yelping with pain and squinting at the damage, Amy feels a wave of fear flow through her stomach and she starts pounding loudly on the steel with a tightly closed fist.

'Jamie?' she shouts through the door.

The sound of her banging rings through the air until it's cut off by another whir, this time much closer. Amy stops her fist in mid-air and draws her eyes upward to see a second camera above the door. She lowers her head and her short breaths mist up the metal in front of her.

'Jamie, please,' she says quietly. 'This isn't funny.'

Like second nature, she reaches into her back pocket to locate her phone. It's empty. She forgot in the panic that he took it from her. Why, though?

Amy turns her back to the door and shields her face from the voyeurs above, studying her surroundings through her fingers. The corridor in front of her has bright white walls and pink vinyl floors ending in wide steps. On the left is the living room and on the right is the dining room. Next to that is a large white marble kitchen area complete with an island and stools. The surfaces are bare. As she walks away from the steel door, she feels a lump forming in her throat. This is the worst proposal she could ever have imagined.

Amy peers around the corner into the living room before turning her eyes to the corridor camera. She keeps watching the lens as she quickly darts left and then jumps right, before running into the living room and ducking behind the sofa. Leaning her head against the velvet, she closes her eyes and lets out a huge sigh. *This must be a surprise party*, she thinks. *I just need to pull myself together and be patient.*

Whir. Beep.

Amy opens one eye and finds her face a few inches away from a camera on wheels. This one's attached to a long neck spouting out of what looks like a Roomba vacuum.

Krrrrr . . . click.

Has it just taken a picture of her?

'Jamie! Stop it!' she shouts, as she shoves it away with her foot.

Amy stands up, dusts herself off and walks around the U-shaped sofa, her nails scratching the pink velvet as she does. She slumps onto the gold and silver cushions and stares at the cinema-size TV screen, which takes up half the wall. In front of her is a glass coffee table, with no remote and no instructions as to what she's supposed to do next. She stares at the TV, hoping it will turn on any second to show her family and friends shouting 'Surprise!' Perhaps there's been a technical hitch, or someone's late to the reveal.

'If this is a surprise party, can you hurry up and surprise me, please,' she says to anyone who might be watching.

After five minutes, there's still no reveal. Amy gets up and walks into a room on the other side. It's a dormitory with eight single beds, a wall made of mirrors and another ceiling camera at one end. When it spots her it starts blinking green.

'Bit antisocial, Jamie,' she says loudly. 'Who wants to sleep in a single bed? While being filmed?'

She wanders between the beds, hunting for any clues. Either Jamie's flash mob has gone wrong, he's made a terrible mistake with a hotel booking or he's bought this place for her, him and their six future children.

Whir. Beep.

The noise is beginning to grate.

She takes a seat on the end of a bed, throws herself back on the mattress and stares at the ceiling. Suddenly, it dawns on her and she sits back up. She knows what this is!

Leaping up, she runs under the camera, jumping up and down and clapping her fingers together like a seal.

'I've worked it out! It's that fitness boot camp you were talking about last year!' she shouts. 'You didn't have to blindfold me, I would have come if you'd just asked – I'm not that bad.' She laughs, knowing full well she would have gone straight to the Krispy Kreme counter at Fulham Broadway, just like she did after his gym gift.

'Amy, please go to the Chat Room.'

Robot voice is back.

Amy hurries through to the living room, pausing briefly in front of three posters she didn't notice before.

IT'S NEVER TOO LATE
TO BE A SIZE 8!

ARE YOU SELFIE-READY?
SMILE BRIGHT, WITH RIGHT WHITE

BRING BACK YOUR BEAUTY
WITH BULL SEMEN!

Why didn't she think about the boot camp earlier? It all makes sense now. That's why she didn't need a jacket.

There are two doors off the dining room. One is labelled the Chat Room; the other, the Therapy Room. She grabs the Chat Room handle and pushes the heavy door open with all her weight. It's dark inside, but the light streaming in from the dining room reveals one enormous single armchair that looks like a throne. She fumbles around for a light switch, finds nothing and steps forward, letting go of the door. It slams shut, leaving her alone in the pitch black. Inching further with her arms outstretched, she finds the armchair and quickly sits down, tapping her right leg as she nervously waits for her big boot camp surprise. Now that she knows what this is, she's finding the whole experience quite exciting. Maybe even fun. Yes, she's disappointed there will be no proposal with pina coladas on a paradise beach. Yes, she's embarrassed to admit to Sarah that she was wrong. Again. But whatever this is, Jamie has gone to a lot of effort. She can't deny that. When Jamie's determined, nothing stops him.

Whir. Beep.

A small green dot starts to flash in front of her and just as she leans forward to look closer, an explosion of light blinds her. She bends into her lap to shield her eyes. After a few seconds, she slowly sits up to face a screen that's appeared in front of her. Her heart pounding, she rubs her eyes and blinks.

She breathes out. It's a photo of her and Jamie, taken at a wedding they went to in Italy last year. It's her favourite – not just because the downward angle hides her chins, but because they look so happy together. A video begins and soft violin music fills the air. The photo switches to another one of them taken in Devon, their first trip away together. Then another at the Edinburgh Festival. Then another in Norfolk. The lump in Amy's throat returns, but she laughs it off when she sees him photobombing her on a gondola in Venice.

SCREECH!

Amy jumps out of the seat and slams her hands against her ears as a nails-on-chalkboard noise erupts from the TV. The photo rips in half and big writing fills the screen. With her fingers still in her ears, she reads.

AMY WRIGHT!

You've been left . . .

ON THE SHELF

'Hello?' she says quietly.

The TV flickers. And then, there he is. He's sitting on an identical armchair, wearing the same clothes that he left her in.

'Is it ready?' Jamie asks someone behind the camera. 'Can I talk? Can she see me?'

'Jamie?' She starts waving at the screen, wondering if he can see her.

He looks into the camera. There are beads of sweat on his forehead and he starts rubbing his nose and coughing as if he's preparing to make a speech.

'JAMIE?' she shouts.

'Amy. I can't see you. I can't hear you. But that's going to make this easier for both of us. Well, mainly me, I suppose.' He laughs awkwardly and looks at the person behind the camera.

'Make what easier? Hello? Jamie?' Amy stands up and moves closer to the screen.

Jamie shifts in his chair, looks down at the floor and sweeps his hair back before fixing his eyes on the camera.

'Amy. Piglet. You must be wondering what's going on.'

'No shit, Jamie,' she whispers.

'Amy, last month I had an epiphany.'

Oh my God, he is going to propose! 'Yes, I'll marry you, Jamie! Stop sounding so nervous! Please, just get me the hell out of here.'

'I've been trying to hide how I feel about you, but I just can't anymore.'

'I love you too!' Amy shouts and throws her hands in the air.

'We're over.' Jamie stares blankly at the camera, through the lens and at her.

That wasn't what she was expecting. In fact, it couldn't be further from what she was expecting. Amy's hands are still in the air. Her jaw is somewhere on the ground.

'What?' Amy whispers, suddenly feeling faint.

'I don't want to get married.'

'Oh my God.' Her breath is shaky.

'And I don't want kids.'

Amy tries to gulp for air as she falls onto the chair and puts her fingers back in her ears. She jumps up and grabs the door handle, but it's locked.

'Let me out! I want to get out of here. Jamie, we need to talk!'

'I want to make this as short and painless for you as possible, so this is me ripping the plaster off,' he carries on coldly.

'How could you do this to me?' she cries, as she spins around, trying to find an escape route.

'And you probably want to know where you are.'

Amy collapses back onto the chair, puffing, and looks up at the screen. How could he just destroy her whole future like that, in seconds?

'You're on the set of a new TV show called *The Shelf*. And we are both being watched by a studio audience in west London.'

The screen flickers to show a huge crowd of people standing in a room, who shout and wave at the cameras when they see they're on screen.

'What. The. Fuck,' Amy whispers.

'I saw an ad for the show in *LAD* and I thought we'd be the perfect couple for it. At a crossroads in our relationship – you thought we were going one way, I knew we were going the other.'

'What crossroads? How could you do this to me in front

of hundreds of people? You are such a tosser!' She knew he could be cruel, but she never thought he would go this far. She folds herself into her lap, hiding her face from the cameras. She needs to get out of here.

'Before you say no, Amy, and I'm sure that's what you're thinking, please just think about what this could do for us. Well, as individuals, I mean. You could get writing offers and I could get Headplace exposure. Plus, if you play your cards right on the show, you could win a million quid. A million quid, Piglet! That's life-changing.'

Amy moves closer to the TV screen to stare deep into his eyes. Is this really happening?

'Amy, I'm actually doing you a huge favour. You'll prob-ably thank me later. One, we don't have to have a long drawn-out break-up, which neither of us would want. Two, we get publicity for our projects. And three, instant million-aire! Just remember the good times when you win, Ames. You know I've always wanted a Rangie.'

Then he laughs.

He actually bloody laughs.

'Fuck you, Jamie!'

'Goodbye, Piglet, good luck and go get 'em.'

Jamie gives her a wink, a grin and a thumbs up, and then the screen turns black, leaving Amy alone in the dark. She sniffs loudly and wipes under her eyes and nose with her sleeve. Then she remembers she's being watched and hides her face in her hands.

She can't believe she didn't see this coming. Well, not

this. How could anyone anticipate being dumped on TV? Do her parents know where she is? Can she leave now, or has she been abducted? Whatever this is, it can't be legal.

A hidden door next to the TV bursts open and light pours into the Chat Room. Amy squints and sees the silhouette of a man in the frame.

'Jamie?' she whispers, desperately hoping this has all been a terrible practical joke.

The silhouette walks towards her and holds out a hand.

Four

The silhouette switches on a light and Amy comes face to face with her mystery rescuer. He's tall and blond with a bushy beard, scruffy overgrown hair, thick-rimmed glasses and soft eyes.

He is not Jamie.

'Hello Amy, I'm Sam. Executive producer on *The Shelf*.'

'Where's Jamie?'

From behind Sam, a skinny young man with a ponytail slides past them. She turns around and sees the back of the TV screen with wires falling out, a camera in the corner of the room and the armchair. Mr Ponytail starts to switch ribbon cables around. She feels invisible.

'Jamie's gone, Amy. I'm sorry.' Sam puts one hand on her arm and quickly removes it when she scowls at him.

'Where's my phone?' she growls.

'Look, I know you're feeling confused right now, but I'm here to help clear things up. It's really not as bad as it seems. You might even feel excited by the time everything's revealed. This is big. You're going to be a star. Come with me and we'll grab a cup of tea. We have to be quick – the next contestant is on her way and Jack here needs to finish prepping.'

Amy turns behind her to look at Jack. He's kneeling on the floor, staring at her.

She hates them both.

Sam leads Amy out of the Chat Room and into a giant warehouse, where a swarm of people are running to and fro wearing walkie-talkies. Cameras are being wheeled around, and at one end of the vast room she sees a sign for STUDIO AUDIENCE. As she follows Sam closely across the room, she dodges beeping equipment and rattling trolleys.

'Sam, the studio audience are expecting some action in thirty, you need to hurry up,' says a brusque woman as she speeds past, without a glance in Amy's direction.

They make it to the other side and enter a small room. There's a sofa and a coffee table with paperwork on it, and a man in a pinstripe suit is standing on the far side of the room, facing away from them.

'This is Harry. He does the legal stuff.'

'How do you do?' he says, turning around stiffly and holding his hand out. When she ignores it, he switches it to a signal for her to sit.

'I'm here to answer any legal questions you might have about the show.'

Amy glances down at the paperwork and sees her name on both documents. How? When? Of course she doesn't have any legal questions – she has no idea where she is or what she's doing. She'd struggle with her name, she's so confused.

Sam mutters into his walkie-talkie for someone called Polly to bring tea, as Amy sits down.

'Hey, sugar?' he asks, and for a horrible second, she thinks that's what he's calling her.

'No.'

'No sugar, Polly, cheers.'

Sam drops into the seat next to her and spreads his legs. Harry wipes his chair with a handkerchief before sitting down and smiling at her like this is the most normal thing in the world.

'Amy,' says Sam, 'as Jamie mentioned in his break-up video, he's nominated you to be on a new reality show called *The Shelf*, which is about to launch on Real TV. Right now, you're sitting behind a studio in west London.'

Amy buries her head in her knees when she hears Sam say 'break-up'. She feels sick. And very alone.

A knock on the door interrupts them. Sam stands up to open it and takes a paper cup of tea from a young woman, who gawps at Amy. She doesn't move as Sam closes the door in her face and continues talking to Amy at the speed of light.

'I know you're feeling a bit down in the dumps right now – sorry, horrible turn of phrase – but please, just hear us out. You're our very first show contestant. Ever! And *The Shelf* is going to be bigger than *Bake Off* by a million. You aren't just going to be famous in the UK, Amy – you're going to be famous around the world. We're in talks to run this in the States, Australia and South Africa. You're going—'

'Wait, slow down.' Amy cuts him off and puts her hand up to her face. 'Are you telling me I haven't just been dumped in front of hundreds of people, but I've just been dumped in front of *millions* of people?'

Harry the lawyer leans forward.

'Amy, Amy, Amy.' He slowly laughs and shakes his head. 'We haven't broadcast anything yet. We couldn't do that without your permission. The break-up was watched by our studio audience, that's all. There's three hundred of them. It was a pre-recording run. Now we just need you to stay on the show, and give us the official thumbs up to broadcast what just happened by signing this paperwork.'

'No. Can I leave now?' Amy stands up, and Sam grabs her arm, pleading with her to sit down again.

'Amy, before you decide, just give me another few minutes to explain the concept of the show. It's an amazing opportunity for you.'

'You don't know anything about me!' Amy hisses.

His walkie-talkie crackles and a voice tells him that they're starting in twenty minutes.

'Amy, I know more about you than you think. Our

researchers have done their legwork. You're an excellent writer, and I know you want to start a blog. I don't know what you want to write about, but I do know blogs need followers to get money. We're offering you ten thousand pounds just to participate, even if you're only here for a week. Sure, this seems like a nightmare now, but it could make all your dreams come true. It could be incredible.'

After a long pause, she lowers herself back down and he lets go.

'OK. Firstly, it's like *I'm A Celeb* meets *Big Brother*, but better. And with an all-female cast. Six women who, like you, thought they were in happy relationships. But weren't. Our next contestant is about to be dumped, just like you were an hour ago!' Sam grins.

'Is that supposed to make me feel better?' she asks them, looking over at Harry, who lowers his head.

Sam inches closer. 'What you'll learn on *The Shelf* will do you the world of good. How to be happier. How to be the best version of yourself. How to make smarter choices when it comes to men. And on top of that, there's a one-million-pound cash prize waiting for the winner at the end of the month. I think you've got a really strong chance at being crowned The Keeper.'

'The Keeper?'

'You know: "She's a keeper". To be crowned The Keeper, you have to prove that you're union material by completing all your tasks successfully and winning the heart of the public.'

She frowns. 'Marriage material?'

'Marriage material. Capable of doing things or behaving in a way that would create a happy union. Are you calm and easy to live with? Are you interested in making a house a home? Are you charming company? Are you good with children?'

Amy stops him with her hand. 'Oh, I'm sorry, silly me, I didn't realise the Chat Room is an actual time machine! Are we in 1955? Should I measure my hips to see if I'm ripe for childbearing?'

'Sorry, bad first examples. I promise we'll apply those to the men, too. If this show is a success, we're hoping to bring out *The Shelf* for men later this year!' Sam says cheerfully, looking at Harry and then back at her.

'And what will their tasks be – building sheds and scratching their balls?' she asks.

'No, I imagine they'll be like the female challenges. The tasks are meant to prove that you can compromise, make sacrifices, be selfless. To be a better half, whether you're female or not. Do your best, beat the other girls, and you'll win over the public.'

'Women.'

'Sorry?'

'We're women, not girls. For God's sake, have you been living under a rock?'

'Yes, women, sorry. All well over eighteen.'

'And what if I don't win?' she asks.

'Look, Amy.' Sam sighs. 'You've been dumped either way. Stay on the show, you've got ten thousand pounds guaranteed. Stay on the show and win, you've got a million pounds and you're on the cover of *OK!*. But leave now and you're on your own with nothing. Seriously, what have you got to lose?'

She raises her eyebrows. 'My dignity?'

'No one cares about dignity anymore!' Sam laughs. 'My God, have you seen *Naked Attraction*?'

Harry leans forward again, looking concerned. 'Amy, we have ten minutes before the next contestant arrives. And there is one clause in this contract that I'm obliged to draw your attention to. During the show, you will receive a number of therapy sessions, which will require you to talk openly about your past, your relationships, your life goals. Therapy sessions, as I'm sure you know, are usually highly confidential. By signing this contract, you agree to waive your rights to this. Session highlights will be broadcast. By signing this contract, you understand and accept this condition.'

Amy stares at him for a few seconds before turning to Sam.

'Sam, how long has Jamie been planning this?' she asks, her voice a little softer. She feels exhausted.

'We ran an ad in the back of *LAD* a couple of months ago. Jamie submitted a form online, gave us your whole backstory, along with some photos, and he was shortlisted for an interview. He came in and told us all about you, your relationship, your family and your personality type. He even showed us some footage of you so we could see what you were like on camera. We thought you'd be perfect on the show.'

'What footage?' she says, immediately worried.

'A video of you doing the running man in a living room.'

Oh, God.

It was after Beck and Adam's wedding in Guildford last summer. She and Sarah had worked their way through a magnum of champagne and taken their freshers' week dance routine back to their Airbnb. Her cheeks turn red; Jamie had promised he wouldn't show anyone.

She hangs her head. 'Please don't put that on TV.'

'You're endearing, Amy. You're real. That's why we chose you. We think the public will feel the same.'

'I want to call my mum.' She sniffs. 'Can I have my phone now?'

Sam and Harry look at each other.

'We've got your phone,' says Harry. 'And we can give it to you now, but you need to sign a non-disclosure agreement that you won't post about the show on social media. You have five minutes to call whoever you want to explain what's happening to you. And if you decide to stay, you'll obviously have to leave your phone behind.'

'I just want to know what she thinks. Wait, what? I won't have a phone?'

''Course not. We can't let you take phones in there, love. We're sealing you lot off from the outside world. No social media for a month. Heaven, if you ask me. Think of it as a digital detox. And tell your mum it's a boot camp for your mental well-being. It's scary now, but when you leave in a month you'll look back on this experience and realise how good it's been for you. It will put you in a much better position to find real love, Amy. To find the man you're meant to be with.'

'Well, maybe he doesn't exist.' She sighs.

'He does! You were just choosing to stay with the wrong guy. And from what I've read, you were so fixated on getting married that you couldn't see he wasn't right for you. Now, you've wasted two years of your life – do you really want to waste another two?'

'I wasn't fixated on getting married!' she snaps, as Sam kneels in front of her.

'Amy, you have two choices. You can take the leap and change the course of your life for the better. Or you can leave and spend the rest of your life dreaming about what could have been. Imagine who you could become if you stay. You have five minutes left to make your decision,' Sam says as he stands up.

'You will need to sign one of these documents,' Sam continues. 'The first gives us permission to broadcast you and says you'll stay on the show for as long as you're a contestant. The second says you don't give us permission to broadcast you and you'll leave through the back door, never to hear from us again. We're going to wait outside the room while you make your calls and consider your choice. Once you've decided, call Harry back in and sign the paperwork. And after, I'll walk you back to the Chat Room where you can press either the Stay or Go button.'

Sam stands up, opens a filing cabinet in the corner and takes Amy's phone out, as Harry hands her the non-disclosure agreement. She signs it and then they both leave the room.

It's suddenly silent apart from Amy's loud breaths. Her chest is tight and her face is burning. She switches on her phone with shaky hands and feels her throat lump growing again.

She goes to Recents and presses *Mum*. Knowing her, it'll be on silent.

Please answer, please answer.

The phone rings out to voicemail. She switches to her dad's number but the same thing happens. She leaves a message.

'Mum, Dad,' her voice wobbles. 'Something's happened. Don't worry, no one is hurt. I don't have long to explain, but Jamie broke up with me. On a TV show.'

She swallows her lump and tries to sound positive, so they won't worry if she decides to stay.

'It's called *The Shelf*! It's like *Big Brother*. I'm at the studio now and they want me to stay here for a month. If I stay, I could win a million pounds! Anyway, I don't quite know what to do and I'm still in shock. I was just giving you a quick call to see what you think. And if I stay, I won't have access to my phone for a while, so it's also a goodbye for now. Please don't worry, I'll be fine! You'll either see me later, or . . . on TV, I suppose! Ha, weird!' She fake-laughs. 'OK, bye. Love you.'

She hangs up, sighs and carries on scrolling through Recents. Seeing Jamie's name makes her feel sick and angry. She hovers over Sarah's number for a few seconds and decides against pressing. Sarah won't answer when she's at work. And if she does, she will spend Amy's remaining two minutes shouting about why she should leave immediately. And Amy isn't sure she wants to hear that. She needs to weigh up her options alone and make her own choices.

On the plus side, she could win a million pounds. Freedom. Experiences. A first-class ticket to Asia. Time to start her blog. And she has been on an eat-sleep-work conveyor belt for the last six months. It's not like she has a job to go to tomorrow. And she's been wanting to take a proper break from freelancing for ages. Being here means no more narcissistic creative directors and dickhead clients for a whole month. This could be the trigger she needs to do something more with her life. It is exciting.

Something to tell the grandkids she'll probably never have.

And then the anxiety hits. She is all alone. Single at thirty-two. What will her friends think of her? Sarah will be disappointed. Jane will think she's a tragedy. What will the other contestants think of her? What will the public think of her?

She's furious with Jamie. But she's angrier at herself for sticking her head in the sand when she saw the signs. What would she do if she left now? She could break into Jamie's, pour her foundation all over his bedsheets, get arrested, thrown in jail, take drugs, turn to the streets, lose all her teeth.

Calm down.

A chance to win a million pounds.

A chance to change my life.

A chance to start again.

A chance to show everyone I can be someone.

A chance to be me.

She closes her eyes, exhales and feels her nerves morph into excitement.

What have I got to lose?

Harry breaks the silence by opening the door, creeping in and sitting opposite her. Without saying a word, Amy takes the pen, signs the paperwork and seals her fate.

'Ready to go back in?' he says.

Sam hurries Amy back along the studio floor and guides her into the Chat Room. When she reaches the armchair, she turns to face him one final time.

'I really hope you've made the right choice, Amy.'

The lights go off, the TV turns on and a countdown timer starts on the screen. When it reaches one, her face flickers onto the screen. She sweeps her hair back through her fingers, wishing she'd been to the bathroom. She looks like a sunburnt hamster.

'Hello, Amy. Welcome. You've got an important decision to make.'

A piercing siren sounds and two big signs appear on the screen. One says STAY and the other says GO.

'Amy. Please make your choice.'

Amy draws a deep breath, closes her eyes and states her decision.

KAPOW!

Firework graphics fill the screen and pop music roars through the air as the STAY sign lights up in neon and the cameras turn to the studio audience, who are going wild. The Chat Room lights up and confetti pours onto Amy from a bucket on the ceiling. She covers her head and can't help but laugh as she looks at herself on the screen through the paper shreds and glitter.

Back in the studio, the cameras zoom in on Adam Andrews, former tween star of soap *West London Free* and reality show fail *The Comeback Kid*. The show had stopped airing after three episodes in which he failed every audition he attended, including one to play himself in a documentary remake of the soap. He never made it on TV again, apart from a D-list celebrity appearance. But he did make it online. His memes from the reality show are so popular that he has his own keyboard extension.

Pinch yourself. Adam Andrews knows who you are, even if he is a digital D-lister.

'Amy is a stayer, but will she be The Keeper?' he shouts into the mic. 'Stay tuned for our next contestant: Jackie!'

The room turns black and the door beside her automatically unlocks.

'Amy. Please return to the studio house and make yourself at home.'

She takes a deep breath and stands up.

Five

All Amy's packed is a week's worth of holiday clothes and a straw hat the size of a picnic rug. She fiddles with the lock on her suitcase, which was magically sitting in the hallway when she returned.

'No coats required.' She remembers him grinning.

Twat.

She debates who's a bigger twat, her or him, as she drops onto the sofa, curls up into the cushions and strategically hugs a silver pillow to hide her belly rolls from the camera. She cringes as it dawns on her that she could be spending the next month in a bikini in front of millions. Of course, things would be different if she was the size 8 she'd planned to be at the start of the year. And every year since she was sixteen, for that matter. At least she's wearing her trusty flight outfit. Skinny black jeans and an oversized jumper. Thank God for this season's baggy trend. Who cares that Jamie hates it.

With no social media to fill these long minutes and occupy her thumb, Amy chews nervously at her broken nail. She abruptly stops and lowers her hand, remembering when Jamie told her she was filthy for doing it. He must be watching her. Picking at the cushion threads, she wonders if he feels guilty. Perhaps he'll rush through the front door any second now with a thousand apologies tumbling from his mouth.

Oh, shut up, Amy, scolds her inner voice. Jamie doesn't say sorry. He's an arsehole. An arsehole she was prepared to spend the rest of her life with. An arsehole who's ripped up her playbook and left her alone at thirty-two with no prospects of marriage or kids.

If Sarah was here, she'd drill some sense into her. She'll be furious when she discovers what's happened. Maybe more furious with Amy when she finds out she's been choosing to stay with an arsehole over being single at her age. For confirming what she's suspected all along.

'Have you ever looked at this age concern from a different angle?' Sarah once said to Amy. 'Do you ever worry: *Oh no, time's running out to travel the world, watch what I like, eat my lunch without sharing and enjoy the simple and silent pleasure of being alone?* Do you ever stop and think about what you're giving up?'

Sarah's jumped from boyfriend to boyfriend since they graduated and was always adamant that she'd 'never settle', even if it meant sacrificing having a family.

Amy had broached the subject of loneliness once. Did

Sarah never feel lonely being single? Sarah had snorted half a gin sour out her nose. 'How could I ever feel lonely, Ames? My life is full of people. Friends, family and, most important of all, me. For a guy to be with me, they have to be happy to fit into my life. I'm not self*ish*, I'm self*first*. Every boyfriend has expected me to fit in with their lives, and they didn't like it when I expected the same. Obviously, not all guys are like that. Jamie isn't like that, is he?'

'No, he's pretty good,' she lied, remembering Jamie telling her she was a distraction. Why couldn't she be braver?

Amy closes her eyes and imagines Sarah sitting here on the pink sofa next to her.

'Amy, I'm so angry with that twat, and with you for not telling me the truth. But you're here now, you've made your choice. And this could be the best thing that's ever happened to you! Jamie is pig shit – be happy he's out of the picture! I'd like to send him a thank you card for setting you free. Where can I get anthrax? Now listen. You are only thirty-two. You don't need to rush into anything. Hell, you wouldn't need to if you were seventy-two! Live life for yourself for as long as you need. If you meet someone that wants what you want, great. If you don't, those are the cards you've been dealt. And if you still want kids, head to a sperm bank. I hear Danish guys are trending. You don't need a relationship to have a kid. If there's no one to pick up little Bertie from the nursery when you're working late, then I can help. I'll send my driver.'

She imagines Jane sitting on the other side of her. The boohoo face, the head tilt. She'd probably make Amy feel like it was her fault. She imagines Jane's head shaking with one eyebrow raised, the unspoken *What are you doing wrong that you can't seem to keep a man?* She sees her discussing Amy with all their old school friends: 'What's wrong with Amy?'

Amy can't imagine any of her other friends being there for her. They'd be too busy planning baby showers or first birthdays, which are the only parties she's ever invited to now. And they're just the worst. At the last one, she was forced to do a 'mums and bubs' dance to *Peppa Pig Hits*, without a baby. To mask her misery, she'd made the mums laugh by jiggling a wine bucket on her hip instead.

They might lend her one ear, with the other on a baby monitor, offering a few standard words of comfort like 'there's plenty of fish in the sea'. They wouldn't hear her reply: 'But the sea is full of rubbish and things that kill you'. They wouldn't *really* want to be burdened by the heartache saga of their last single friend. She knows because she's been one of those smug bastards for the last two years. Single over thirty is like an illness that's too awkward and depressing to talk about.

As she wonders who's going to watch the show, she sees something race towards her from the corner of her eye. She screams as she jumps a metre into the air, lands on the back of the sofa and falls over the other side, where she lies, cursing under her breath, in a crumpled heap on the floor. If the producers have released a rat into the house for comedy effect, she's going to sue them for a sprained ankle as well as emotional trauma. Trembling, she peers over the sofa and exhales in relief.

Krrr, click!

It's the Roomba again.

'Ugh, sod off!' she barks into its tiny glass face. 'And stop taking pictures of me from below my chin! Everyone knows it's the worst angle!' She mutters that last bit quietly as she crawls back into her sofa nook.

Turning her back on the Roomba – which is now silently staring at her like a needy one-eyed puppy – she looks down at her black jumper and notices it's covered in glitter, with a brand-new motif. An upside-down face of make-up, which has been daubed on her chest along with all her tears. She needs to clean up before the next arrival. It should help her feel a little more human in this hideous hospital lighting. *Men must have designed this set*, she thinks.

Amy swings her legs to the floor and stands up. She rolls her suitcase behind her as she limps her way to the bedroom, the wheels making tiny squeaks with every turn and providing a fitting soundtrack to the tragedy that she is. Alone, abandoned and hobbling her way to a small single bed – all she needs to do now is walk into a door frame or stub her toe to complete her public humiliation.

In the bathroom, Amy searches the walls for cameras or

mics. She can't see any, but that doesn't mean they aren't there, hidden somewhere in this heavy decor. It's enough to trigger a seizure, with floor-to-ceiling gold-and-black marble covering every surface. Three showers, one bath and three sinks. She hopes to God they aren't expected to wash at the same time. There are two types of women in this world: those who get naked in the gym changing room, and those who get naked in the gym changing room toilets. Amy is definitely one of the latter.

If she's going to be on TV, her face needs a good scrub and some surface work, but at least she did all the pre-holiday hard graft in Jamie's flat. As the sink fills with hot water and steam clouds the glass, she leans over and splashes her face, instantly feeling the ugliness of her morning wash away. She pats her face dry and feels happier for a fleeting second, watching the glitter spiral down the plughole.

Ten minutes later and Amy's still deep in thought, sweeping a third layer of mascara onto her eyelashes. She's deliberately taking her time, embarrassed to perform the clumsy dance of her regular make-up routine. For her final act, she applies a layer of sheer pink lipstick that she got from the cover of *Heat*. It's been lying lidless in her make-up bag for at least two years.

Would I watch this show if it wasn't happening to me? she wonders. *Would* The Shelf *be my next* Love Island?

She likes to think she'd hate to see women being dumped for entertainment. But the truth is, she's a sucker for a TV craze. If she was on the outside, she'd be one of the millions tuning in, and she'd hate herself for it.

Amy's chosen the bed that's furthest from the door and next to the wall. Rather a wall than a stranger, is her logic. After unpacking her clothes into an assigned wardrobe, Amy waits. Not for long.

Ping!

Ping!

Ping! Ping! Ping!

She pokes her head into the living room to see the TV has come to life and there are words scrolling down the screen. It's a comments feed.

Oh God.

Isn't it too soon for public commentary?

@ultimanufan Give us a smile love, you could win a million quid! #theshelf

@thebirdsloveabitofhim I would #theshelf

@imlukeyman Oi Amy, watch out for that #cameltoe #theshelf

Amy shoots her eyes to her crotch and covers it up with her hands.

@imlukeyman Haha made you look! #madeherlook #theshelf

@playwithsarahj Jamie is such a tosser! Why kiss her like that? Cruel #theshelf

The last message makes her feel better until she remembers that kiss. His smile. His hair. The familiar smell of Dior Sauvage floating around him. Him just being there, in her life.

Stop it.

She leaves the TV and wanders through to the kitchen. She'd love a cup of tea, but after spending a minute trying to find the fridge, she gives up, conscious she looks like a twit. She'll never get used to the world watching her every move. She walks outside through the giant bifold doors that wrap around the studio house.

The doors open onto a neon green plastic lawn that's home to three large garden gnomes. Their heads turn in unison as she moves past, as if gnomes could get any creepier than they already are. When she looks closer, she spots cameras in their eyes and jumps back. Her face must have been the size of the moon in that shot.

There are two social seating areas on either side of the garden. One looks like a Tiki bar and the other like an après-ski chalet. There's also a long, thin swimming pool that takes up one side of the garden and makes her cringe when she thinks of the public seeing her near naked. What will the comments say then?

At the Tiki bar, she slides her fingers into her back pocket before it dawns on her. It's empty. And it will be for a while. She drops her head onto her folded arms on the counter and wonders how long it will take to stop automatically reaching for her phone. Her security blanket. Her window to the world. To Jamie. What would she be looking at now? She'd be zooming in on his recent pictures, trying to find any kind of evidence to suggest this was coming. Maybe there'd be something in his eyes.

How can I ever trust a man again? Will I ever even meet a man to distrust again?

She and Jamie built a life together, and now that he's smashed it to pieces she has to rebuild it from scratch. On her own. Exhausted, she takes a deep breath through her nose and exhales for five.

BANG!

The silence is broken by the slam of a door and heels clicking loudly across the floor. She sits still and tries to stare through the glass door as shouting erupts from the living room.

Amy gets up from her seat and tiptoes across the garden and back into the kitchen, where she stops in the dining room doorway and approaches the sofa.

A tall, powerful-looking woman is shouting at the TV screen with her arms folded tightly across her chest. She's wearing a skintight red dress with gold heels and has an enormous beehive of braids coiled on her head, adding half a metre to her height. Her neck, ears and wrists are dripping in beads. She oozes glamour.

'Oh, get fucked!

'Fuck off!

'What the fuck do you know, @essexboy2000? Fuck all, that's what.'

She turns around and towers over Amy. Unfolding her

lithe arms, she takes Amy's hand in long, slim fingers as she grins with brilliant white teeth shining through bright red lipstick.

'All right, love? I'm Jackie! What the fuck have we done?'

Six

All six contestants are sitting awkwardly on or around the sofa, struggling to speak through sobbing or spitting venom. They've just finished picking at a salad delivery, which was discreetly dropped off in the fridge earlier.

What are you supposed to say to a stranger who's just had the plug pulled on their whole future? Amy had chosen an inappropriate 'Lovely to meet you' with Jackie, an unconvincing back pat and a 'Well, it could be worse' with Hattie, a chef from Southampton, and an awkward 'So, how would you spend a million pounds?' with Kathy, a quiet fifty-two-year-old mum from Bristol.

'On myself!' she chuckled, shifting in her seat to lean across the coffee table. 'My kids are busy living their own lives in London now. If I shared it with them, I wouldn't see the little shits for the rest of the year. Bless. I love them really.' She smiled before glancing at the camera, her eyes glistening in the light.

For the fifth and sixth contestants, Amy resolved to give a knowing nod that simply and silently said 'I feel your pain'.

'How many people do you think are watching us?' whispers Hattie, who's clearly feeling insecure about being on screen, constantly trying to sit where the camera can't see her and hiding her tummy with folded arms.

Jackie continues, 'No one's going to watch this show, it's a bunch of sexist wank. I give it a week before it's cancelled and we're out of here.'

Whir. Beep.

The cameras turn on Jackie.

'Exactly. Who the fook would wanna watch our motley crew of miserable outcasts?' says Lauren, a DJ from Newcastle with a bleached-blonde pixie cut and a nose piercing. 'A reality show about funerals would be more upliftin'.'

'I don't know, Lauren,' begins Kathy, staring blankly into the distance. 'People love seeing other people fall. It makes them feel better about their own lives.'

The housemates have made a policy to avoid looking at the comments feed in front of them, which is proving impossible for most of them. Over the last hour, it has become clear that the public are taking a sick pleasure in being cruel, and the continuous string of emotional outbursts are exhausting. But for some housemates, the temptation is too much. Just a few moments ago, Amy's heart almost burst when she asked Gemma what she did for work.

'None of your fucking business, mate.'

'Sorry, I was just trying to make conversation,' replied a red-faced Amy.

'Sorry, babes, I wasn't talking to you, I was talking to this creep asking me how often I work out. Fuck, I wish I had my phone. I'd properly give him a piece of my mind.'

The comment does make sense. Gemma looks like she's made of pure muscle. She also seems to love the spotlight, and has reapplied her lip gloss in front of the glass doors at least ten times since they arrived an hour ago.

The screen suddenly switches to a countdown clock, starting from five.

4 . . . 3 . . .

Amy feels sick.

2 . . . 1

'Here we go,' says Lauren.

The TV goes blank momentarily before Adam Andrews' giant face appears, his eyes the size of side plates they're so big on the screen.

'All right, girls?' He winks.

A bass-heavy dance track starts blasting and the cameras quickly pan out to the studio audience, who are going wild and throwing their hands up in the air like they've joined a religious cult.

'Ugh, I hate it when men call us *girls*,' mutters Amy. 'It's so gross.'

'It's better than what my ex Dylan used to call me,' Hattie replies quietly with a straight face. 'Hattie the Hippo.'

'Don't worry, I've been Piglet for the last two years.'

'Hippo was actually a compliment compared to what the boys used to call me at school. I'll give you a clue – it begins with F and rhymes with Hattie.'

Amy leans over and gives her a side hug.

The camera focuses on a group of four young men wearing matching white fedoras, tuxedo jackets and tangerine skin. When they see they're in the spotlight, each one unbuttons his jacket to reveal a word printed across his oily six-pack.

GEMMA – IS – A – FITTY!

They pump their arms and thrust their hips in time to the track.

'Where do they find these people?' mutters Jackie.

'OH MY GOD!' screams Gemma, leaping out of her chair. 'Those are the lads from my gym!'

Gemma breaks out into exactly the same dance routine, her glossy pink filler-plumped lips pursed in duck-face mode.

'Sick!'

She jumps back onto the sofa, looking around at the other housemates, smiling sweetly, with her chewing gum lodged in her veneers.

'OK, calm down everybody,' Adam laughs as he addresses the audience at the front of the stage and they start to simmer down. 'Wow, you lot are loving this, aren't you? Well, there's even more to love coming up right now, because it's time to meet the stars of the show. ARE . . . YOU . . . READY?'

The audience scream a collective 'YES!' followed by a chorus of woo-hoos.

'I think I'm going to be sick,' says Hattie, whose hands have started to shake uncontrollably. 'What have I done?'

Lauren takes one of them and clasps it in her lap.

'I'll take that as a yes then, shall I?' Adam looks out, his Tangoed face basking in the glow of the adulation. 'Well then, let's go!'

The camera zooms out as he runs over to the studio sofas.

He's not alone.

'Holy shit.' Jackie sits up.

'Jason, you little fuck!' Gemma shouts. 'Look at him, sitting there like he's fucking cock of the woods!' She flips him a bird.

'He can probably see you, Gemma,' says Kathy.

'Do I look like I give a fuck? I hope he can.' Gemma adds a second bird. Lauren joins her in solidarity with her one free hand, the other still holding onto Hattie.

Gemma's face relaxes into a smile.

'Cock of the walk,' Amy says, and then immediately regrets it when Gemma shoots her a look.

Jamie's in the middle. He's changed into the shirt Amy bought him for Christmas last year. Well, technically she didn't buy it. He exchanged the one she bought him for this. She never did get his gifts right. She watches him lean back with his arms behind his head, loving every minute of his moment in the spotlight. This is the best thing that's ever happened to him. The best thing that's ever happened to him is the worst thing that's ever happened to her. What the hell kind of relationship has she been in for the last two years? She wishes she could jump through the screen and rip that shirt right off him. But she also wishes he would stand up, admit that he's made a huge mistake and come and save her from this living nightmare.

Fat chance, she thinks as he smiles and waves at the audience. His crow's feet wrinkle up. He disgusts her.

'OK everyone, let's begin. So, over there,' Adam points to the camera, 'we have our lovely contestants, fresh off the love train and ready to make some life changes!'

The screen switches to the living room camera. No one moves. No one smiles. It switches back to Adam, who's pulling a sad face.

'Oh dear! Chin up, girls, you're on telly! Now, let's meet the men responsible for those slapped arses – sorry, I mean faces. Give it up for the exes, everyone!' He starts clapping with the audience. 'Let's meet our first contestant.'

Please not me please not me please not me.

'Jackie Adu!'

A huge picture of Jackie laughing at the camera fills the screen, with graphics on the side. It couldn't be further from the image of her now. Amy can see her chest start to rise with deep breaths.

Name: Jackie Adu
Age: 38
Location: London
Profession: Solicitor
Status: Married, no kids
Description: Selfish

The screen switches back to the sofa and the cameras zoom in on a tall man who's towering over Adam, despite sitting down. He doesn't look as pleased with himself as Jamie. He almost looks humble. But who is Amy to judge? She thought Jamie was The One, and look where that idea landed her.

'Aaron! Tell us. Why did you leave Jackie on *The Shelf*?'

'Hi everyone, hi Jackie.' He gives a half-hearted wave, looking into the camera. 'I'm Aaron Adu, Jackie's husband. Estranged husband now, I suppose. The truth is, I left Jackie on *The Shelf* because she doesn't understand what marriage is.'

'What do you mean?' Adam interjects, looking comically sincere.

'Well, she doesn't consult me over big decisions that impact our lives. She keeps secrets from me. She puts her father's needs before mine. And she doesn't want kids, even though I told her I did when we got married.'

Jackie shifts in her seat, radiating anger. 'And I told you I *didn't* want kids when we got married,' she says through her teeth.

'Broken promises.' Adam shakes his head.

'I don't feel proud of myself for putting her on here,' Aaron continues. 'But I do think *The Shelf* will teach her to value what's most important in life when you're married. Isn't that the whole point of the show?'

Jackie rolls her eyes and shouts to the camera.

'I keep secrets from you, Aaron? *Me*? This morning you told me we were taking my dad out for lunch. Now look where I am. Hello? Can you hear me?'

'I don't think we're on sound, love,' says Lauren. 'They don't want to hear our side.'

'Tricky situation, Aaron, but it sounds like you've done the right thing. Now let's move on to Jason!' shouts Adam over the audience applause.

The screen flashes a picture of Gemma posing on the side of an infinity pool. The audience start to coo and whistle.

Name: Gemma Burns
Age: 30
Location: Cheltenham
Profession: Personal trainer
Status: Long-term relationship
Description: Distant

'Jason, my word, you must have a very good reason to leave *that* on *The Shelf*! Explain yourself, sir! Why is Gemma "distant"?'

Jason is pure beef. He has a neck as wide as his head and tree trunks for arms. The high pitch of his voice is a shock.

'Steady on, mate. Gemma Burns isn't "that". She's my girlfriend. I mean, ex-girlfriend. I think. Is she? And yeah, she's beautiful. Inside and out. But I was forced to leave her on *The Shelf* because she needs an intervention. All she does is stare at her phone all day, posing for pictures or replying to comments. It's been months since we had a proper conversation. Whenever I try and talk to her she doesn't even bother looking up from the screen anymore. It's like her followers are more important to her than her friends or family. I miss her. We all miss her. She needs to wake up and realise that she has a problem and that I didn't sign up for going out with the back of a mobile phone.'

Adam shakes his head. 'Sounds like a classic case of being taken for granted.'

'Yeah, but she . . .' Jason backtracks. He doesn't seem cocky at all, despite Gemma's comment earlier. 'She's a good person. She's just lost her way a bit. She's got caught up in this whole influencer world, and that's what I have a problem with.'

'Well, you didn't seem to have a problem with it when we got those free flights to Magaluf last month, Jason, so why don't you make your mind up?' Gemma screams, leaning forward with her arms crossed tightly.

Amy makes a mental note not to cross her.

'Next up is – drum roll, please – Jeremy!'

Kathy groans at a black-and-white photo of her on her wedding day. It must have been taken at least thirty years ago.

She sighs. 'Look at me. So bloody naive. An absolute fool.'

Name: Kathy Hegarty
Age: 52
Location: Bristol
Profession: None
Status: Married, two adult kids
Description: Bitter

The camera switches to a small, middle-aged, twitchy man with large sideburns and an earring in his left ear. He looks like a bad-tempered ferret.

'Jezza. Bitter? Ouch! That's gotta leave a bad taste in the mouth.'

'Well, it does, Adam.' The ferret shrugs. 'I put Kathy on *The Shelf* because she was refusing to leave. I told her weeks ago to pack her things. She just ignores me. If she has nowhere else to go, that's her problem, not mine. She needs to accept our kids have moved out, I have moved on and Susan's moved in.'

'Who's Susan?'

'The love of my life, Adam, that's who. Anyway, Kathy's ruined what was supposed to be a happy time for us for too long. Susan is really upset. Mine and Kathy's relationship is over, and I'll be filing for divorce when she gets out. I'm hoping *The Shelf* will help her accept reality.'

Amy shuffles towards her. 'Kathy, I'm so sorry.'

Kathy looks at Amy with a surprisingly calm face. 'Don't be. I knew about the affair for ages. He's such a cliché, leaving the dumpy old wife for the sexy young PA. Pathetic, really,' she whispers.

'Sounds like you're takin' it like a total boss,' says Lauren. She hands Kathy a tissue. 'I'd have gone fookin' apeshit.'

Oh, God.

Name: Amy Wright
Age: 32
Location: London
Profession: Copywriter
Status: Long-term relationship
Description: Desperate

It's Jamie and Amy on the beach in Cannes earlier this year. Their last holiday together. Jamie is bronzed, shirtless and showing off his six-pack. Amy is covered from head to toe in a variety of mismatching sarongs and Factor 100 sun cream, having burnt herself to a crisp the day before. She looks ridiculous. She can't believe he's used that picture. His last stab.

Bring it on, Jamie.

'Moving on to Jamie! Tell us, where did you meet Michael Jackson?' Adam guffaws. The audience crack up and Jamie fake-laughs. Amy knows it well. 'Just kidding. Tell us about your relationship with Amy.'

'Hi everyone.' He sits up, spreads his legs and rests his elbows on his knees while clasping his hands together in his classic *let me explain something to you* pose. 'I'm Jamie O'Connor, CEO of new executive search agency Headplace.'

Someone in the audience wolf-whistles. Something stabs Amy in the gut.

'Ha, thank you. Anyway, I'm Amy's ex-boyfriend. Don't get me wrong, Amy is a lovely girl. Just . . . for someone else.'

Who, Jamie? And why the fuck has this only just dawned on you?

'I left Amy on *The Shelf* because she was always putting pressure on me to move in, get married, have kids. I could not have been clearer when I told her I didn't want any of it. She just kept on pushing, pushing, pushing. I suppose it's the natural programming of most women. It's not their fault – it's just nature.'

He's said that to her before. She thought he was teasing.

'I hope Amy learns to listen on *The Shelf*. I wish her luck. For more information and all your executive search needs, visit Headplace.co.uk or email jamieo@headplace.com.'

Amy stares at the screen, unflinching.

'You all right, love?' Lauren leans over to rub her knee.

'Desperate?' Amy replies, before clearing her throat. 'It's like he's talking about a completely different person. It's like he was in a completely different relationship. It's all total lies. Pressure? We never once had a conversation about it, I swear to God,' she says. 'I'm not mad, I promise.'

'We know you're not,' says Jackie. 'It's just classic male bullshit.'

'How about I make everyone a cup of tea?' Kathy stands up and looks around.

'Kathy, please do not leave the living room.'

Hattie suddenly throws her head into her lap. The rest of them look up to see a photo of her on screen. It's terrible. It's a selfie of Dylan, who looks like a prize prat, laughing at Hattie asleep on the sofa in the background. It isn't flattering. Her mouth is hanging open.

Name: Hattie Jackson
Age: 33
Location: Southampton
Profession: Chef
Relationship status: Long-term relationship
Description: Boring

'Chefs work long hours!' she shouts from between her knees, barely audible.

Dylan is a filthy-looking man-child, sitting on the studio

sofa in a Fortnite hoody and baggy jeans, with his greasy black hair slicked down over his forehead.

'Hattie, how old is Dylan?' Jackie asks the question on everyone's mind.

Hattie sits up, her face bright red.

'Thirty-four. Why?'

'No reason,' she replies.

'Dylan, Dyl, Dyl Boy, Dylo Pad . . . What's going on, man? Tell us why you left Hattie on *The Shelf*.'

'Yeah, all right bruv, you can call me Big D.'

Vom.

'Hattie's got a heart of gold, no denying. I've got a few back troubles and I can't do much around the house. She does most of the cleanin', shoppin', making tea 'n shit – sorry, stuff. I can't swear, can I?'

'No.'

'Sweet. Sorry. But the deal is, right, she's just got well boring. She's always moaning 'n shhh . . . stuff. You know, the little things. We never 'ave a laugh anymore. It's always like: put your mug in the dishwasher, or turn the telly down, it's three a.m. It's like she's sixty-three, not thirty-three. And if I wanted a grandma, I'd just move in with mine. At least she'd make me biscuits – do you know what I mean!' He laughs. Like a dolphin.

'I've told him before,' Hattie says quietly. 'I cook all day. The last thing I feel like doing is making you biscuits. I make him dinner, isn't that enough?' she asks, looking around the sofa.

'Cooking dinner is more than I do, babe!' Gemma pipes up. 'Silly bugger should've counted his blessings while he had them, if you ask me.'

'Ah, fookin' hell,' mutters Lauren.

Name: Lauren Hawk
Age: 36
Location: Newcastle
Profession: DJ
Status: Short-term relationship
Description: Easy

Lauren's photo looks like a promo picture, showing her behind the decks in a nightclub.

'Bloody hell, babes, you look well cool.' Gemma nudges her. Lauren smiles, shrugs and looks down, almost sheepishly.

'Now, bad news everybody,' Adam says to the camera. 'Lauren's partner – or should I say *ex*-partner – has chosen to remain anonymous.'

The audience boo.

'Don't worry, he's written us a letter instead. Let's see what Mr Anonymous has to say.'

He waves a card around.

'I left Lauren on The Shelf *because she's a liar. She's not the kind of woman I thought she was. I want to be her someone special, not just another number in her little*

black book of bed-hopping. She wouldn't know what marriage material was if it slapped her on the arse. She thinks she's all that because she gets behind a set of decks a few times a week. But she's thirty-six, not twenty-six. Long past it. She needs to learn that no one is going to put a diamond ring on a washed-up local club DJ who's been with the entire male population of Newcastle.'

'Mate, you forgot female population, too.' Lauren laughs. 'Christ, when did I ever even say I wanted to be marriage material? You are so fookin' pathetic.'

'Mr Anonymous wants you to be marriage material more than you do,' Jackie replies.

'Yeah, I know. DAVID DICKSON needs to learn how to handle rejection better!' she shouts at the camera.

A gong sounds on the TV.

'Ladies and lads,' Adam says as he stands up and walks to the stage, 'a round of applause for the exes, please!'

Behind him, Amy sees Jamie turn to the others and shake their hands. He's giving them his business card. Tosser.

'And of course, a big round of applause for our six brave contestants. Selfish Jackie! Distant Gemma! Bitter Kathy! Desperate Amy! Boring Hattie! And last but not least, Easy Lauren! Welcome on board this life-changing journey to better yourselves! After the ad break, we'll be taking a tour of the house and showing you what our girls have in store for the next four weeks.'

It's getting hard to hear Adam over the cheers. He takes a few steps closer to the camera until his face fills the screen, as if he's talking to just them.

'Aren't you girls lucky?' he whispers, and winks.

Seven

@**jaydenrom** Jackie − 4. Amy − 7. Hattie − 3. Gemma − 10. Lauren − 6. Kathy − 2. #theshelf

@**beckyblack_12** See y'all in 4 weeks. #theshelf is LIFE! #bestnewshow

@**bigbennoj** What a bunch of whingers. No thanks #Iwouldnt #theshelf

@**yourmatemike** I'll grab a Gemma and Amy sandwich to go please #theshelf

The comments feed cuts off and Adam's back on screen, standing in front of what looks like a model of the house.

'Welcome back to *The Shelf*, everybody! Now, in front of me is a model replica of house. You've got the Chat Room, where housemates can reveal all their secrets and feelings, and secret feelings . . .'

He pauses as the audience cry 'Ooooohh!'

'. . . Then you have the fancy AF dining room, with more

than enough chairs for our contestants to eat, drink and dance on top of into the wee hours.'

Adam starts vossi-bopping. At least, that's what Amy thinks he's trying to do. The audience crack up and a few stand up to join him. It's a cringeworthy few seconds that Amy hopes she'll never have to witness again. He stops abruptly and points his finger back to the model.

'In the corner we have the Therapy Room, where our celebrity therapist will be guiding our girls through their spiritual, emotional and physical journey of relationship enlightenment. Now let's move on to the kitchen, my favourite room in the house. This giant fridge will have a regular supply of all the essentials and, my favourite feature of all, this prosecco tap!' He gawks at the lens as he gestures towards a feature in the corner of the kitchen that Amy thought was just decorative.

'The fridge will also be packed full of healthy stuff to make sure our girls get their five-a-day. We wouldn't want them piling on the pounds while they're in there, would we now?' He wags his finger at the lens. 'And to make sure that doesn't happen, here's our state-of-the-art gym! Notice that it's right next to the kitchen. Perhaps it'll make them think twice when they open that fridge door!'

'Twat,' says Jackie.

'Mostly the girls will make their meals themselves. But they'll deserve nights off, too. So they can also win take-aways on some of our special challenges, in partnership with our friends at Foodfix. But they'll only get special treats if they've been very good girls!' He laughs and points his finger at the camera again. 'And ladies, Hattie, if you *do* have any dietary requirements, I'm sure we can accommodate.'

Hattie looks at the others and shrugs.

'Why the fook did I agree to this?' says Lauren under her breath.

'Let's move on to the garden!' shouts Adam, before anyone has time to answer.

'Feast your eyes on our cosy après-ski chalet and sizzling Tiki bar, where things could get seriously heated in due course. And if they do, then a dip in the long pool will be just what the doctor ordered! And girls, a stern reminder that you're under surveillance out here, courtesy of the all-seeing eyes of our trusty Gnome Patrol!'

The camera zooms in and out on replica gnomes on the table, before Adam grabs one and throws it into the audience. A group of them scramble to fetch it.

Gemma shakes her shoulders. 'Those gnomes are well creepy, the way their eyes follow you around.'

'Their eyes are camera lenses,' Amy replies.

'Fuck's sake,' Gemma whispers.

'Let's head into the living room!' shouts Adam, moving around the table. 'Now, there are a few things you should know about this living room. One, there's a giant television. They're gonna be living a life of luxury, I tell you. But we aren't here to watch them just Netflix and chill. This TV is for the girls to watch my ugly mug chat with guests on our live shows, and of course introduce our challenges. But it also has another very special purpose.'

He walks up to the camera and mists up the glass with his breath.

'Ew,' says Amy. 'I don't remember him being this irritating on *Celebrity Thumb Wars*.'

'The TV will also run a live commentary feed called The Wall. The Wall will keep our girls updated on what the world thinks of them, twenty-four-seven! So, you'd better behave in there, ladies!'

Text runs along the bottom of the screen, giving details of how to comment and what to hashtag.

Amy dreads what they'll target. Her nostrils? Her eyebrows? Eyebrow, if she gets lazy. How normal and boring she is? All of the above? She makes an unlikely promise to herself that she won't look at any more comments unless she has to.

Adam beckons the camera with his fingers into the model bedroom and bathroom, and describes how there are eight single beds and a bathroom, which has no cameras or mics. The crowd boo.

'Why do you want to watch us take a shit? Sickos,' says Gemma.

'Why are there eight beds when there are only . . .' Hattie nods her head around the group. 'Six of us?'

'Probably thought they'd get two more to stay,' says Jackie, with a shrug.

83

'What? You mean someone refused to take part?' Lauren replies. 'Shockin'.'

'And now for the important part,' Adam continues. 'What the girls can do to win this freakin' thing and be crowned The Keeper for the first time in history!'

The crowd cheer as he moves over to a screen, which lists a set of instructions for the next four weeks.

'Hush up and listen closely, peeps. First, our housemates will have regular sessions with our show therapist, who'll help them identify their problem areas and create positive change to steer them back on course. They'll also undertake weekly challenges, where the public will rate them on their performance. The housemate with the highest rating wins the challenge and gets a prize for themselves or for the house. Finally, they have a few mystery dates lined up along the way. The public will rate them on their style, behaviour and charm – just a few of the things we'll be watching out for.' He grins. 'Don't go away – we'll be back right after this ad break.'

The screen pauses on a close-up of the instructions.

How to Win *The Shelf*!

- Embrace your therapy sessions for positive life changes!
- Throw yourself into the challenges and learn how to love!
- Welcome your mystery dates! You'll be surprised what they'll teach you!

- Smile for the viewers! They have the power to keep you in!

'Ladies,' says Jackie quietly, as she gets up and stands in front of the TV. 'We did choose to stay on here, so it's not like we can complain about it now. But we could play the game a little differently to how they want us to. We could challenge every challenge, point out the blatant sexism and tell the audience how wrong this all is. They can't stop us from doing that. They can't fire us – otherwise they won't have a show. But we'd have to be in it together.'

'They could just choose not to vote for us, though, couldn't they?' Hattie asks.

'But that's up to the audience, not the producers. As long as we don't break the rules, we'll stay. And then we just need to get the audience on our side. I mean, surely everyone can see how terrible this show is? Getting them on our side won't be that hard, will it?'

They don't have time to answer.

'Everything all right in there, ladies?' calls Adam, looking into the camera.

The housemates nod in unison and wave at the cameras.

'Lovely stuff. Now, let's talk about the most important part of the show! The votes! Every week, the public vote to keep their favourite contestant in. The contestant with the fewest votes is booted off. And that brings me nicely on to another fancy gadget we have in the house – The Tracker! Girls, please make your way to the dining room.'

The audience murmur.

As they drag their heels next door, the TV screen in the dining room flickers on. The Tracker looks like a league table. Amy can't help but feel a little relieved that she's in the middle. Gemma's at the top, which isn't surprising. Lauren's coming last, which is a surprise. Amy thought she'd be a hit.

'The Tracker shows the girls how they're being rated by the public at any point in time. It's a continuous feed, which gives the girls a steer on how their behaviour is being judged. It can detect positive and negative emotions. It's very clever.'

'Unlike you, you wally,' Jackie mumbles.

'If the public think a girl is being bossy, for example, not naming names' – he coughs an audible *Jackie* and the audience crack up – 'the Tracker will identify those negative feelings online. That will probably take them down a notch.'

Jackie shakes her head.

'If they're being sweet, that'll probably give them a boost. The Tracker helps make each of the girls aware of how they're acting, and is a handy reminder to keep their attitudes in check. Don't say we don't have your back, ladies!

'At the end of the month,' Adam continues, 'two girls will go head-to-head in the epic show finale. The girl with the most votes gets a cash prize of one million pounds, ongoing therapy sessions, a fitness membership, a makeover, a holiday and a year's subscription to dating club Love Market.'

The audience cheer.

'And the girl who just misses out? Well. She doesn't go home completely empty-handed. She leaves with a month's worth of self-healing on the house and a healthier attitude towards relationships!'

Adam turns to the crowd and lifts his arms.

'And that's a wrap, folks! Tune in tomorrow to find out what's next in store for our contestants!'

The screen cuts out and silence fills the air.

'Lads, it's eight o'clock,' says Jackie. 'And high time we tested that prosecco tap.'

*

It's just gone 10 p.m. when Amy tiptoes into the bedroom and crawls under her covers. Gemma, who went to bed an hour ago, stirs lightly. The last time Amy slept in a bed this narrow was when she was ten. She thinks back to Jamie's California king, where she was this time last night, trying to fall asleep without making a sound.

'It's your huge nostrils,' he would say. 'What? It's a compliment. Fearne Cotton has a massive pair, and she's a belter.'

Amy would pretend to find it funny, then stare at everyone else's nostrils the next day wondering if hers were bigger than average. He would continue to joke about it, along with her bingo wings, wobbly thighs and double chin.

87

When she first developed her nostril complex, about three months into their relationship, Amy was genuinely worried that Jamie would dump her because he couldn't bear the thought of being kept awake for the rest of his life. She'd spent hundreds of pounds on every expensive gimmick available, including a mouth guard that made her look like Hannibal Lecter. They eventually settled on an app that played rain to drown out the sound of her breathing. Of just being there in the room.

She wishes she was at Amuse Bouche. In any normal break-up, she'd weep over a glass of wine and grapple with Sarah for her phone. Then she'd go home, gorge on pork dumplings and watch *Kardashians* reruns while swiping Love Market to make herself feel momentarily better. That's how you get over break-ups. You don't get over break-ups on national TV in the company of five strangers who you have nothing in common with apart from being dumped in public.

Of course, the producers aren't holding her hostage. Amy could walk right now if she wanted to and still get the participation fee, which would more than cover a trip to Thailand. But something at the back of her mind makes her want to stay. Maybe she doesn't really want to go back to her drink-dumpling-reality-TV-binge routine. Perhaps she wants to do something completely different that breaks the endless cycle. Maybe she wants to prove to the world that she can do this. And let's face it, one million pounds is probably worth all this humiliation.

Worries flood her mind.

What the hell *am I doing? Is this the worst decision I've ever made in my life? Am I going to die alone?*

Can Gemma hear me breathing?

Eight

WAAAAAAAAAH, WAAAAAAAAAAH!

It's so loud. So very loud. Fucking blaring, in fact. Amy jumps out of bed and looks around the room, confused. What is that? A fire alarm? She sees the others running around the room, trying to find the source of the sound. Someone turns on the lights, blinding them all for a second.

A second wail hits the air. *WEEEEEEEEEH, WEEEEEEEEEH!*

'What the fuck is happening!' shouts Jackie, standing on her bed.

WAAAAAAAAAH, WAAAAAAAAAAH!

Kathy shouts something inaudible.

When the noise abruptly stops, they inch towards the bedroom door and peer out towards the living room.

'Oh my God,' whispers Jackie.

WEEEEEEEEEH, WEEEEEEEEEH!

90

'It's six o'clock – what are they doing to us?' Gemma shouts as they all move into the living room together, apprehensively.

The housemates stand transfixed, staring at the cots that have magically appeared next to the sofa. There are six screaming babies, each with the name of a contestant on their bib. Not real babies, of course. Creepily realistic dolls that have been set to cry mode, with no stop button that any of them can find. The housemates have woken up on *Love Island*, except they couldn't be further from paradise here.

WAAAAAAAAAH, WAAAAAAAAAH!

Amy scans the cots and finds her doll. Ben Wright. She looks inside, picks him up carefully and examines him underneath to see if she can turn his volume down. Nope. Unsure what else she can do, she holds him at a distance in front of her.

This must be our first challenge, she thinks as she scans the room to see what everyone else is doing and if she should be copying them. Jackie's holding her doll upside down by one leg, Gemma has hers in a headlock as she marches towards the kitchen with an offer to make everyone tea, and Hattie has her hand over her doll's mouth as she stumbles back to bed, bumping into the bedroom door on her way.

'Hold up, Gem, there's a note in my cot,' says Lauren, unravelling the paper. '"Congratulations, housemates. Welcome to motherhood. It's Day Three and time for your first challenge – Oh, Baby! – where we'll be putting your natural maternal instincts to the test".'

'And if we don't have any?' asks Jackie rhetorically.

Lauren shrugs and continues. '"For the next few days, you are accountable for the health and well-being of your tiny tot. Inside your cots, you'll find everything you need. Nappies, formula, wipes and blankets. The rules are simple. Set a routine that supports their physical and emotional needs. Sleeping, feeding, sicking, pooping and feeling loved".'

'But . . . they're plastic.' Hattie looks around at the others anxiously. 'How do we know if we're doing it right?'

'"We'll be watching and rating your response to this huge life responsibility",' Lauren continues. '"And finding out just how suited you are to the task". Fookin' hell. That last bit was me.' She drops the piece of paper and picks up her baby by the back of the head. 'Christ on a bike, why does mine look like Phil Mitchell?'

She starts to bounce him around. 'All righ', darlin', I'll 'ave a pint a' larga an' a packet a' fags,' she mimics in a sandpaper Cockney twang.

✳

Amy's chewing mindlessly on a piece of underdone jam toast, watching Ben snore in his cot.

'Since when do babies snore?' she asks the room.

A blob of jam falls from the toast and lands on his

forehead. She quickly licks her thumb and wipes it off, checking up at the cameras and jumping at the sound of the tannoy overhead.

'*Contestants, please take a seat on the sofa. The show is about to start.*'

A familiar theme tune sounds and they look at each other. Amy glances at the clock and inhales sharply.

'Is that what I think it is?' asks Gemma. 'Are we about to be on . . . ?'

'Welcome back, viewers at home, and a very good morning to those of you who've just joined us!' chirps Jenny Mackenzie, host of Real TV's live audience Saturday-morning show, *Put the Kettle On*. 'We have a very special segment in store for you this morning! Let's give a big hand to the host of new hit show *The Shelf*, Adam Andrews!'

Adam's on the sofa, looking twice as orange as yesterday.

The screen cuts to the living room, and Hattie is the only one who responds, with a half-hearted wave.

'And, of course, to our contestants! Oh, Adam, they all look a bit shocked, don't they? Are they all right?' Jenny giggles, covering her mouth with her hand.

'Well, Jenny, I would be too if I woke up to find a new-born baby in my living room!' He laughs too hard and slaps her on the knee.

'It's only Day Three and *The Shelf* is already hitting the headlines – you must be delighted. Now, tell us a little more about this first challenge. What's it called – Oh, Baby?'

Adam switches his face to serious mode. 'Bang on, Jen. So, *The Shelf* is all about giving girls who are unlucky in love the chance to prove they can be long-term prospects – that they have what it takes to be a life partner. And one of the essential qualities to being a life partner is a willingness to self-sacrifice. Care for the physical and emotional needs of someone other than themselves. Nothing puts that to the test quite like motherhood, does it?'

'Perhaps not. So, what do the girls have to do to win the challenge?'

'To be honest, Jen, we just want them to be themselves. Look, most of them have zero experience with children. How they care for these babies will be a window into their characters. Some are born to handle motherhood, some aren't. And knowing this will help them find the right match – and path – in the future.'

'And someone who can help assess their characters is just behind the cameras, isn't he?' Jen comments, and cranes her neck.

'That's right!' Adam waves furiously. 'I'd like to introduce you to a man you'll soon be seeing a lot of! He's our resident therapist, a shoulder for the girls to cry on and recently published author of UK bestseller *Are You in a* Real*ationship?* Dr Howard Hicks!'

'Who?' says Kathy.

'Never heard of him,' replies Amy. And it seems no one else has either. The audience's claps are muted at best as a small, middle-aged, balding man with thin-framed round spectacles walks timidly onto the set, taking a cautious seat on the sofa and waving coyly at the crowd.

'Dr Hicks, welcome to the show.' Jen smiles. 'It's brilliant to have you here. Tell us, what's that book of yours all about?'

Dr Hicks pushes his glasses up his nose and answers slowly. He looks uncomfortable in the spotlight.

'Well, Jenny, firstly, thank you for having me here. *Are You in a* Real*ationship?* is all about getting couples to consider how *real* their relationship is. Are you being truthful with each other? Is your relationship love or habit? Couples are meant to read it together. It will either end their relationship or make it stronger. Either way, the outcome is positive. It's meant to encourage honesty while preventing hostility or blame.'

Dr Hicks stares at the audience and smiles as a lone cough sounds in the background.

Amy looks around, wondering if anyone else thinks the book sounds quite good. Jackie's fixing a braid, Kathy's staring into space despondently and Gemma's flossing her front teeth with a strand of hair.

Just me, then.

'Wow, that sounds like a bestseller to me, doesn't it?' Jenny nods at the audience, who take that as their instruction to cheer.

Dr Hicks turns pink and waves away the cheering.

'So, tell me, Doc,' continues Jenny, after hushing them down, 'what will you be getting up to here on *The Shelf*?'

'OK, Jenny,' he shuffles forward on the sofa, 'I think the concept of *The Shelf* is an extremely interesting one, and I'm going to be fascinated to see how the housemates develop during their time on the show. I think we're going to see some very surprising results—'

'Uh-mazing,' interrupts Adam, sounding insincere.

'I'll be hosting regular therapy sessions, trying to understand why they're on the show in the first place, hoping to guide them out of this predicament they find themselves in and helping them to be stronger candidates for long-term love in the future.'

'And what about all that dirt you'll dig up?' Adam laughs, looking at the audience and winking. They snigger collectively.

'Yes, well, that's not quite my intention,' Dr Hicks responds, pushing his glasses up on his nose again. 'But I'm sure we'll hear some interesting stories. Perhaps a few that we can all relate to as well.'

'And tell me, Dr Hicks, do you have any predictions on how the contestants will cope with the motherhood challenge? How do you think our new mums will do in there?' Jenny's smiling so hard her eyes are almost closed.

He shakes his head. 'Oh, I couldn't possibly comment, Jenny, I haven't spent any time with them.'

'Go on, just take a guess, Doctor Howard!' Adam squeals and Jenny nods furiously in agreement.

'Please, I can't, really – it would be deeply inaccurate and unfair.'

'Spoilsport! Well, Jen, I can tell you that I'm guessing Kathy will cope best – obvs, been there, done that, got the saggy' – he pauses for effect and looks sideways at a wide-eyed Jenny – 'T-shirt.'

Jenny rolls her eyes and waves him away. The audience murmur, and Dr Hicks stares at Adam with a hard frown.

Amy turns to Kathy, who has folded her arms across her chest.

'Ignore him, Kath.' She leans over. 'He says things like that for a cheap laugh, not because it's true.'

'He's a fookin' dick, mate, don't even think about it,' adds Lauren.

They turn back to the screen.

'. . . if that baby isn't burnt to a crisp, missing a limb or face down in the bin by the end of the challenge, I'll present the next show in a pair of Speedos!'

Just under the surface of Jenny's stiff smile is a grimace. Dr Hicks shakes his head and mutters something.

'Who are they talking about?'

'Me.' Jackie turns to them, smiling. 'Don't worry.' She lifts her hand up to stop Gemma from comforting her. 'Appreciate the concern, but he's right. Although he did miss out "floating at the bottom of the pool with a rock tied to its leg".'

'"Head cut off in a freak chopping accident".' Lauren laughs, and Jackie joins in.

Jenny continues. 'Nah, I think Jackie will be all right.

She's a great role model for any young girls watching this show. Outspoken, ambitious—'

'Selfish,' Adam cuts her off. 'She's Selfish Jackie, isn't she?'

'That's simply one opinion from a hurt partner who is bound to lash out,' Dr Hicks adds.

Adam tries to respond but Jenny cuts him off. 'Well, I suppose we'll see in three days!'

The cameras zoom in on her.

'That, ladies and gents, is all we have time for! Thank you for watching, and don't forget to tune in to Real TV every night at nine p.m. to see what the girls have been up to!' she shouts and waves at the camera.

When the camera zooms out, Dr Hicks and Adam can be seen having a heated discussion on the sofa, as Jenny freezes her smile, pretending it isn't happening.

The camera feed cuts out and the room is silent.

But, of course, it doesn't last long.

An ominous gong chimes through the air.

'*Amy. Please go to the Therapy Room at nine a.m. tomorrow. Dr Hicks will be waiting.*'

Nine

Amy's nose is whistling as she waits anxiously for the arrival of Dr Howard Hicks for her first therapy session. She can't decide whether to sniff or blow into a tissue. She isn't sure which the public would find most off-putting. Taking a tissue from the box on the coffee table in front of her, she fake-coughs and quickly sniffs afterwards. It works, and she relaxes. Jackie's looking after Ben for the next hour, and Amy is delighted to have the peace, quiet and freedom, despite feeling nervous about what she's going to reveal to Dr Hicks and the thousands watching.

She leans back and looks around her, absorbing her surroundings. This is the first time she's been to therapy. Are all therapy rooms this soulless? This beige? Three posters on the wall are making her feel hostile.

TODAY IS A NEW DAY

No shit.

CHOOSE HAPPY

What if it's not a choice?

BE YOUR OWN SUNSHINE

I'd rather be a fork of lightning.

There are three succulents lined up on the coffee table in front of her. Of course, she reaches forward to touch one, pricking her finger in the process. She gasps. *I wonder how he'd interpret that?* A physical manifestation of her self-destructive tendencies? She doesn't need therapy; she already knows what's wrong with her. She needs a night out with Sarah and three bottles of wine.

The door opens and Dr Hicks enters the room, shutting it quietly behind him and smiling at Amy as he approaches the table.

'Good morning, Amy. I'm Dr Hicks. How are you?'

Amy stands up and shakes his small, clammy hand as he takes a slow, creaky seat in the vintage leather armchair in front of her.

'Fine, thank you,' she responds, feeling anything but.

Behind his glasses are twitchy little eyes.

'Well, actually, I'm still a bit shocked,' Amy adds when he doesn't say anything back.

'Of course. This is an unusual situation, to say the least.'

He picks up an iPad in front of him and taps the screen.

Whir. Beep.

Amy shifts around in her seat. It squeaks against her thighs, making the atmosphere even more awkward. Her denim beach shorts aren't made for massive leather sofas. Her thighs look like two huge pieces of rolled-out, unbaked dough. When she spots this, she puts a cushion over them.

'Try to ignore the camera,' Dr Hicks says, still looking down but sensing her discomfort. 'Today is the easiest session. It's just a little chat about your background – who you are and why you're here. Is that OK?'

Amy nods, unsure if he can see her.

'My advice is to try to be as open and direct as you can. That way we'll get the best results from these sessions. Don't think about who's watching you.'

Her parents. Her friends. Never mind her – how are they going to feel if Dr Hicks mines something from her subconscious that hurts their feelings?

What about work? What if she can't get a job after this?

'Oh my God, no way! It's that nutcase from *The Shelf*!' says an imaginary HR director, pointing at his screen to show an imaginary team who've gathered round his imaginary desk in an imaginary office. They pretend to stab each other, laughing.

Amy, if you win this, you'll never have to work again.

Besides, she can't back out of this session now. She's signed the contract. She has to spill everything. She has to tell the world about her relationship, even though she's spent the last two years avoiding the subject, and with the very person she is in a relationship with. Was.

'Amy Wright, thirty-two, only child, a copywriter.' Dr Hicks interrupts her thoughts.

'That's me,' says Amy, pinching the skin on the back of her hand.

'Tell me, Amy, why do you think you're here today?'

He puts the iPad down on the table and rests his fingers in prayer mode under his chin.

'Because I'm a . . . complete dickhead?' She shrugs her shoulders and fake-laughs. If she doesn't fake-laugh, she'll cry, for real.

He raises one eyebrow. 'What makes you think that?'

'Well, I've wasted two years of my life with the wrong person, and now I have to start all over again.' She can feel her cheeks heating up.

'Start what all over again?'

'I don't know, trying to find someone to do life with?' Her stomach cramps when she thinks about how desperate she must sound.

You're such a loser.

'And what does that mean to you? *Do life*?' he asks.

'Living together, marriage, kids, holidays, seeing things, having experiences – I don't know, doing normal stuff that normal people do at my age.' She sniffs and pinches the bridge of her nose.

Please don't.

Her eyes glisten and she bites her bottom lip to stop it from shaking.

No no no no no no no.

The silence is pierced by a loud gulp.

Dr Hicks stares at her, which isn't helping. He knows that she's about to cry. He probably wants her to. It'll make great TV.

Here it comes.

She grabs a tissue and quickly wipes away a tear racing down her cheek. But she can't hold it in anymore. Letting go of her lip, she grabs a fistful of tissues and starts wailing.

'Why are you crying?' asks Dr Hicks, without moving an inch. He just sits there, staring at her. Not helping. Not caring.

'I hate myself, I'm so pathetic.' She gulps for air in between sobs, grabbing more tissues to hide her ugly crying face from the camera. When she lowers her hands one of the tissues sticks to her eye. She quickly snatches it off.

That's the shot. I'm going to be a meme.

'I'm so sorry, I didn't think I'd get so emotional,' she says, before blowing her nose and hoping to God it doesn't go everywhere when she removes her hand. 'I thought I was over it. I didn't even feel that sad when Jamie dumped me – I just felt angry. These are angry tears.'

'It's perfectly natural to cry. And it's perfectly natural to feel angry. But who are you angry with?'

'Him . . . Me.'

'Why?' he asks.

103

She inhales and exhales deeply through trembling lips. Lowering her head, she picks the tissues apart.

'I thought I had it all sorted. I thought I was going to get married. I thought I was going to have kids. I thought I was going to be just like all my other friends who are already miles ahead of me. Now I'm thinking, there's no hope. I'm single again. I've lost two years of my life and I'm never going to find anyone else. I'm going to end up forever alone, with no children, no family and no friends. And the thing is, I probably deserve it. I could see Jamie wasn't right. I saw the signs. The great big neon billboard signs right in front of my face saying: *He is not the one! He doesn't make you happy!* I'm angry because I've let myself down and I've ruined my chances of having a happy, normal life. What's wrong with me? Why do I have such bad taste in men?'

'Amy, do you think there's something wrong with you?'

'I don't know!' Her voice is wobbly again, but now her tissues are torn up and she has nothing to bury her face in. Her fingers dig into her eyes. 'I'm ugly, I'm fat, I'm old, I'm boring? I have bingo wings, big nostrils and I breathe loudly?' she says, rapid-fire.

'Would your friends describe you that way?'

'No. But they're probably too busy to know what I'm like anymore,' she snivels. 'For all they know, I could have run away with the circus, married a traveller and popped out three babies. Actually, if I had three babies they'd sit up and see me again. Kids are the ticket to their grown-up club.'

'Why are they too busy?'

'They're planning baby showers, first birthdays, redoing their basements, booking family holidays. I know it's not their fault, that's the life they're supposed to be living. That's the life *I'm* supposed to be living. But I just keep on making terrible life choices that take me further and further away from that.'

'Do you compare yourself to your friends a lot?' he asks.

'No,' she fibs.

'And what about social media – do you use it?' He picks up his iPad and types something. 'I see lots of women your age who think their friends are living better lives than they are because of what they see on Instagram and Facebook.'

'Not really.'

Yes! All the time! is what she should say. What she should say is, 'It's my go-to when I'm waiting for anything. Thirty seconds for the kettle to boil? That's enough for a few stories. Pedestrian light gone red? I have to check what everyone else has been up to in the last thirty minutes. Walking up the stairs and watching my step? Boring! I need to know who Sarah's with at that bar, I don't care if I fall and break my neck.'

The truth is that her screen is what greets her in the morning and what tucks her in at night. And the script never changes.

1. Open Instagram
Flip through stories, then scroll. Feel depressed you aren't

where @lottietheexplorer is. Feel more depressed when you
see that Jane's new kitchen is the size of your flat.

2. Open Facebook
Scroll through a sea of sponsored posts about weight loss.
Click on a link to a listicle about the world's most fashionable
pets. Hate yourself for wasting your life.

3. Open the Mail Online
Hide your screen from Jamie. Avoid anything about *Love
Island*. Finish on an article about D-list celebrity weight gain.
Pledge to delete the app tomorrow.

Suddenly Dr Hicks' iPad is in her face, interrupting her
daydream.

'Amy, I want you to explain what you're doing in this
picture.'

It takes Amy a few seconds to register what she's seeing.

'Where did you get this?' she asks, confused.

It's a picture of the bouquet toss at Angela's wedding
three years ago. In the foreground are a group of women
reaching out with feverish eyes and howling mouths, clam-
bering over each other trying to catch it. Amy is not part
of the group. She's standing on the outside looking bored,
with one arm firmly down and the other holding a glass
of champagne. Amy remembers that wedding reception
vividly. Well, not the actual reception itself. More like the
next day, when everyone had messaged her about getting

off with Angela's lechy fifty-year-old uncle on the dance floor. She had wanted to die. It was the last in a series of hazy and questionable choices she had made in the aftermath of her break-up with Ben. She was the only single woman at the wedding, she wanted to feel wanted that night and after two bottles of wine, he would do. She didn't drink for a month after that.

'Our researchers found it,' Dr Hicks continues. 'I want to know what you were thinking at that moment,' he says.

'I was thinking that bouquet tosses make women look really pathetic. Like we're all desperate to get married. Like we're all rivals, racing each other to the altar. I didn't want to be part of it out of principle,' she says, composing herself.

'Interesting.' He takes the iPad away from her, placing it on the table between them and staring at her again. 'And you say you *do* want to get married?'

'I didn't want to catch the bouquet because I think it's embarrassing. It doesn't mean I don't want to get married.'

He nods as he taps the screen.

'Amy, I have one last question for you.'

'OK.' She's gathering up her tissues.

'Did you love Jamie?' he asks.

'Yes,' she responds, a little too defensively.

'What did you love about him?' he asks.

Her mind goes blank. What did she love about Jamie? *Good skin. Nice smile. Clean teeth. Stacks the dishwasher. Makes supper. Has a job. Doesn't live in a cardboard box. Clever.*

'He was clever,' she says. 'Sorry, I mean he *is* clever.'

'Is intelligence important to you in a life partner?'

'Yes, of course.'

'Why?'

'Well, it makes having conversations a bit easier, I suppose,' she says.

'What did you and Jamie talk about?'

'Lots of things. Life. His business. Current affairs.'

The truth is that conversations with Jamie had entered drought status months ago. Their interactions revolved around whether there was milk in the fridge, what they fancied for supper and if Jamie was going to the gym. Occasionally they'd branch out into discussing Headplace. Jamie would ask Amy for an opinion on a logo; she'd choose her favourite and he'd choose anything but her favourite. She'd learnt long ago not to bring up her own work. His standard response would be, 'I'm not sure, Piglet. Just do what you gotta do,' which didn't even make sense half the time. He hadn't always been like that. At the start, he was involved. Interested. He helped her with her CV, he put feelers out for contract work, he even read some of her copy and showered her with praise. But after a year of investing in the effort, he could sit back and relax. He'd caught her. She was going nowhere at her age, and he knew it.

'Amy?' Dr Hicks leans forward.

'Yes, sorry?' She blinks, coming back into the room.

'I said, did you ever talk about your relationship?'

'Sometimes,' She responds. *Never*.

'And when you did, what did you talk about? Can you give me an example?'

'He gave me a key to his flat recently, and told me I could come and go as I pleased,' she says. 'Well, as long as I gave him some notice.'

Dr Hicks stares at her.

Yes, thank you. I realise how stupid that sounds now. But the key proved our relationship was serious. You don't give someone a key if you're about to break up with them.

'And did you talk about what the key meant for your relationship?'

'No, I didn't think we needed to. It was symbolic.'

'Did you ever discuss your future?' he asks. 'Marriage, kids, that kind of thing?'

He did refer to her as 'wifey' once when she went through a phase of packing their lunches. She wasn't doing it to be 'wifey', she was doing it to save money. The comment had both irritated and pleased her. Irritated her for making her feel servile, and pleased her because he was thinking about her like that. And then she was irritated with herself for feeling pleased.

You can't say that in front of the cameras. You will look like such a moron.

'He called me "wifey" once,' she says.

Oh, Amy.

Dr Hicks stares at her again.

She sighs and rubs under her eyes, conscious of the mascara smears on her cheeks.

'No, not really. Sorry, it's quite hard to think of examples on the spot when I'm being watched. I need more time. I need a break.'

'OK, Amy. I think that's enough for now.'

'That's what I just said.'

He picks up the iPad and starts tapping, leaving Amy to wonder if she has to apologise to anyone. She doesn't think she's said anything offensive, but she should probably apologise for being such a blubbering mess.

'I have some homework for you. I'd like you to work on it before our next session in a week.' Dr Hicks stands up and walks over to a printer on the other side of the room.

Amy looks at what he's wearing from behind. Brown cardigan. Brown cords. Brown loafers. His clothes are worn and his few remaining tufts of hair are unkempt. He must be in his late fifties. No wedding ring, but then not all men wear them.

'I can't believe Pete wears a wedding ring,' Jamie had said, laughing as they clambered into a taxi after leaving a supper at Jane's last year – the last supper they'd been to as a couple. 'How pussy-whipped is he?'

Amy hated that expression, and had asked Jamie before not to use it.

'Why wouldn't he?' replied Amy, feeling her toes curl.

'Women wear rings. Real men wear Rolexes.' He raised

his eyebrows and lowered his chin in the look that said, 'You're so silly'. Amy had a love-hate relationship with that look. It was so arrogant. Why did she find it so sexy?

'Real men shouldn't be worried about whether they look like real men,' she replied, gazing out of the taxi window at the raindrops racing across the glass. 'They should wear what they like. I just think if women wear wedding rings, it makes no sense for men not to.'

'Since when did you become such a little feminist?' he said. 'Is pocket-rocket Piglet on a mission to smash the patriarchy?'

'No.' She was getting goosebumps. She couldn't tell if it was because he was making her skin crawl or because he was kissing her neck. 'Piglet's on a mission to prove that you're a sexist pig.'

Then he'd oinked into her ear, making her laugh and ending the conversation.

How could she have let a comment like that pass? When did she become so sloppy with her standards? What had happened to her? Twenties Amy would have stopped the cab, hopped out and skipped off, confidently telling him never to call her again. What happened was that she hit thirty and found The Fear. The fear of not finding The One. And if she didn't want to die alone, she'd have to accept unacceptable behaviour.

The printer hums into action and breaks her train of thought. Dr Hicks returns to his seat with a single sheet of A4 paper and three questions on it.

Amy Wright, Day Four,
Session One: homework

1. When did Jamie make you feel happy in your relationship?
2. When did Jamie make you feel *un*happy in your relationship?
3. Name what you need to feel happy in a relationship.

Amy reads the list of questions, as Dr Hicks hands her a pen.

'We'll discuss your responses next week.' He takes a seat and starts clicking on the iPad again. 'Goodbye, Amy. Good luck with the baby.'

'Thanks,' she says, as she stands up and all the tissue bits scatter across the floor.

Ten

'YOU CAN HAVE HIM BACK NOW!' shouts Jackie from behind fake-baby Ben's moon head, with his glassy eyes and a mouth that's covered in crust.

'Where's yours?' asks Amy, amused, grabbing him and holding him at arm's length.

He stinks.

'Under a blanket where she can't be seen, heard or smelt!' Jackie tuts, walking away. 'Why the fuck you'd ever want a baby in real life is beyond me! Do you hear me, Aaron? Why would you want to live this fucking nightmare?'

Jackie slumps onto the sofa and lets out a big sigh.

'Don't tell me you want one of these?' she asks Amy.

'I do. One day. I'm an only child, so I always thought that having a family would be fun.'

'Ah.' Jackie raises her hand for a high five. 'I'm in the Only Child Club, too. Did Jamie ever use it against you? Aaron always said I had "only child syndrome". Which meant I was selfish and spoilt. Apparently, I don't care about anyone else except me and my dad.'

'Jamie used to tell me I had only child syndrome because I was needy, which wasn't true at all. I think he just wanted something to use against me. Did your parents spoil you? I feel like mine did, a bit.'

'Parent. It was just me and Dad growing up. Mum left when I was a baby. He didn't have much to spoil me with, but I suppose we were very close. Didn't let many people in. That's what bothered Aaron.' She looks down at her lap. Amy sees her swallow. 'I hope Dad's going to be OK with me in here. I see him every day, you know, now that he's getting on. I shouldn't be here. God, maybe I am Selfish Jackie.'

She inhales deeply and exhales hard. 'I just hope staying was the right decision for us. Me and Dad, I mean. Not Aaron. Cold-hearted bastard doesn't know the meaning of family – he can fuck right off.'

'Why did you decide to stay?' asks Amy gently.

'I think I just needed an escape from reality for a while. And the truth is, we need the money. This show might be about helping me find a long-term relationship, but I couldn't give a shit about letting another man into my life right now. Our lives, I suppose. I have to include Dad. We've been really struggling. I lost my job last year, which meant I couldn't help Dad out as much as I used to. I want to win this for him. Give him a better life. Pay him back for everything he gave up for me. I just don't know how

I'm going to pretend to be "a keeper" when I'm the oppo-site. I was thinking I could get some publicity out of it afterwards, even if I don't win. Sorry, probably a bit too much information. And Aaron thought I was good at keeping secrets. The arsehole doesn't know me at all.'

'Well, if your dad has a TV at least he can watch you every day. I'm sure he's really excited for you.' Amy smiles, giving her a side hug.

'He sounded excited. Well, more like confused, actually. I called him before I came on to make sure he was going to be OK. Didn't have a clue what I was on about, but I told him what channel to watch and at what time. We're a tight unit, me and Papa. I'd never let anyone or anything get between us.'

*

The next night, Ben won't go to sleep. Again, the little shit. He has kept her up for three nights running now. It's 1 a.m. and Amy has been pacing back and forth with him for over two hours. Everyone else went to bed long ago, and she feels deranged with tiredness.

Surely real babies can't cry for this long, this loudly? She considers entering the Chat Room to report that Ben has a glitch. How do actual parents do this with actual kids? She thinks of Jane and the twins and feels guilty that she ever felt Jane was milking it with the 'it's hard being a mum' thing. And Jane has twice the torture. Amy can't do this. She'll never be able to do this. She's struggling with just one, and he isn't even real.

'How are you doing?' a voice whisper-shouts from the bedroom door, making Amy jump.

Kathy tiptoes into the living room, checks on her angelic baby Ruth and walks over to Amy with her arms outstretched, offering to take Ben.

'Ugh, thanks – my arms are killing me,' she says as she rubs them and sits down. She takes a sip of her tea and spits it back into the mug when she realises it's ice-cold. She can't even have a cup of tea. 'How the hell did you do this, Kathy?' she asks.

'If anyone tells you that parenting is all giggles and sunshine, they're fibbing. It's the toughest job I ever had. Although I suppose that isn't saying much because it's the *only* job I ever really had.'

Ben's wailing is turning into a soft whimper and it sounds like he's settling down.

'Well, I obviously don't have the touch.' Amy sighs. She feels useless.

'Don't worry, they're just testing you.' She throws her eyes to the ceiling cameras. 'They don't need to test me, I've done this before. This challenge is all a bit wasted on a woman of my age.'

'Maybe you're here to show us what to do. Although I have no idea what you've just done to get him like that.'

Ben has stopped crying completely and is now breathing heavily, deeply asleep.

'I love being a mum, but it wasn't my dream. I wanted to be a nurse. Then Jeremy came along and our first kid happened. Then our second soon after that.' She sighs, carefully lowering Ben into his cot. 'What makes me angry is that I somehow knew we'd end up divorced. I just had this funny feeling. He never thanked people who gave way for him. In the car. He always thought he was better than everyone else and could buy his way around. You know the type?'

Amy knows exactly the type. One of her biggest bugbears about Jamie was how he never made way for people. When he walked down the street, he would always walk in a direct line, making everyone move out of his way. No apology, never 'excuse me'. Amy would dart around to help people get past and he'd just carry on walking. They'd often end up walking separately, with him striding ahead. Once, she stopped to see how long it would take him to notice she wasn't there. He got so far that he couldn't see her anymore, then sent her a text telling her to hurry up.

Their conversation has given Amy a good blog idea. 99 Red Flags, a site where women can submit their personal warning signs to watch out for.

'Anyway,' Kathy continues, 'I met Jeremy just after I qualified as a nurse. It was all very whirlwind. Engaged after six months, married after a year, pregnant after a year and a half. His car dealership was going well and we decided I didn't need to work. That it would be better for the family if I stayed at home and looked after things there.'

'Well, that works for some families,' Amy adds, thinking how boring she'd find it.

'I didn't know what I was doing, I wasn't old enough to make that choice. My parents thought it was a good idea too, but they were a different generation. We were happy for a long time, and I forgot about being a nurse. We were comfortable. I felt secure and I loved being able to spend so much time with my kids. They needed me, and that felt good. Of course, when they became teenagers, they didn't need me so much anymore. And neither did Jeremy. He'd opened new branches across the country and was away most of the time. It was like I'd reached early retirement. It seemed too late to start a career. I just ended up floating around the house with nothing to do and no one to look after. We had a huge fight once about him being away so much. He told me I'd become needy and boring. That I was no use to anyone anymore, and I might as well be put on an iceberg and floated out to sea.'

Amy has to stop herself from laughing in shock about how outrageous that sounds. How could Kathy have stayed after that?

But then again, how could Amy have stayed after Jamie told her *she* was boring? It happened to her, too. And she stayed.

'There were a million other warning signs, but I just ignored them. I had no money and no real experience. Besides, he wasn't always bad. When he came home the next day there were flowers and chocolates. We went out for supper and he told me I looked nice, which was the first compliment he'd given me in years. He did seem sorry for what he said. So I just carried on, hoping that when he retired we might be able to pick up where we left off in our twenties. Then about eighteen months ago, the insults continued but the apologies stopped. Next I started smelling a perfume that wasn't mine. Then I found a hairband in our car that didn't belong to me or our daughter. And then three months ago he told me our marriage was over, that he'd met someone else who suited him more. That he was happy. And that he wanted me to start making plans to move out. After thirty years. I knew it was the end, I just didn't know where to start.'

Amy wonders what she would have done in the same situation. She'd like to think she would have risen to the occasion, thrown Jamie out, got an expensive makeover and met a handsome billionaire. But the movies aren't real. She'd probably have moved in with her parents and spent the next three months stalking his new girlfriend on Facebook.

'Did you take a baseball bat to his car, Beyoncé-style?'

'Surprisingly, I reacted quite calmly. I'd known about the affair, so I was waiting for him to come clean. Just looking at him made me feel sick. But I also didn't want to move, because I had nowhere to go. So I refused to give him the divorce and he couldn't evict me because the house was in both our names. I know it sounds spiteful, but I did enjoy seeing his face boiling with rage when I carried on as if everything was normal and the conversation had never happened. As if there wasn't a new woman suddenly living in my house, sleeping in the spare room above the garage that Jeremy had been sleeping in for over a year. And then, this show happened. Can you believe, he told me he wanted to have a family lunch with the kids? It was for my birthday, the bastard. Anyway, I'm actually delighted to be here. This is the most exciting thing that's ever happened to me, and the only chance I'll have to get my hands on a million pounds. But it's not just that. I want to prove I can do this on my own, and that I can be somebody without them.'

'Well, I think it's amazing that you're being so calm about it all. When Jamie dumped me on here I was a complete mess.'

Amy has a flashback to weeping and screaming in the Chat Room in front of everyone.

'I wouldn't worry about it. Others would be the same. Amy, you have your whole life ahead of you. At least you didn't waste any more time with your ex. Otherwise you'd have ended up like me.'

'Doesn't look too bad,' says Amy.

'Well, I did get two beautiful brats out of it. They don't even seem to care that it's over, they're too busy spending their salaries at bars.' Kathy moves towards the bedroom. 'But I do love them really.'

Ben starts whimpering as Kathy leaves and Amy puts her head under a pillow, praying for him to shut up. Kathy's right. At least she only wasted two years of her life – not one second more. She wouldn't put it past Jamie to upgrade to a younger model in ten years' time. He always wants people to think he has the best. Maybe that's what this is all about. Maybe he's met someone else. If she had her phone she could hunt for clues. She hates him right now, but the thought of him being all over someone else still makes her feel sick.

Eleven

Amy's wiping vomit off the kitchen floor for the third time that morning. The yellow goo has also spilt onto her flip-flop and oozed its way in between her toes. If it were real, she'd be sick herself. She's baffled by how the producers have created these anatomically functioning moulds of plastic. The fake formula the housemates feed them comes out one of two ways, and Amy has become a reluctant master at cleaning up both.

Some of the housemates aren't adjusting to mock mother-hood as well as others. Earlier that morning, Amy saw Jackie hosing down Alice's bottom with a garden hosepipe, holding her by the top of her head. Gemma has been using Bel as an arm weight. 'She's a dumb-Bel, get it?' she'd cackled, before continuing with her bicep reps, kissing the baby on the forehead with every lift. 'This would make the best Instagram story, wouldn't it?' she'd added, before putting Bel down on the sofa and slumping next to her with a big sigh. 'God, I can't believe we've been here for almost a week already. I am missing out on so many stories right now. I'll never get to see them, either. And I'll have, like, the biggest backlog of comments, too.'

The others are handling it a little better. For Kathy the challenge is second nature. She soothes, feeds and puts Ruth to sleep without so much as a sigh, scream or an entire bottle of Sauvignon blanc. Hattie is a total helicopter parent and has her baby Sophie attached to her hip twenty-four hours a day. It landed her in trouble on The Wall when the public accused her of suffocating the doll in the middle of the night. Tears and apologies followed.

To Amy's surprise, Lauren seems to have the magic touch, despite coming across as the least maternal of them all. Seb is by far the calmest baby in the house.

When Amy asked her if she was lacing her formula with whisky, she'd just shrugged. 'I suppose when you're a DJ, you just get used to being tired. And I remember my sister telling me that having a baby is all about sticking to a routine. So I just do the same thing over and over and over again. It's fookin' boring, but it seems to work.'

When Ben isn't crying, he's vomiting. And when he isn't vomiting, he's crying. When Amy complains about it out loud, there are some very helpful suggestions from the public.

@allyal1984 Two words Amy – duct tape! :)))) #theshelf #badparenting

@lovaboyv247 Have you tried breastfeeding? Get your
boobs out! #theshelf #funbags

'God, men are gross,' says Gemma as she lunges past the
screen, holding Bel at chest height.

'Ed Sheeran seems nice,' says Amy, as she puts Ben down
to go to the loo.

'And Benetton Cumbercross!' shouts Hattie from down
the corridor. Amy starts to correct her, then stops. It's close
enough.

When Amy returns to the sofa, she finds Ben crying on
the floor. She scoops him up and looks nervously at The
Wall. Of course, her blunder hasn't gone unnoticed.

@samirmu200 Ha! Amy's an idiot. Wouldn't let her look
after my pet goldfish! #theshelf
@erina Everyone knows you can't leave a baby alone!
EVER! Thought she'd be better at this . . . #theshelf

'I was gone for a second! God, how are mums supposed
to wee? I don't want to hold him while I do it, it's just
weird.'

She takes Ben into the bedroom for his mid-morning
sleep. It's become one of her favourite times of day in this
human zoo, along with his afternoon sleep and his night
sleep. She's beginning to realise that she'll never be a Hattie,
playing peek-a-boo with Sophie for two hours non-stop.
Or a Lauren, doing the same thing on repeat every day. Or

a Kathy, devoting her entire life to two children who'll end up leaving anyway.

Maybe motherhood isn't all it's cracked up to be.

Maybe everyone is pretending.

At least Amy's got off lightly with her bathroom blunder. Jackie's copping an earful for how she's been handling Alice.

> **@frenchiefanatic_2** She's not a pair of trainers you fuckwit! #jackie #theshelf
>
> **@candykan90** Child abuser! Take that baby to social services! #jackie #theshelf

'Who's moderating these?' Amy says, loudly, so that she can pretend not to hear Ben wailing from the bedroom as she comes back in. 'Comments like this could send someone over the edge.'

'Real TV don't give a shit, Amy,' responds Jackie, throwing Alice up and down in the air like a ball. 'All they care about is ratings. If someone does go over the edge, that's a bonus.'

'Sickos,' says Lauren, rocking Seb on her knees.

'Amy! Ben needs something!' screams Hattie from the bedroom.

'Uuuggghhh,' Amy groans into her lap.

'You OK?' Gemma asks. 'Want me to go?'

'No, it's fine, I'm just so tired.' She rubs her red, itchy eyes. 'Am I the only one here who hates their baby?'

'Bel's a right bellend.' Gemma smiles, pleased with herself. 'I came up with that earlier. Just think of the money, Ames.'

125

When Amy gets to Ben, he's lying in another pile of puke. She'll be glad to see the back of this smelly little plastic prat when the motherhood challenge is over.

As she walks through the living room with Ben on her hip, a thread on The Wall grabs her attention.

@tonytalks65 Amy needs to man up and grow a pair! #lol #theshelf

'Ugh, that's exactly the kind of idiot comment Jason would make,' says Gemma, lunging. 'Bet he would have run for the hills if I'd dumped him on here. It takes guts to stay.'

@smashthepat She has a pair already **@tonytalks65**. They're called boobs. You're not funny #sexismisneverfunny #theshelf

@tonytalks65 Oh boy, here we go. Why can't women laugh at themselves? Go on, give us a smile **@smashthepat** #feministscanttakejokes #theshelf

@smashthepat We'll laugh when you say something funny. Warning: it has to be intelligent. Something you might struggle with **@tonytalks65** #theshelf

@tonytalks65 What's wrong, **@smashthepat**, a bad bout of PMS? Or just Mad Cow Disease? #funny #haha #theshelf

'Oh shut up, you tosser,' Gemma mutters.

Twelve

'There's a circle of yoga mats in the garden,' says Hattie, staring out through the glass and sipping on a tea, later that day. The others join her at the garden door with their babies in one hand and their mugs in the other.

'Yoga makes me fart,' comments Lauren. 'My apologies in advance, lads.'

Gemma laughs, giving her a side hug. 'I fucking love you.'

Doooong.

Jackie jumps back from the window, dropping Alice on the floor.

'Shit!' she says, bending over to pick her up and simultaneously spilling hot coffee over her scalp. 'Shit shit shit!' she stammers, rubbing the doll's head with her sleeve. Alice starts crying.

'Is that the front doorbell?' asks Kathy.

Doooong.

'Coming!' shouts Hattie, making a move towards the door.

'I can take her, Hatster,' Jackie says, putting her mug down on the side table and grabbing her baby Sophie's arm, which promptly pops out of its socket. Hattie shrieks and looks horrified.

'Oh my God, sorry, little mate.' Jackie laughs, throwing Alice towards the sofa behind her and ignoring her wail as she flies through the air. 'I'm rubbish at this, aren't I? Maternal instincts, my arse.' She sticks her tongue out as she reattaches the limb the wrong way round and creates a zombie Sophie with a dislocated arm, a near-detached head and a low moan.

Doooong.

'Hello? Anyone home?' a muffled voice shouts through the door.

Doooong. Doooong. Doooong.

Hattie reluctantly leaves Zombie Sophie with Jackie and hurries to the front door, while the others gather expectantly in the living room. They hear the front door open, followed by a loud chorus of greetings in a familiar voice.

'Is that . . . Hugo Jones?' whispers Amy.

'Sounds like him,' says Gemma, rolling her eyes and throwing herself onto the sofa with Bel on her lap. 'He's such a knob,' she sighs. 'I met him at an influencer conference last year. He tried to explain to me how I could grow my following by targeting. Like I didn't know that already. How else did I get to twenty thousand followers? Patronising moron.'

'Is he the "drop calm" bloke?' asks Lauren.

Celebrity mindfulness coach Hugo Jones – or HuJo – became famous by sparking *#dropcalm*, a movement that went viral last year. The idea is to stop whatever you're doing and, wherever you are, meditate for one minute and then post it on Instagram. HuJo amassed a huge fanbase, with people everywhere sitting cross-legged in newsagents, on train platforms and – most irritatingly – in tube carriages at peak rush hour. One woman even made the headlines by drop-calming at a funeral, with her family weeping in the background. He's since scored a weekly meditation show on morning TV and a daily *Metro* column. And when he isn't posing shirtless on his rooftop terrace overlooking Primrose Hill, he's being papped with pop stars on beaches in LA.

Amy's too embarrassed to admit she follows him, even though she only does it passively. *Not now, HuJo,* she thinks, every time she scrolls past a post asking her to 'find a meditation minute'.

Hattie runs back to the living room, puffing.

'It's . . . it's . . .' She bends over and rests her hands on her knees, breathing hard.

HuJo glides into the living room behind her with a yoga mat under his arm.

'HuJo!' he finishes her sentence. '*Namaste,* ladies.' He softens his voice. 'How are we all this afternoon? Feeling blessed?' He holds his palms together and takes a bow, his topknot bouncing forward and hitting him on the forehead. It reminds Amy of a ball sack.

129

He's greeted by a mixture of unenthusiastic hellos.

'Oh dear, girls, are we not feeling grateful for today?' He looks around. 'What are all these frowns?'

'I am,' says Hattie, smiling. She's standing next to him and looking star-struck.

'That's the spirit, Hattie. Now, everyone, follow me. I'm here to make happy happen!'

A second later, all the babies fall silent and switch off at once.

'God, you are fookin' creepy,' says Lauren, putting Seb into his cot.

The housemates take their seats on the yoga mats outside and HuJo removes his shirt. Being naked from the waist up for a mindfulness session seems unnecessary.

'First of all, ladies' – HuJo arches his back, stretches his arms and flexes his six-pack – 'thank you for being here with me today.' He shuts his eyes and inhales through his nose.

'Do we have a choice?' mutters Gemma.

HuJo opens his eyes.

'Choices are exactly why I'm here. Do you want to know one of life's biggest truths? We can't always choose what happens to us, but we can always choose how we react. Today I'm going to teach you, girls, how to stop overre-acting. I call it *Keep Calm*.'

He looks around at the group, expecting a response. He's disappointed.

'Now, when I say keep calm, what do you think I mean?' he continues.

'Ooh, I know! Keep Calm and Carry On!' shouts Hattie, excitedly. 'My mum got me the mug for Christmas!'

'My mug says: Stay Angry and Smash Balls,' replies Lauren.

He ignores the sniggers.

'I'm jokin'. It's actually a flag above my bed.'

Still nothing.

'What I mean by calm is C-A-L-M,' he spells out the letters. 'C is for Consider your reaction. A is for Answer with a smile. L is for Let it go. And M is for Make it better. Being C-A-L-M is the key to responding with the right level of emotion in every situation. Especially in relationships. It's about disciplining your minds, ladies, regulating your moods and controlling your natural urges to lose your rag.'

'Every situation?' says Jackie, looking cynical.

'Every situation,' he repeats. He stands up and walks around like he's circling his prey. When he reaches Jackie, he leans over and starts to rub her shoulders. Jackie instantly squirms away and spins around, with virtual laser beams shooting out of her eyes.

'I'm sorry, Jackie, you just seem on edge. Maybe motherhood is making you tense. I was just trying to relax you. Apologies, I should have warned you.' He crouches down next to her, uncomfortably close.

'It's not about warning me, mate – it's about asking me. And the answer is always going to be no.' She carries on glaring at him as she shuffles away.

HuJo nods his head, straightens up and returns to his mat.

'Well, that response brings me nicely on to what I was about to say. I've created C-A-L-M especially for women. Women are wired differently. You respond with your hearts, not your heads. You're emotional. You find it easy to feel hurt, stress, anger, upset and jealousy. You find it easy to . . . overreact.'

'So, we should be doormats?' Jackie interrupts. 'Is that what you're saying?'

HuJo closes his eyes, breathes in for a few seconds and exhales loudly through his nose.

'Many women have thanked me for saving their relationships. Will you give me a chance to save yours, Jackie?'

Hattie shoots her arm up. 'Are you keeping C-A-L-M right now?' she says, leaning forward.

'Yes, Hattie, I am. Do you see? If I had overreacted and shouted at Jackie, I would have made the situation much worse.'

Jackie tuts and folds her arms.

'Now, girls, today I'm going to ask you to recount personal situations where a partner has made you feel upset, and you responded emotionally. Then, we'll discuss whether this was an overreaction, an under-reaction or a just-right reaction. Close your eyes, clear your mind, breathe and reflect.'

Amy closes her eyes and thinks about everything Jamie used to do that upset her. How he stared at other women,

132

making a joke of it instead of trying to hide it. How he made time for the gym, but not for her family. How he stopped inviting her to the pub with his friends. How his eyes would follow her fingers if she reached for a biscuit, then get annoyed if she got upset and say he was just teasing. How he'd ask what Funsponge Amy had done with Fun Amy. It's like a Netflix menu – too many choices and impossible to pick one.

'Shall we start with you, Hattie? Tell us about a time when you felt upset with a boyfriend.'

Hattie's cheeks turn pink as she glances around the group.

'Well, Dylan cut up all my fitted clothes a few months ago. He told me I was too big to wear anything tight and he didn't want people staring at me. He said it was for my own good, but they were some of my favourite clothes. They were memories. He even threw out the dress I wore to our school leavers' dance.'

The group gasp.

'What a control freak, Hattie,' mutters Gemma. 'I would have cut off his knob.'

'And obviously, Gemma, that would have been an over-reaction. How did you react, Hattie?' HuJo asks.

'I locked myself in the bathroom, made a bed in the tub and cried myself to sleep. We only have one bedroom. I crept out of the house in the morning, went to Mum and Dad's for three days and didn't reply to any of his text messages begging me to come back. When I did go back, we just carried on as if nothing had happened.'

133

'So, that's also an overreaction. Now, what Dylan did was wrong. But your response was wrong, too. You threw a tantrum and then you sulked. It was childish.' HuJo spreads his palms on the mat. 'You wouldn't be able to do that if you had a real baby, now would you?'

'But when I try to argue with him, he gets so angry,' Hattie replies. 'It's scary. He screamed so loudly once, the neighbours came round to check on us. He won't let me talk, he won't ever listen. My voice isn't loud enough. I'm not tough enough. So, I give up.'

'Well, then, my advice is don't respond immediately. Wait until he's cooled down, go into the kitchen, make yourselves some tea, let it pass. That would have been the C-A-L-M reaction, not storming off in a sulk.'

'I didn't storm off, I went and hid quietly. He was the one who ranted downstairs for an hour.'

HuJo pretends not to hear her and turns to Lauren, who's been picking at the grass, sighing and looking bored.

'Lauren. How about we move on to you next?'

'Oh God,' she says, leaning back on her hands. 'My ex went mad when he found out how many people I'd slept with. He told me he couldn't date a woman who'd slept with more people than him. He said real ladies don't open their legs for anyone, and that I wasn't marriage or mother material.'

Another gasp from the group.

'And now you're all wonderin' how many people I've slept with, aren't you?' Lauren laughs.

The group snigger.

Amy wishes she could be more like Lauren. She's unapologetically herself and doesn't seem to give a shit about what people think of her.

'And how did you react?' asks HuJo.

'I told him he had a small willy and that was probably the reason he'd only slept with two women. And that he wasn't husband material because he's a boring shag. And just a reminder – and a warning – his name is DAVID DICKSON and he works in IT,' she calls out to the camera and joke-winks. 'I've got your back, ladies.'

'Are you proud of your reaction, Lauren?' HuJo asks, coughing and looking uneasy.

'Yeah, I am, actually.'

'Well, throwing immature insults at someone about his penis size is just as bad as storming out in a sulk like Hattie did. Why take the bait? Be the bigger person. You should have smiled, said you were sorry that your past makes you incompatible and then left with your head held high.'

'Wait, so she has to apologise, take being slut-shamed on the chin and move on?' Jackie scowls. 'That's bollocks. Lauren, I would have responded in exactly the same way. That was a completely normal reaction. Can I also just point out,' she goes on, raising her hand, 'you're teaching us how to react to situations, instead of teaching men not to be complete shitheads and cause those situations. Seems like the wrong way round, doesn't it?'

The housemates mutter in agreement and turn to HuJo, waiting for his response.

He ignores them. 'Adults talk, children throw tantrums and name-call. We're all adults, aren't we, girls?'

'We aren't robots! Being calm in those two situations is impossible!' cries Gemma. 'How can we smile when we're called fat sluts? We can't turn round and be all, "Oh, I'm sorry you feel like that, I'll just let it go and be on my way"!'

'OK, Gemma, let's move on to you,' says HuJo, less smiley than he was at the start. 'What's your situation?'

Gemma leans forward, her elbows resting on her knees.

'So, I was sitting on the sofa the other night watching telly, just minding my own business. I was on Instagram, trying to think of a caption for the selfie I took wearing this new red lipstick I got sent. Suddenly, Jason turned round and went apeshit for no reason at all. He said, "Did you not hear what I just said?" And I said, "What are you on about?" And he said, "I want a herb garden like the one on the show", and I said, "Sure, why not, let's get one". That's what I thought he wanted to hear, but he didn't speak to me until bed. Then in bed he started going on at me about how I care more about my followers than I do about my family, and that I'm addicted and how it's not good for me and it's not good for us. He told me that my mum had said something about it, too. He said that I can't be two seconds away from my screen. So, I said, it's not my fault, I have like a thousand notifications every time

I look at my screen, and how can I ignore that? I have to respond to my followers, because that's what they want and they'll stop following me if I don't reply. He told me that he's sick of being ignored, and that my friends are tired of seeing me posting instead of being present. And then I said, well, maybe they're just jealous because I've got twenty thousand followers. Then he said, they don't give a shit about that, they're just sick of talking to someone who just looks at her screen the whole time. So I said, well, are you sick of all the free shit we get, like that Peloton bike? And then he turned over, muttering that if I uploaded the red lippie selfie, then it's obvious I don't care about his feelings or our relationship. I did feel bad, but this is my job. What was I supposed to do?'

The group tries to process the 'he said, she said' saga.

Kathy breaks the silence. 'So, did you post it?'

'Yeah, I had to, I was being paid, wasn't I? I captioned that red lippie gets me in the mood for some red-hot lovin'. Then in the middle of the night we made up.' She laughs and joke-winks.

'So you weren't prepared to compromise at all on what you were doing, despite the fact that it was upsetting him?' HuJo asks. 'Is that a lesson you'd like to teach little Bel when she's older?'

'Look, I know I spend a lot of time on my phone,' Gemma continues. 'But I have to – it's what pays the bills. I'd never tell him not to go into work every day. And my job isn't exactly a nine-to-five, is it? Instagram doesn't work like that. He can come crying to me when he stops enjoying his free trainers.'

Amy sees both sides of their argument, to be fair. Jamie had been spending much more time on his phone recently. It wasn't just leaving it face up on the table at dinner – it was during sex, too. He never used to do that. 'Just in case so-and-so calls,' he'd say. 'I need to show I'm always available.' But why would so-and-so call at 9 p.m. on a Sunday?

When HuJo lands on Amy, she talks about the time Jamie accepted an invite to one of Jane's dinner parties and then at the last minute refused to go, saying that he had work to do. Amy had to go alone, again, surrounded by couples, and then cover for him, again. When she called him on her way back, he didn't pick up. She tried a second time, still nothing. And then he called her, drunk, from a nightclub at 1 a.m. She didn't say a word on the phone as he told her he was networking, and then sent him a single message telling him he was selfish. He didn't reply. Ever. And when there was still no reply the next evening, despite two blue ticks, she began to get worried he'd fallen into a ditch or been stabbed. So she called him, and he picked up like nothing had happened. All he mumbled on about was how ill he was.

'Then somehow he managed to charm me into bringing him a Whole Foods takeaway, a Pret green juice and some paracetamol. I'm such a sucker. And we never talked about the text I sent.'

'OK, so that's like a major under-reaction, isn't it?' says

Gemma. 'I'd have stormed over first thing in the morning and made his headache much worse.' Gemma turns to HuJo, who's keeping quiet.

'Well, I just thought that would make me look needy,' Amy replies. 'I didn't want him to think I cared that much.'

'And that's what keeping C-A-L-M is all about. I think your reaction was suitable for the circumstances you describe. You made your feelings known with the text message and you let it go. And you even did something nice for him the next day, which makes you the bigger person.'

'Or the doormat!' says Jackie. 'No offence, love. But your reaction gave him an open invitation to do it again and again.'

'Jamie should have thanked his lucky stars to have a girlfriend like you, and not me,' adds Gemma.

'Amy, how long did you stay together after that?' HuJo asks.

'Eighteen months.'

'Exactly.'

Jackie mouths *what the actual fuck?* to the rest of the group.

At the end of the session, which seems to reach no agreed conclusions, HuJo distributes some C-A-L-M bracelets around the circle.

'Remember, girls, if you find yourself in a situation where you're feeling emotional, just glance down at your bracelets and remember not to overreact.' He looks at them. 'And don't forget – we're watching you. Maybe the calmer you are, the more points you could win on the show.'

No one responds. No one puts their bracelet on. And after a few proseccos that night, to celebrate being back to a baby-free house, the mantra is rewritten by a hiccuping Jackie.

Consider your wants.
Answer to nobody.
Love yourself.
Meet your needs before others'.

*

The housemates are having an early supper of chicken, green salad with no dressing and a side of cauliflower rice. 'It's Keto!' Gemma explains as she presents her speciality dish at the dining room table.

'Is it me,' Jackie whispers to Amy, out of everyone's earshot, 'or does this cauliflower rice taste like the inside of a shoe?' They laugh, then hush as Gemma comes back, looking delighted with her efforts.

'Does anyone else miss the babies?' Hattie asks.

'NO,' the rest of them chorus in reply.

Doooong.

The women look at each other, frowning.

'Fingers crossed for pizza delivery!' Jackie shouts, as she gets up and walks towards the corridor.

140

'Oi!' shouts Gemma.

Jackie laughs as she throws open the door, the other contestants watching from the dining room table.

A petite woman with glossy blonde hair tumbling over her shoulders steps into the corridor and stretches out her arm.

'Hello, Jackie. I'm Flick. Contestant number seven.'

WEEK TWO

Thirteen

Felicity Brimble, Flick for short, has glowing skin, shiny blonde blow-dried hair, sparkling eyes and a waist the size of Amy's left thigh. It's only 8.30 a.m. and she looks like a perfectly manicured miniature supermodel in a long-sleeved little black dress and nude heels, with a touch of blusher, a suggestion of mascara and a dab of lip gloss.

Flick's arrival last night was strangely uneventful. It felt like she was delighted to be here. There was no drama, no tears. She briefly introduced herself, unpacked her immaculately folded clothes, showered and went to bed wearing a face mask. While the housemates agreed it was odd, they all felt relieved. They were finally baby-free and looking forward to savouring an early night of uninterrupted sleep.

This morning, Flick trots across the living room and lowers herself at a sideways angle onto the sofa, crossing her legs tightly. Amy notices she doesn't have a single patch of cellulite, and subtly moves a pillow over her own thighs.

'I can't believe I've missed out on over a whole week here!' Flick says, swishing her hair over her shoulders and smiling to reveal celebrity-white teeth.

'Uh-huh.' Jackie laughs as she leans over the back of the sofa. 'You do realise you're on *The Shelf*, right? The world's worst TV show? I'd say it's a blessing you missed the first week.'

'What? I love it!' Flick smiles. 'I've been watching you girls all day, every day since it started.'

'I can't believe you're thirty-four,' says Kathy. 'You don't look a day over twenty-one!'

Flick blushes a soft peach colour. 'Gosh, I don't think so, Kathy, but thank you.'

'Do you do your own make-up, babes?' Gemma asks, leaning in to her face. 'How do you get your eyebrows so neat? What's your trick?'

'Hours of practice, lovely. I'm a bit of a perfectionist,' Flick whispers back, like she's pretending to think it's a flaw.

Amy is finding it hard not to stare at her. She's slightly star-struck, but she's also suspicious. Flick was dumped less than twelve hours ago. In public. Where's the crimson face and snotty tears? So far, the only thing to spring from Flick's eyes is a look of shock when Lauren burped loudly in the kitchen earlier.

'Did you take the week off work or something?' Amy asks.

'No, I work from home, so you've all been keeping me company in the background. You know, Amy, you really shouldn't bite your nails.' She laughs and wags her finger.

Amy titters back so Flick doesn't feel awkward.

'So, Flick, what do you do from home?' Kathy asks.

'Let's see,' she says, playing with her hair. 'I'm a cook, cleaner, gardener, PA, interior designer, bookkeeper, nurse, therapist, driver.' She looks around the group. 'I'm a stay-at-home mum. Of sorts.'

'With all those jobs you must make a fortune,' Jackie shouts, walking towards the kitchen.

'I was a stay-at-home mum of two.' Kathy laughs. 'For all my sins!'

'For all your sins?' Flick turns to her, looking worried.

Kathy is taken aback. 'Not really. Sorry, I was only joking.'

'How old are your kids?' Amy asks, changing the subject to remove the tension.

'Well . . .' She looks at the floor. 'That's why I said *of sorts*. I don't actually have any kids. Yet. I'm working on it!' She smiles.

'Mimosa, anyone?' says Jackie, coming back with a tray of prosecco and a carton of orange juice.

'Just the juice for me, thanks,' Flick says.

The housemates pause and look at each other, surprised.

'You're gonna need to drink on here, my love.' Jackie shakes her head. 'It's the only way to get through it.' She throws back one of the flutes and replaces the prosecco with juice.

'I'll be fine,' Flick replies. 'I'm not a big drinker.'

'So, Flick,' Lauren says, reaching for a flute, 'tell us about the twat who put you here.'

'Oh no, he's not like that. Actually, I'm still in a relationship. His name's Simon, and we've been together for about four years. We met at my old practice. I'm a paediatrician. Was a paediatrician. I don't practise anymore. I saw the ad for the show in *LAD* and decided to apply for myself. I want to get some pointers for the areas where I'm lacking.'

Kathy looks around at the others, who also seem confused. 'Isn't the whole idea that we're dumped here?'

'That's what they said when I first applied,' Flick replies. 'But then they called me back a few days ago out of the blue. They told me they'd changed their minds and that it would be fun to throw in a curveball, one week into the show. So here I am. A curveball!'

'Why were you reading *LAD*?' asks Gemma, her nose wrinkling.

'I read it all the time. It helps me figure out what men want. I read the other day that men hate it when women wear too much make-up.' Her eyes linger on Gemma's pink lips and painted eyebrows.

'Yeah, I think I'll stick to *Cosmo*,' says Gemma.

'Flick.' Jackie leans in, looking worried. 'You do realise how evil this show is, don't you? You do realise it's run by a bunch of men who want to brainwash us into thinking we need to better ourselves?'

Flick stares at her for a few seconds, then smiles. 'Careful, Jackie, men hate it when women say they're feminists. Besides, I think we could all do with some fixing. If I was single, I'd feel really lucky to be here. *The Shelf* is going to give you all the best chance of finding – and keeping – a good man, like my Simon.'

'Not sure I want to, thanks, love,' says Jackie.

'Then why bother?' Flick asks.

'For the shits and giggles, obviously.'

'So, Flick' – Kathy turns to her – 'why did you chooe to be a stay-at-home partner?'

'I did it to save our relationship. Even though Simon and I were working together, we had long hours and worked weekends. We struggled to even share a meal. We only saw each other to say good morning and goodnight, or to mumble a professional greeting in the surgery corridor. And when we did spend time together, all we ever talked about was admin and DIY. I mean, what's the point of being in a relationship if you never spend proper quality time together?'

'Sounds like the perfect relationship to me,' Amy jokes, hoping Jamie hears her.

'Well, I hated it. With me at home, the time we have together is about us, not about what needs fixing in the house, because I've already had the time to sort it. We couldn't be happier.'

'Looks like it, what with you in here 'n all,' says Lauren.

'How come you had to stay at home, not Simon?' asks Jackie pointedly.

'Well, the surgery had been my whole life, all day and every day for over five years. I was looking forward to having a break and doing something different for a while.'

'Being a stay-at-home mum, wife or girlfriend is fine, if that's what you want,' Kathy says. 'As long as you don't put all your eggs into that one basket, believe me. And as long as Simon doesn't treat you like a round-the-clock maid.' She downs the rest of her mimosa and shakes her glass at Jackie for a top-up.

'Simon works really hard to support both of us,' Flick says defensively. 'The least I can do is offer him a home-cooked meal in a clean and comfortable house. I don't think that's too much to ask. If it makes him happy, it makes me happy.'

'Well, that's it, Flick,' Kathy replies. You work really hard to support him, too, don't you? The only difference is, you don't get paid.'

Amy feels her pulse rise. 'Flick, you just said to Jackie, "why bother?" But why are you on here, then? First you say you need some self-improvement, but then you say you two couldn't be happier. So which is it? How can you be in a such a perfect relationship if you're here, with us?'

'Seems a bit unfair to the rest of us,' Hattie adds.

'I said we couldn't be happier, I didn't say we were perfect. Relationships need constant work.' Flick shrugs her shoulders. 'Why are any of you here? If it's just for the money and fame, that's not fair either. None of you is taking this seriously, as far as I can tell. All you do is sit around hating men, trashing the tasks and refusing to admit you have flaws.'

'We all have our own reasons for staying, but we also want to show everyone how much scrutiny and pressure we get on the outside,' Amy replies, trying her best to sound as calm as Flick. 'And I'm really sorry, Flick, but you're not helping the cause. But I suppose if your goal in life is to be the perfect 1950s housewife, that's your choice.'

Amy sighs, looking around the rest of the group for some support.

'Well, that's the thing. It *is* my choice.' Flick looks down. 'And I'm happy.'

'Yes, you keep saying that.'

'So if you win,' Jackie says, 'Simon gets the million pounds?'

'No, *we* get the million pounds.'

'Well,' says Jackie, smiling at her. 'Sounds like he's got it all under control.'

Fourteen

Amy wasn't the world's best fake mum, but she wasn't the worst, either. Jackie probably took that crown when she marched into the garden and flung Alice into the pool to stop her from crying as she was trying to cook. Flick sprinted after her, but it was too late. Alice didn't cry after that. Hattie wanted to hold a funeral, but Jackie told her she was going to try cryogenics and shoved her into the freezer next to the fat-free frozen yoghurt.

No more vomit-wiping, feeding, changing, reading, singing, worrying that she's killing Ben or feeling like an idiot every time the public call her out for slipping up. Last night, without Ben, was blissful. She actually slept.

In the Oh, Baby! test, the most brutal comments have always come from real parents, who seem to spend their entire time watching and judging them. No matter what the housemates do, there's always been someone who's 'frankly disgusted' and delighted to tell them they're doing it wrong. Like the comment yesterday morning.

> **@mamofchamps** What fucking retard would put a baby on a counter while she makes a cup of tea? #amy #theshelf

'Great example to set for your kids! Hope you enjoy visiting them in prison when they're older,' Amy had shouted back.

Giving it back to @mamofchamps and now a mini-confrontation with Flick – Amy is never normally this bolshy, especially without the protection of online anonymity. Maybe Gemma, Jackie and Lauren are rubbing off on her. Whatever it is, she's getting a kick out of it.

Being sucked into the world of competitive parenting is one of the few but real fears Amy has about babies. She was once exposed to the horrors of it through one of Jane's coffee mornings, when she was duped into thinking it would be just the two of them. Having the twins there was enough of a downer, but it was made worse when they were joined by Jane's entire NCT class, who formed a loud swarm that forced everyone else to leave. The entire two hours was a shouting match of one-ups about what Roo, Delilah and Zebedee had achieved in six months of being squeaking blobs. She remembers sitting there, being ignored and wondering why they weren't more supportive of each other. You could see they were all struggling, from the exhaustion in their eyes and the fake smiles. No one wanted to admit they were finding it hard. That's not what good parents do, is it?

One of her colleagues came into the office last year with a newborn, and Amy felt obliged to go over and start cooing. Her colleague wasn't a Jane; she was honest. She told Amy that she hadn't slept in two weeks, that she was bored and terrified she'd made a huge mistake. That parenthood was a massive let-down, and to hold off for as long as possible. Then she made Amy hold the baby while she went to talk to the others for a suspiciously long time. The baby was sick on both shoulders and left Amy with two shattered eardrums.

Amy looks over at Flick, who's been staring out of the window despondently for the last few minutes.

'You all right there?' Amy asks.

'I'm OK. I'm just sad I missed out on the baby challenge. The one thing I really wanted to do. You girls were so lucky to experience that.'

'Don't worry. Who knows, on here? They might make a comeback. Like a scene from a horror movie.'

'I hope so. I'd love to see the look on Simon's face. Me with my own baby.'

The rest of the housemates join them on the sofa. Everyone looks relieved, even those who took to motherhood like ducks to water.

The screen flickers on and the opening sequence starts.

WEEEEEEEEEH, WEEEEEEEEEH!

'Good evening, Yummy Mummies! Bet you won't miss that sound, will you?' shouts Adam. He pops out from behind an audience member and runs down the aisle wearing a giant nappy, the audience in hysterics behind him.

'He really is such a fookin' tit,' mutters Lauren as Adam hops onto his chair in front of the six cots.

'What a first challenge, ladies and gents! We threw them straight into the dark depths of motherhood for four days, and for some mums, it was a piece of cake . . .'

Footage of Kathy shows her rocking Ruth to sleep to the sound of a lullaby, followed by *aaaaahhs* from the audience.

'. . . for other mums, it was no picnic!'

Cue footage of Jackie putting Alice in the freezer to the theme tune from *Psycho*.

'Here to tell us how the mums performed in their roles are celebrity paediatrician Dr Michael Macpherson and author of *Mother Nature: The Modern-Day Guide to Traditional Parenting*, Clarissa Fenton-Brown!'

The audience cheer as the two guests come on stage and peer into each cot with a mixture of adulation and disgust, before taking a seat on the stage sofa.

'So, Dr Mike and Clarissa F-B, tell us what we're desperate to know: who were the best and worst mothers you witnessed this week?'

'For the worst, it was a close call between Jackie and Gemma,' says Dr Mike through a thick white moustache. 'Women are born with maternal instincts. It's in their nature, no matter what they say.'

'Not mine, Dr Shit Moustache!' Jackie shouts at the screen.

'But I have serious doubts about some women's capabilities,' he continues. 'Jackie has to take the crown for the worst mother I've seen this week. Well, probably ever. Not only did she kill Alice and stuff her body in a freezer, but she also broke poor Sophie's arm. Very distressing indeed.' He shakes his head and his moustache vibrates.

'I have to agree with Dr Mike, Adam,' interjects Clarissa. 'Appalling behaviour. And unfortunate for Hattie, who had been doing so well up until then. She'd nailed her routine.'

Hattie beams.

'Well done, Hattie!' shouts Gemma, slapping her on the back.

Jackie laughs. 'Why can't people get that it's just a doll, for Christ's sake!'

'Come on, Jackie, this was never about them being dolls.' Flick blinks her big eyes at a bewildered Jackie and turns back to the screen, slowly sipping her warm water infused with lemon juice. 'It was much more important than that.'

'What are our thoughts on the only experienced mother in the group – Kathy? Dr Mike?'

'Ruth here is in rude health.' He chuckles. 'A perfect pulse, a radiant glow, no scratches that I can see. A beautiful bouncing baby. Well done to the mother. Top job.'

'Kathy couldn't have shown more patience and care with her baby. But I can't give her full marks. Take a look at this, Adam.' Clarissa points to the big screen.

The TV cuts to grainy footage of Kathy rocking Ruth to sleep. The camera zooms in to show Kathy wiping tears from her cheeks.

The housemates swivel their heads around to look at her,

and Kathy brushes it off, shaking her head. 'It was nothing, I was just tired. Weren't we all?'

'What do you mean, Clarrie?' Adam says, holding the microphone next to her.

'Babies are sponges, Adam. They absorb negative emotions, stress, psychological strain. Kathy shouldn't have been crying so close to the baby. Mothers – if you feel the tears coming, hide yourselves away. Motherhood is a hard job, but it's also *your* job. You accepted the role. It's the most important responsibility you will ever have. What happened to the British stiff upper lip?'

'And how did Amy take to the responsibility? Clarissa?'

'Amy is a typical new mum. Clueless, but kind. Feeding him too much, putting him to sleep too much, no routine at all. It's no wonder she was whining about being tired. Amy has the potential to be a good mum, but she needs to put a lot of legwork into learning what it takes before she does.' Clarissa looks sternly at the camera.

'Of course I'm clueless,' Amy protests. 'I've never looked after a baby in my life!'

'Ignore them, babes.' Gemma pats her on the leg. 'You did brill.'

'So that leaves me with one final question,' Adam continues. 'Who was our Mam of the Match? Our Mother of the Week?'

Dr Mike walks behind the sofa and lifts Seb out of his cot, who has a beaming face. 'I couldn't fault little Seb. He is glorious. Lauren says she hasn't done this before, so she's obviously a natural. That girl needs to find a mate and do the world a favour!'

'I'm not livestock, you old perv!' Lauren shouts at the screen.

'Interesting observation, Doctor,' says Adam. 'Clar?'

'I'm with the doctor on this one. Flawless parenting from start to finish. Lauren stuck to a routine, fed Seb the perfect amount, was there when she was needed but was sure not to mollycoddle. She's going to be a fantastic mother!'

'Well, you might think so, Claaar, but I'd rather stick a metal spoon in a live socket,' says Lauren, leaning back. 'One night babysitting a month is enough for me.'

The audience whoop as Adam tosses Seb up in the air, with Dr Mike running to catch him in the background.

'Ladies and gentlemen,' Adam screams into the mic, 'I'm delighted to announce that we have our motherhood challenge winner! It's only bloody Lauren the Legend, isn't it?'

'Well done, love! What do you think you'll win?' asks Gemma.

'A bottle of Grey Goose would be nice.' She looks up at the screen. 'And maybe a singing telegram to David telling him about my excellent mothering skills.'

'Or a giant luminous billboard outside his office,' adds Amy.

'Don't forget to mention his wee willy winky,' winks Kathy.

'Well, it would be unfair to the female population not to.'

When the prize arrives, it's hard not to laugh.

'Are they actually fookin' jokin'?' Lauren says, deadpan, as she holds up a £1,000 Mothercare voucher.

'I'll take it!' Flick cries.

*

Flick is all The Wall can talk about.

On the one side, there's fury that she's encouraging outdated gender roles.

> **@emilyg238** Another small step for man. Another giant leap backward for womankind. Thanks a lot Flick, you utter fuckwit #theshelf
>
> **@alicedecker94** I'm a woman and my place IS in the kitchen. At the table, waiting for the boyfriend to make me a sandwich #theshelf

On the other, there's support for it.

> **@oldbarrymorgan** My mam loved her kitchen! Happy childhood! Still married after 50 years! #theshelf

The *#imwithflick* hashtag is beginning to trend on Twitter, and there's talk of making T-shirts with different slogans.

> THE FUTURE IS FLICK
> I'M WITH FLICK
> BE MORE FLICK

The back-and-forth on the screen and on the sofa has left Amy feeling desperate for some alone time. She forgoes supper with the housemates and has an early shower followed by a full-on pamper. With no cameras and only the bedroom mics catching louder sounds, the bathroom feels like the only escape here.

With a cool sheet mask on her face that makes her look like a yeti, she smothers herself in body lotion and locks herself in the loo with a compact and a pair of tweezers. Her chin hairs have resurfaced, and she'd hate for them to be the next hot topic on The Wall.

In bed, she can hear the rest of the housemates continuing the discussion after supper and responding angrily to each comment. She feels bad she isn't out there defending the cause, but she's tired and she's had enough confrontation for one day.

As she drifts off, the bedroom door opens and slow footsteps cross the floor into the bathroom. She opens one eye and sees Flick crying quietly on the floor of the bathroom through the door she didn't mean to leave ajar. When Flick sees Amy in the mirror, she looks startled. She stands up, straightens her skirt and shuts the door without saying a word.

Fifteen

'Knock, knock! I thought you'd like a cup of tea,' Flick says at the bedroom door the next morning.

Amy sits up abruptly and rubs her eyes. When she opens them and blinks her way out of her sleep fog, she's embarrassed to see she's the only one still in bed. She runs her fingers through her hair and looks for a sign that Flick might want to talk about how she's feeling. Amy doesn't feel qualified to give her any advice. But perhaps she can offer a practical solution, like 'stop looking at The Wall', or just a quiet shoulder to cry on and an ear for a rant.

'I've made everyone scrambled eggs on toast. Shall I put yours in the warmer for you?' She takes hold of Amy's hand and squeezes it. It's like they didn't have that moment last night.

'Thanks, I'll come through in a minute.' Amy pulls herself up and turns around to make her bed.

'Can I show you a trick?' Flick asks.

'Sure.'

Flick trots over to her bed on the opposite side of the room and pulls out a spray bottle from a box underneath.

'Have you heard of Amanda Jackson, from *The Wife House*? This is one of her best tips.' She smiles. 'Lavender-infused water. The water helps remove creases and the lavender gives your sheets a lovely calming scent to help you sleep.'

'Why did you bring it with you?' Amy asks.

'I like to use my own cleaning products. Now watch.'

She sprays the sheets and pulls them across tightly, tucking them under the mattress and running her hand across the top to iron out the creases. Then she stops to admire her work, with a look of pure joy on her face.

'Thanks.' Amy half smiles. 'Fancy doing that every morning.'

'See, Amy? Being friends with a 1950s housewife isn't so bad after all, is it?'

After her shower, Amy finds everyone on the sofa staring at The Wall like they've been there all night. Hattie's standing with her face two inches from the screen, Jackie and Gemma are playing thumb wars on the sofa, and Kathy is trying desperately to dodge their flying fists and save her coffee. It looks like a scene from a weird dream, and Amy has to rub her eyes to remind herself that it isn't. This is the reality of her life right now. Eating breakfast with a bunch of randoms under a device that constantly reminds her of how likeable or not she is. She squints. She's still floating around the middle of The Tracker.

In the dining room, Flick is putting Amy's eggs down on the table. Then she takes a seat opposite. When Amy realises that Flick's going to watch her eat the entire meal, she wolfs it down. It's delicious, but what else would you expect from a woman who lives in a kitchen?

'Amazing, thank you.'

'Sweet corn and parsley. Simon's favourite.' She smiles.

'Lucky Simon.'

It's slowly dawning on Amy that Flick's mission in life is to look after people. She was a doctor, and now she's a mother without children. It's sweet, but suffocating.

Doooong.

'Oooooh!' cries Gemma, leaping out of a squat and running towards the front door. The housemates stand and move towards the corridor in anticipation of another new arrival.

Gemma opens the door to a chorus of excited greetings.

'HIYA!!'

'Hi, babes!'

'Oh my *God*!'

'Woo-hoo!'

A feverish troop rushes into the house, wearing make-up belts and dragging beauty cases behind them. Amy knows exactly who they are and starts grinning for the first time in ages.

'Oh my God, this is mental!' Gemma screams, jumping

up and down like an excited puppy. She runs back to the guests and starts hugging them one by one. 'I can't believe it, you're my absolute favourite!'

'Oh, hi, ladies!' says Katie Carroway, lead star and head-mistress of *Beauty School Squad*, the TV show where cosmetology students compete to give makeovers to busy mums who've 'lost their lustre'. She parts the frenzy to reveal herself to the cameras in an army-green military jacket, leather leggings and red ankle boots. Her signature silver bob shines under a matching red beret.

'Now, let's see what we have to work with here,' Katie announces as she walks around the housemates, running her eyes all over them. She stops in front of Hattie and reaches up to her temples, brushing her fingers through her hair, shaking her head in disapproval.

'Oh, no, this won't do at all. None of this will do, ladies. You all need a lot of work. But you can stop fretting, because that's why we're here. As the official glam army on *The Shelf*!'

Her students start cheering as she walks up the stairs and addresses the room.

'Ladies, ladies, ladies!' She looks around and wags her finger in all directions. 'Or should I say lazy, lazy, lazy! That's what you are. I'm sick of women giving up after the big three-oh. Beauty is a long-term investment in yourself. In your confidence. In your love life, if you want one. But it's also a commitment. When I look at you, I weep.'

Amy wants to burst out laughing when she sees Gemma

looking comically insulted, with her mouth hanging open.

'Do you know what I see?' Katie continues. 'I see women who've quit the race. I have to be cruel to be kind. I know that you're all stunning beneath that orange skin' – she looks at Gemma – 'that insane hair' – she looks at Hattie – 'and those forehead ferrets' – she turns to Amy, who frowns and strokes her eyebrows. 'I mean, big eyebrows are in, darling, but they still need some shape.'

Amy feels crushed as she lifts her fingers to her brows to search for any loose strands. She imagines Jamie laughing at her on the other side of the screen and suddenly feels hot.

Jackie folds her arms across her chest and coughs loudly. 'I think I speak for everyone when I say we're quite happy with how we look, thanks very much.'

'Um,' says Gemma, 'speak for yourself, Jacks, I want a makeover!'

'Me too,' mutters Hattie. 'My hair *is* insane.'

'I'm with you, Jacks. I don't need a makeover,' Lauren states matter-of-factly. 'This is a face for radio, anyway.'

'Jackie and Lauren,' says Katie, 'I make lots of women feel more fearless and more powerful every day. Make-up isn't supposed to *hide* your natural beauty, it's supposed to highlight it. I like to think I have the power to give any woman the spunk of a supermodel but in their own skin, and a boost of self-esteem to win those daily battles. Lauren, so your face isn't on TV. But I bet your voice sounds better when you're feeling sure of yourself. And Jackie, you were wearing red lipstick when you first arrived. Doesn't it make you feel fierce?'

Jackie shrugs her shoulders. 'A bit.'

'Of course it does!' Katie shouts. 'Ladies, there's no shame in wanting to be the best version of ourselves with a sweep of lipstick or the flick of a straightening iron. Now come on, soldiers, we've got a lot to teach you for tomorrow night.'

The group look at each other.

'What's happening tomorrow night?' says Amy on behalf of them all.

Katie waves her army into the dining room to start setting up their stations. 'Whoops, I've said too much! My lips are sealed.'

∗

Katie has assigned one student per housemate, and the women are lined up in a row on dining room chairs. In front of them are mirrors on wheels that are covered in sheets. Amy hates salon mirrors, which is the main reason she only goes to the hairdresser twice a year. They make her look like a drowned rat, and when there's nowhere else to look it's two hours of torture. Perhaps she could suggest a sheet covering at her next appointment.

'OK, ladies, we're going to start by pointing out your problem areas. Brace yourselves for brutal honesty. My students will say exactly what they think of your current look, and I'll judge them for their analysis. After that, we'll start the reset process and beautify you with all the tools we have at our disposal. Shall we begin?'

First in the firing line is Jackie. Her student is a timid-looking little redhead with a shaky voice.

'OK, Matthew. Tell me what Jackie needs,' barks Katie.

'Um, her braids have become tangled and they're starting to split, which is making them look matte instead of shiny. She needs an oil-based gloss to bring back some shine, but I need to make sure none of it lands on her skin, which is oily. She has bumps all over her T-zone, so her skin looks uneven. I'm going to apply a tea-tree-based toner and use a water-based foundation during make-up.'

'Excellent assessment!' Katie cries, patting a relieved-looking Matthew on the back.

Katie marches on to Hattie.

'Good God, Jarryd, what have we got here?'

Jarryd whispers something into Katie's ear. She bends down afterwards.

'Have you been cutting your own hair, Hattie?' asks Katie, softly.

'Yes.' She stares at her lap. 'I watched a YouTube video.'

Katie and Jarryd look at each other.

'OK, Hattie, we're going to show you what an amazing difference a professional cut makes to your confidence.' Katie smiles. 'Now, Jarryd, what else are you thinking?'

'I'm going to give Hattie a short crop cut, Michelle Williams-style, and apply a frosted chocolate gloss to help lift her natural olive complexion. Her skin is a little grey at the moment. I'm going to fix it with an iridescent gold sheet mask, and find her a yellow-based foundation serum to transform her skin from dull and glum to a dewy glow.'

'That sounds dreamy. Is that OK, Hattie?' Katie squeezes her shoulder.

Hattie nods and gives a shy smile.

Katie continues along the line, practically bypassing Flick.

'Darling, it looks like you had this done a few days ago. I'm not even sure *I* could get your hair as bouncy!' she cries, tossing the hair around in her fingers.

'I had it done professionally before I came on.' Flick smiles as she strokes it. 'And I blow-dry it every day at home.'

'You can tell. Not a strand out of place!' Katie admires her from the back. 'Oh, to have the time for a morning blow-dry. I envy you! Now, what about your face?'

'I don't like wearing too much make-up, so just as natural as possible, please. No lipstick either. Or too much blush. Men don't like kissing clowns.' Flick laughs.

'Oh.' Katie stands up. 'Maybe they'd like to kiss my arse instead?'

Flick's wide eyes follow her down the line to Amy.

Amy's been dreading what they're going to say about her chubby cheeks and bushy eyebrows.

'I can't see any major problem areas, Katie,' says her student, Rachel, looking at Katie and twisting her fingers around Amy's scalp. 'But her look is just a little . . . bland.'

'Yes, I can see she doesn't have a strong visual identity,

but there's plenty to work with. So, what's your plan?'

'I'm thinking a hair reshape with lots of layers to frame her face and streamline her apple cheeks.'

Translation: hamster cheeks.

'And natural make-up hues with browns, not pinks and oranges, to give her that effortlessly chic Parisian look. Think Audrey Hepburn in *Breakfast at Tiffany's*.'

'Wonderful, Rachel, nice work. Can't wait to see the end result.'

When Katie moves on to Lauren, she's cut off before she can start.

'Love, you can't touch anything. Especially the lid.' Lauren smiles, but with a stare that says she's not to be messed with. 'This look is pure me, and I don't need a rebrand. No matter what that lot say.' She nods to the cameras and scrapes her hair back.

'Not even the—'

'Nope.'

'Eyeli—'

'Nooo.'

'Can I just show—'

'Woah woah woah. Put that wand down and step away from my eyeball, mate.'

'Very well, then. That gives us more time for . . . Kathy!' chirps Katie, turning to the end of the line, folding her arms and shaking her head. 'Heaven knows we need it, team.'

Kathy frowns.

During her session, Rachel guides Amy through

everything she's doing. How to contour her face, shape her eyebrows without thinning them and use dabs of highlighter in the middle of her lip bow for definition. Despite the insults she delivered earlier, she's being quite sweet to her, and Amy does appreciate all the tips. She loves make-up, but her method is usually slapping it on and hoping it sticks.

Soon it's time for the big reveal, and the housemates are instructed to close their eyes while the sheets on the mirrors are pulled down.

There's a collective inhale, followed by a still calm, as each woman leans forwards to the mirror to inspect the new her.

Gemma starts gasping. 'I feel like a princess!' she says, with a waterfall of dark curls falling around her face. 'Fuck, I wish I had my phone.' She throws her arm into the air and starts pressing her palm with her thumb, pretending to take selfies for ten seconds.

'Don't sell yourself short! You're a queen!' shouts Katie, as she hugs her from behind.

Amy isn't really listening. She's completely engrossed in her own reflection. Her chins are now just a chin.

'Rachel, I love it, you're a miracle worker!' She beams, swishing her hair around.

'It's not the first time I've been told that!' Rachel responds with a grin as she runs her fingers through the back of Amy's new style. Then she crouches down to Amy's ear and whispers, 'You're my favourite. Lots of people on the outside think so, too, I promise!'

Amy leans back into her chair with a sigh of relief. She looks over at Flick, who hasn't said much since the reveal. Nor does she look that different. Her student Ollie gave her a facial and followed her instructions for how she wanted her make-up applied.

'Holy shitballs, Hattie, you look fucking *amazing*!' shouts Gemma.

The housemates all turn to look. Gemma's right. Hattie looks like a completely different person. Her eyes are bright and open, her skin looks polished and healthy, and her hair has been chopped into a sleek, slick cut.

She smiles but looks embarrassed as she strokes the back of her head.

'What do you think, everyone?' asks Kathy.

Kathy looks like she's just stepped off the cover of *Vanity Fair*. She has dramatic smoky eyes, dark brows and a nude lip. Her blonde hair is slicked back and blonder, transformed into a chic Emma Willis-style crop. She stands up, walks behind the chairs and does a twirl, while the housemates all cheer.

'Oh please, who am I kidding.' She laughs. 'I don't think a smoky eye is going to change the fact that I turned invisible when I hit fifty.'

'Rubbish!' cries Katie. 'Is Cindy Crawford invisible? Is Julianne Moore invisible? Age isn't a barrier. It's a limitation you put on your own mind.'

Kathy looks at herself in the mirror and smiles.

'Check you out, Jacks,' says Lauren.

Jackie looks like a goddess. Her braids are glossy, her skin is luminous and she's wearing the same red lipstick she wore when she entered the house.

'Yeah, I feel good. As long as we aren't competing for best in show.'

'But Jacks, I don't wear make-up to be competitive. I wear it to be confident. To be me,' replies Gemma, pouting in the mirror. 'I love this look. Mwah.'

The debate is cut short.

'Housemates. Please go to the living room.'

There's a text message on the TV, under the heading **Mystery Date No. 1.**

Gemma, fancy a pint at The Secret Garden tomorrow night? See you at 6. Don't be late. Dylan

Excited chatter fills the room when suddenly Lauren breaks the buzz.

'Hold on. Hattie's ex is called Dylan, isn't he?'

They all turn round to look at Hattie. She's staring at the screen, biting her nails.

Sixteen

'I've slept on it and I'm not doing it! No way. Sorry, not sorry,' Gemma shouts up at the camera the next morning. 'I'm not giving that complete twat any of my precious time.' Gemma falls onto the sofa next to Hattie. 'Mates before dates, babes,' she says with a fist bump.

'He isn't a complete twat,' mutters Hattie.

Gemma looks at her, surprised. 'Hat. He called you fat and cut up your clothes.'

'Well, maybe he's sorry now.'

'Gemma, please go to the Chat Room.'

'So, first they tell us to forget the ex and then they torture us by parading them under our noses,' rants Jackie from the sofa. 'Anything for good TV, right? Mystery dates, my arse.'

'I feel sorry for the housemate who ends up on a date with Jeremy. He chews with his mouth open and spits when he talks.' Kathy laughs, playing with her fringe in the reflection of the glass door. She's lost in thought for a few seconds and turns around, smiling. 'In fact, whoever dates him can pass on a message. Tell him I said thank you. Being here has brought me back from the dead. I'm no longer Kathy, your ex-wife. I'm Kathy – me. And I'm so happy that I'm seeing myself again for the first time in twenty-five years. And take out that ear piercing. It makes you look like such a prick.'

The housemates laugh.

'It really does,' says Amy.

Kathy nods her head and shudders.

'My message to Jamie would be: what the fuck was I doing with you for so long? A week ago I was so angry you'd wasted two years of my life, but now I can go wherever I like, travel whenever I want and watch all the trash on TV I fancy. And I can go to bed without having to watch you watch yourself do yoga in the mirror.'

'Hmmm . . .' Jackie pauses. 'I would say: I'm sorry you felt you came second to Dad. But I'm even sorrier I thought you'd stand with me, not against me, when shit hit the fan. But being here has opened my eyes, and now I see that I can support myself. I don't need you. I never did.'

'My message is: I never came,' Lauren whispers.

They burst out laughing as Flick enters the living room. 'What have I missed?'

'Gemma's going on a date with Hattie's ex tonight,' explains Jackie, pointing at the TV screen. 'So Gemma's going to use the opportunity to pass on a message to him in person.'

Flick stares at the screen.

'Do you think all the exes will come on the show? I just can't imagine Simon would want to. Or have the time. I'd love him to be here, of course. But I suppose he isn't my ex.'

'What's your message to him?' asks Amy.

Flick takes a seat slowly on the back of the sofa and brushes her hair off her face.

She smiles. 'I hope I'm making you proud.'

Jackie lets out a snort.

'OK, so I do have to fucking do this,' shouts Gemma as she returns from the Chat Room, 'or I'll be evicted tomorrow, no matter what the votes are. Dickheads. Hattie, I'm really sorry, babes. I wish I didn't have to.'

Hattie lifts her head. 'It's OK, Gem. I'd like you to pass on a message to Dylan.' There's a resolute look in her eye.

'Sure, babes, anything for you.'

'Tell him he'll never call me names again, or text me incessantly at work or drunkenly rant about me for hours downstairs while I'm trying to get just one hour of sleep before my next shift. I am done supporting a loser who lounges around all day doing bugger all with his life. I want more from mine. This time it's forever. I am not coming back.'

The housemates look at her with mixed expressions of pity, anger and pride.

'We're proud of you, Hats,' says Amy, squeezing her

shoulder. 'Sounds like that might be the best decision you ever made.'

'Hattie, you leave it with me.' Gemma stands up, puts her hands on her hips. 'Now, where are the scissors? I think someone's tie might need a quick trim.'

Seventeen

Amy's back in the Therapy Room, watching Dr Hicks take a painfully long time to arrange his notes on the table. He eventually finds them and looks at her through glasses resting on the end of his nose.

'So, Amy. In our last session a week ago, I asked you to complete an assignment about your relationship. Have you given it some thought?'

'I have.' She swallows. She feels self-conscious about revealing her innermost thoughts to the people who are watching. Although she's more concerned about her friends and family than strangers. And she hopes Jamie is listening.

'Let's start with the first question. When did Jamie make you feel happy in your relationship?'

'I'm better at writing than talking, so I'm just going to read out my bullet points.'

'Whatever makes you comfortable.'

'OK, here goes.' She breathes out and takes a deep breath in.

'Jamie made me feel happy in my relationship when he made me feel like my opinion mattered to him. When he messaged me without needing a reason. When he wanted to see my friends, and when he was the life and soul of the party. When he talked like I was part of his future. When he introduced me to his friends as Mrs O'Connor. When the conversations weren't always about money. When he made me laugh, but with jokes that weren't at my expense. When he wanted to be with me, every single night. When he told me he'd never met anyone that suited him more, and that we would travel the world together.'

She coughs to emphasise her next and final point.

'But I can't remember the last time any of that happened.'

Dr Hicks pauses for a while, smiles at her and taps out some notes on his iPad.

'OK, thank you, Amy. And moving on to the second question. When did Jamie make you feel *un*happy in your relationship?' he asks.

With the same preparation, she puts mind over matter and ignores the tremble in her voice.

'When he stopped inviting me to the pub with his friends, and when he stopped coming to the pub with mine. When he went from being the life and soul of the party to being the no-show. When he told me it was weird how I wanted to see my parents so much, and when he was too busy to come when I went. When the only things he cared about were his business and his body.

'When he forgot where I worked, a few months ago. When he started texting at the dinner table and then taking calls. When there stopped being a dinner table at all. When he only wanted to sleep with me when he was drunk or hung-over. When he stopped greeting me in the morning. And then kissing me goodnight. When he said I was boring. When he joked about my double chin, my bingo wings, my hearty rump steak thighs.

'When he gave me a key to his place, but told me I had to let him know when I was coming round. When he made it abundantly clear that it wasn't an invite to move in with him. When he made me feel like I was his future one second, and then a guest in his home the next. When he called me Piglet.'

Dr Hicks looks at her with kind eyes.

'And tell me, Amy, how does it feel to get that down on paper?'

She flashes back to the steaming-hot shower she took after writing this list. As she scrubbed herself clean, she tried to visualise all her relationship doubts, fears and anxieties being washed down the plughole. She imagined shedding her skin and stepping out of the shower as a brand-new Amy.

'It feels good to get it out in the open. I've spent the last year pretending to everyone, myself included, that Jamie and I were going somewhere, and making excuses for his behaviour. But exposing the truth, accepting the truth and then putting it out in the open for everyone to hear isn't something I feel ashamed of anymore. My only regret is that I didn't do it sooner.'

Dr Hicks taps a few slow notes and looks up at her. 'Don't be too hard on yourself, Amy. It's not easy to break habits. Don't focus on what you did then, focus on what you're doing now. I'm here to help you develop a deeper understanding of who you are and what will make you happy.' He smiles at her. 'Which brings me on to the last question of the assignment.' He looks at his papers. 'Name what you need to feel happy in a relationship.'

Amy clears her throat.

'To feel happy, I need to feel that a relationship has a purpose. To really mean something for both of us. I want someone who makes me feel that my life is richer with them in it, and that I in turn enrich theirs. Take my relationship with my best friend, Sarah. Why can't I find that same sense of togetherness with a partner? I want to be part of an unbreakable team. We don't even have to be a winning team – we can be happy losing together because all that matters is that we're together and we have each other's backs, through thick and thin.'

'Did Jamie ever fulfil any of those needs?'

She sighs. 'No. In the first six months, maybe. Not at the end. Jamie made me feel like I was a kink in the chain, not a cog in the wheel. And all he added to my life was a load of new insecurities. I want someone to tell me that

180

they love everything about me, warts, double chins, bingo wings and all. But am I expecting too much from a relationship? Am I being high-maintenance? Do relationships like that even exist in real life?'

'Amy,' he says, sitting up. 'Treat your break-up like it's given you a blank canvas. On this blank canvas you can paint a new future, full of everything you need to feel happy. Stop caring about whether people think you're demanding. Ignore the critics, and stop looking at what other people are painting. Focus on yourself. Take your time. And stop denying yourself the happiness that's true for you. What does your painting look like?'

'A beach in Thailand?' She shrugs her shoulders and laughs a little.

'Why not?' He smiles back as he stands up and walks over to a screen on the wall. He switches it on and then turns around.

'I'd like to move on from your relationship to talk about your life goals, starting with the motherhood challenge. I watched you closely with baby Ben, and would like to ask you a few questions.' He looks up.

'OK.' She laughs nervously, worried about having to defend her score and the amount of food in Ben's stomach.

'So, what are your life goals?' he asks.

Big question.

She pauses for a few seconds to think.

Start a blog.

Travel the world.

181

Have adventures.
Find love.
Have a family.
Make a home.
Be free.

'Amy?' he interrupts. 'What are you thinking?'

'I'm thinking I want to have it all. But I know that having it all is impossible. I want to settle down, but I also want to travel. I want children, but I also want my freedom. The truth is, when I see babies, I don't feel broody – I feel anxious. They're like little anchors. But I shouldn't feel like that at my age, should I? How can I want a home *and* want to sleep in a tent on the edge of a ravine? It's like I'm two Amys. I have one foot on the plane and one foot on the runway, and I can't work out what will fulfil me more. Right now, I don't feel excited by the thought of buying a house, having a family and climbing the career ladder. But I do when I imagine being a sweaty, squashed sardine on the Khao San Road, trying to hail a tuk-tuk with a laptop in my bag, breathing in all that dust, all those fumes and spices.'

She pauses, imagining being in Bangkok.

Nothing is stopping you from leaving. You could walk out of here. You could be there tomorrow if you wanted.

She blinks out of her daydream.

'But then the bells of doom sound like gongs, warning me that time is running out and that it's too late to chase dreams like that.'

She sighs loudly and digs her thumbnail into her finger. 'The intrepid explorer in me retired years ago. I had my chance and I didn't take it. I chose Jamie, and I have to live with that. I just wish I could stop dreaming of making a quick escape. I'm so tired of hearing the voice in my head tempting me to jump on a plane this instant and leave everything behind. It's not normal. It's blurring my vision and cluttering my head.'

'Amy, normal is a standard that you've set by comparing yourself to others,' says Dr Hicks. 'You could aspire to be the most natural version of yourself. That way, the only point of comparison is you. If you don't feel ready to settle down, then that is you being natural. Perhaps you will change in a few years. Perhaps you won't.'

'But I do want to have kids, Dr Hicks, I just wish I didn't feel rushed into it because of my age. I would make a rubbish mother right now.'

He switches on the screen in the room.

'You're thirty-two, Amy, not fifty-two. There's time for kids, and the worst thing you could do is rush that kind of decision. For the record, I'm inclined to agree that you're not quite ready. Take a look at this.' He smiles as he presses the clicker.

Clip one shows the first time Amy saw Ben screaming in his cot. She recoils, then she pulls a contorted face that's a mix of terror and revulsion. Clip two shows Amy holding Ben on her hip and walking through the bedroom door, hitting his head hard on the door frame, and then looking around to see if anyone saw before picking a splinter out of his forehead. Clip three shows Amy sprinting into the bathroom to rescue Ben from an overflowing sink where he's floating face down. Clip four shows her and Jackie next to the prosecco tap, replacing their baby formula with the contents of a third glass. And then feeding their babies, while collapsing on the floor in hysterics.

'Shall we carry on?' he says, one eyebrow raised comically.

'OK, I get it. But these are plastic dolls. I wouldn't do that to a real baby!' She laughs.

Dr Hicks stops the montage and switches the TV off.

'Yes, of course, I know that. You aren't a monster. But Oh, Baby! was meant to give you a real indication of whether childcare comes naturally to you. Whether you enjoy all that responsibility. How ready you are for it. Now that you've completed the challenge, I have one final question for you. Do you feel ready?'

After a few seconds, she says, 'No.'

'OK. I'm delighted we've managed to end the session on a high by clearing one internal conflict from your mind. Motherhood can wait.'

*

When she leaves Dr Hicks, Amy feels like a weight has been lifted from her shoulders. She makes straight for the bedroom, to find the rest of the housemates helping Gemma choose the outfit she's going to wear on her date.

Hattie looks nervous about what's unfolding.

'Hattie, don't worry, hon,' Gemma says with a serious expression. 'I'm not dressing up for your ex. I just want to show the public how I scrub up!' She smiles, pulling her entire wardrobe out and onto the bed, before picking out three dresses.

'I'm not worried about that – I just hate the idea of you meeting him. I'm embarrassed. You're going to think I was nuts being with him.'

'I think he's nuts for dumping you in here, but I'm glad he did.'

Gemma looks at the dresses. One's a black spandex mini, the second is a pink leather playsuit and the third is a tight white lace dress, the low-cut back of which sits below the top of her bum.

A moment later she's in the final dress, modelling it around the bedroom. 'It's called bum cleavage! It's like boob cleavage, but on your butt! Don't you love it?'

'Darlin', you would look class with a condom on your head,' says Jackie. 'Just make sure there's enough stretch in that dress to pull a punch if you need to.'

'Easy!' she says, as she crouches down in her five-inch heels, punches a left hook then an uppercut, followed by a roundhouse kick.

Flick stands in the corner with her arms folded. 'You can't go out like that. Half your bottom is hanging out! At least put some knickers on.'

Gemma stops and looks upset. 'Yeah, all right, Dad. I

can't wear knickers, it will hide my bum cleavage. And that's the best bit.'

Flick shakes her head and tuts. 'And you wonder why we get catcalled. I can't wait to see the comments on The Wall tomorrow.'

'It's not my fault men can't control themselves. My body, my image, my choice. Boom. Or should I say bum?' she says, jiggling her bottom.

'Well, when I have a daughter, she's never going to be allowed out looking like that.'

'Flick, for fuck's sake, get with the times, hon.' Gemma struts out from the bathroom, twirls and swishes her hair. 'Women shouldn't have to hide their bodies just because men are so basic they can't handle a bit of flesh without getting a boner.'

*

The housemates gather round the TV. On screen, Dylan is pacing up and down in The Secret Garden next door. He's wearing a loose-fitting black shirt with white pinstripes, jeans that are too big for him and shiny black dress shoes. Impossibly, it makes him look even younger than before, wearing his teenage gamer uniform. The producers have gone to town with festoon lighting, candles, red roses and a bottle of champagne resting in an ice bucket. In any other situation, it would be romantic.

For the first time ever, Hattie has crept above position

five on The Tracker. Clearly, this Dylan date has got the viewers talking.

'He's made such an effort,' Hattie says softly. 'I can't remember him ever making that kind of effort for me.'

Amy catches Lauren's eye and Kathy rubs Hattie's back. Hattie drops her head in her hands and sniffs.

'Hattie, my love' – Lauren shifts closer to her on the sofa – 'you are gonna find someone who makes an effort for you every day. I have a good feeling about it, and I have a strong gut. You deserve someone who treats you like a gift, and you'll find them. You're a top prize, and don't you for a second ever think you're anything less. That clown out there is a fookin' idiot, and you don't want a fookin' idiot in your life.'

They all look up when they hear The Secret Garden door slam. Gemma strides in confidently, muttering hello. Dylan scuttles to her chair and draws it back for her to sit down.

'Ah, bless.' Flick smiles. 'Nice to see that chivalry isn't dead.'

As Gemma sits down, Dylan cranes his neck forward and stares down her back, with his mouth open and his tongue visible.

'Oh. Oh dear,' Kathy says, looking over at Hattie.

'Oh my God!' Hattie cries. 'Look at him, he's staring at her like a dog at his dinner!'

'He is a dog, Hattie.' Jackie walks behind her and rubs her shoulders. 'He's a fucking little chihuahua with his tiny lipstick out.'

Dylan eventually moves, taking the champagne bottle out of the bucket as he sits down. After too many attempts to open it, Gemma grabs it from him and pops it open with a karate chop of her hand.

'Wow, wicked trick.' Dylan laughs, then stops when she doesn't. 'You look nice. I like your dress. Especially the back of it.' He winks at her. And unleashes hell.

'Jesus Christ, mate, how fucking old are you?' Gemma shouts. 'Is that the first time you've seen a female arse before? I know it can't be, because you were lucky enough to have that godsend Hattie in your life. Fuck knows how – you were seriously punching. And Hattie is sitting there on her perfect peach, watching you perve down my back like a horny teenager. You know, I'm actually glad she saw you do that. It'll make her realise just how pathetic you really are. Grow up, and show some fucking respect.'

'Good God!' Flick folds her arms and shakes her head. 'How on earth can she be a keeper when she behaves like that? Men would run a mile. Frankly, I wouldn't blame them. She has absolutely no shame.'

'YASSS, Gemma!' shouts Jackie. 'Queen!'

Amy looks across at Hattie. Her eyes are closed. And although her cheeks are still shining from a few sliding tears, she has a smile on her face, like she's listening to the world's sweetest lullaby.

In blissful ignorance that tomorrow, one of them will be gone.

Eighteen

'That woman is on a different fucking planet. Flick is so far away she can't see how insensitive she is being,' Jackie mutters to Amy in the bedroom. They received a singing telegram at breakfast earlier, merrily delivering unpleasant news. Tonight is *The Shelf*'s first live eviction.

Everyone is on edge. Even Zen master Kathy snapped at Flick earlier for saying wives shouldn't put children before husbands, and how she'd never dream of making Simon feel second best when they're married with kids, because doing so would give him a licence to stray.

'But I don't think she's a bad person,' Amy whispers back to Jackie. 'She just doesn't think before she speaks. She forgets who's listening. I don't think that comment was a dig at Kathy. It's like she says these things out loud so that Simon can hear. She did say sorry afterwards. I think she felt terrible.'

'Isn't that worse, though? When you don't even realise that you're saying something wrong? And her apologies are always way over the top. When you say sorry a million times, it isn't because you're sorry for what you did to them, it's because you want to get rid of the guilt. I just think she's setting a really bad example. You've seen what her fans are like on The Wall. Literally the world's worst type of people.' She walks out, leaving Amy alone to think about the riddle that is Flick.

Jackie might have a point. Sometimes Flick can be a bit too much with the gestures, the food, the endless offers of tea. And Kathy snapped at Flick again for her repeated apologies. 'Bloody hell, stop smothering me, I'm fine!'

There are times when Amy wants to grab Flick by the shoulders in a fury and shake the hateful views right out of her. At other times, she feels desperately sorry for Flick and flummoxed by her fixation for Simon's approval. Flick is smart. Doctor-smart. She's a bloody paediatrician! How can she genuinely believe that a husband's needs are more important than a child's? It's like he's poisoned her, and all her toxic views on marriage, relationships and appearance are the symptoms of someone very sick. Whatever the root of the evil, it's horrifying that she has so much support. Since her arrival just five days ago, The Wall has become a bleak breeding ground for racists, sexists and bigots to stick their heads out of their dank Internet corners. Many comments quote Flick out of context and give her words a more sinister meaning than Amy thinks she's intended.

Or at least hopes.

＊

Amy's scrubbing the bathroom with bleach from top to bottom to relieve her stress at the prospect of being evicted tonight. She's found several hairballs, two false nails, a thong and enough hairgrips to start an eBay shop. Even those didn't make her feel as nauseous as tonight's show does.

'Excuse me, Amy!' cries Flick as she almost trips over her, turns on the tap and splashes her face with water. She starts crying into the sink.

'Are you OK?' Amy stands up, not sure how to comfort her. Is Flick a hugger? She gives her a little rub on the back to test the waters.

Flick spins round. Her cheek looks like it's never seen a tear in its life. How does her skin remain so perfect, with such a contorted face? Annoying. But Amy soon switches from irritation to pity when she sees Flick's eyes brimming with tears. When Amy reaches out for a hug, Flick drops all her weight onto Amy's left shoulder. All eight stone of her.

'What's happened?' Amy mumbles into her ear.

'I've been made the mascot of some awful white male supremacist group, Amy! They've put my face on a bloody

T-shirt like Che Guevara! I haven't even been here a week!'

Amy struggles not to laugh at how ridiculous the visual is in her head of Flick wearing a beret on a T-shirt with a fist in the air. Maybe she's in a bonnet with a feather duster.

'They can't do that, Flick. Maybe you could make a statement saying you don't support their views, and perhaps ask the producers if there's anything you can do to stop them. Or Jackie might know – she's a lawyer.'

'Jackie hates me. Everyone does. If I'm not pissing you lot off, I'm pissing half the public off because they think I hate women.' She sniffs. 'I wish I'd never come on here – this was such a stupid idea. Simon and I were perfectly happy the way things were. Why did I have to go and rock the boat?'

'Well, maybe wanting to rock the boat is a sign you weren't as happy as you thought you were.'

Flick stares at the floor for a while.

'Thanks for cleaning the bathroom.' She smiles as she walks out, lifting her head up. 'It looks great. I really appreciate it.'

*

There's one hour left until the live eviction, and the house-mates are dressed up and sitting in the dining room, glued to The Tracker.

Day 12

1. Gemma
2. Jackie
3. Flick
4. Amy
5. Lauren
6. Kathy
7. Hattie

'Housemates, please make your way to the living room. The eviction will begin in fifteen minutes.'

Messages on The Wall are flying in so fast that it's almost impossible to read them before they disappear off the bottom of the screen. Amy's nerves start to swell. The middle isn't the safe zone. She hates to think how Kathy and Hattie are feeling right now. Kathy, who has the chance to make it on her own for once. Who has nowhere to go because her husband and his girlfriend have taken over the house. And then there's Hattie, who is desperate to reinvent herself and learn how to live without Dylan. Who's become quietly dependent on the rest of the housemates for friend-ship, love and support. How is she going to cope on the outside, alone?

@larnimarni Kathy is too old for this show. Time to go #dontvotekathy #theshelf

@superwomanly Hattie is so unhealthy-looking. She shouldn't be on TV #dontvotehattie #theshelf

@jkraze WTF was Gemma wearing last night? Slag!
#dontvotegemma #theshelf

'This is exciting,' says Flick, sitting down on the far side of the sofa.

'Flick,' says Jackie, handing out a round of proseccos, 'we're saying goodbye to someone tonight. I know emotional intelligence doesn't come naturally to you, but try to be a bit more sensitive, yeah?'

Flick catches Amy's eye and looks down. Amy's about to ask Jackie to steady on with the punches, but she's interrupted.

'Good evening, housemates!' shouts Adam Andrews into the camera, as a make-up artist applies the final touches to his face. 'It's 7 p.m. and you know what that means . . .'

A siren screams and the camera pans out to reveal Adam in his dressing room. His hair is gelled back and he's wearing a glitter tuxedo.

'It's *The Shelf*'s first ever live eviction!' he bellows. The show's theme tune starts pumping as he runs out of the changing room, with the cameraman running closely behind. In the studio corridors, he puts his hands up to high-five the runners who are standing back.

'Oooh, there's Sam!' says Flick. 'He told me I had a really good shot at winning.'

'Same,' says Jackie immediately.

Adam jumps off the stage and runs up the stairs through the audience, who are going berserk. The camera continues to follow him out the back door and into the studio car park, where he lifts his arms to greet thousands of people gathered outside.

'Fuck me,' mutters Jackie.

Amy can't believe what she's seeing. How did this show, a show no one had ever heard of two weeks ago, manage to get so many fans so fast? She sweeps the living room and sees that everyone else is in shock, too. The placards reflect the mixed sentiments. And some make more sense than others.

WHAT THE FLICK?

KATHY THE COUGAR!

HATTIE'S GONNA HATE!

Amy isn't sure what the last one meant and, by the puzzled look on Hattie's face, she isn't either.

'Welcome again, everyone, to our first live eviction!' Adam screams as fireworks start crackling across the sky. They're audible from the TV and the garden, which doubles the volume and Amy's heart rate.

'Well, lads,' shouts Lauren at the group. 'This is really fookin' happening, isn't it? We'll be all right,' she says, patting Hattie on the shoulder.

Amy presses her fingers to her ears as she watches Adam kick a sign next to him saying ADAM'S A PLANK, then run back into the studio and down the aisle. He jumps onto his chair in front of three guests sitting opposite him on the sofa.

'Tonight is the night we've all been waiting for,' he says to the camera. 'The first night we give one of the housemates the old heave-ho. With me tonight is a group of our biggest celebrity fans, who are here to place their bets on who'll be the first housemate to face the boot.' He kicks his leg in the air.

The camera pans over to the first guest, Archie Martucci, a former presenter on *Rags to Riches*, a reality show where contestants had to live on the street for a month to win a cash prize. The show had been cancelled last year when one of the contestants went AWOL. Archie gives a thumbs up to the camera.

'Did they ever find that bloke who went missing?' asks Jackie.

The housemates shrug.

The next celebrity guest is Sonia Cole, who blows a kiss to the audience. She's a former Page Three girl turned PR machine who released a tell-all book last year about her numerous affairs with Members of Parliament.

'Ugh, I can't stand her,' mutters Flick. 'Such trash.'

The final guest is a familiar face. It's Katie Carroway from *Beauty School Squad*, who's dyed her hair bright blue for the occasion.

'OK, celebrities, I'm going to ask each one of you who you think is heading off tonight, and why. Archie, go!'

'Well, Adam,' Archie says in a slow and nasal monotone, 'it's got to be Hattie. Who else can it be? She's been at rock bottom since the show began. Hippo just isn't a hit with the viewers. Sad, really. I don't mind her.'

Lauren grabs Hattie's hand and squeezes it. 'He's just a D-lister who's desperate for airtime.'

'He's talking bollocks, Hattie, don't believe it,' adds Gemma.

Adam moves on. 'How about you, Coley, what's your prediction for tonight's show?'

'I wouldn't be surprised if Amy got dropped,' Sonia says in a gravelly voice. 'And I wouldn't care either.'

Amy's heart sinks.

'Ooh! Controversial! What makes you think that?' asks Adam.

'Because she's drop-dead boring! The viewers want to watch a show, not a dead slug! Sorry, love, no hard feelings. I think you're nice, but nice doesn't win.'

Amy glances to The Tracker, terrified she'll have dropped to bottom place. But she hasn't dropped – weirdly, she's moved up one place.

'I have to disagree with Sonia,' says Katie. 'I think the fact that Amy isn't getting involved in too many dramas makes her extremely likeable. What's wrong with wanting someone normal on there?'

'I want tears, bitch-slaps and hair-pulling,' Sonia replies. 'That's good TV. Save the long talks and political debates for *Question Time*. Yawn!'

The audience cheer and laugh.

Katie looks disgusted. 'So, you want a show that makes women look like emotional train wrecks?'

'Bit dramatic,' intervenes Adam. 'OK, Katie, if you're voting to save Amy, who's on your leave list?'

'It has to be Flick.'

'You were all over Flick the other day during glam time!' Adam cries out.

'I don't *dis*like her, I just don't understand why she's here. She's in a relationship. She doesn't need to learn how to be in one. She can't have her cake and eat it.'

The audience burst into cries of 'Ooooohh'.

Flick sighs. 'I didn't force them to put me on here. They phoned me.'

'OK,' Adam continues, 'so you *want* Flick to go, but who do you *think* will go tonight?'

'Hattie, of course,' she says. 'Poor kitten hasn't got a cat's chance in hell of being saved by these viewers.'

'All right, all right, all right,' Adam says, turning back to the camera. 'We've got two-to-one on Hattie leaving the house tonight, but we aren't quite ready to cut her cord yet, folks. Because we have one last, very special guest, that we're saving a spot for on the sofa. He knows her better than anyone else . . .'

'Oh nooooo!' Hattie starts fretting. 'They can't bring Dylan out, can they?'

'Babes!' Gemma replies. 'He's long gone, don't worry.'

'Welcome to the stage for the second time, our very own Dr Howard Hicks!'

Hattie exhales.

The audience cheer as Dr Hicks does an awkward half walk, half run towards the sofa and lowers himself down, smiling and waving at the audience.

'So, Doctor Howard,' Adam asks him in a serious tone, 'we don't have much time. What I would like to find out is what you think the emotional impact of this rejection will be on our first loser. How do you think someone like Hattie will handle it?'

'Well,' coughs Dr Hicks, 'don't forget that Hattie's exit isn't a sure thing. The Tracker in the dining room is simply a social media listening tool. It's an automated system with an algorithm that tracks whether the housemates are being talked about positively or negatively. It's not always accurate. For example, the system can't detect sarcasm. If I was to say "Yeah, *sure* Hattie is going to stay",' he says in a dramatically sarcastic voice, 'then the computer will pick that up as me saying I'm sure Hattie is going to stay. Not the opposite, which is what I mean.'

Adam stares at him blankly and the audience are silent. Someone sneezes.

'So you think Hattie will get the fewest votes tonight?' Adam asks.

'No, that's not what I was saying at all,' Dr Hicks responds. 'I'm saying don't trust The Tracker. It isn't that accurate.'

'OK, gotcha!' shouts Adam, mouthing *Whaaaa?* at the audience, who all laugh. 'So back to my original question: how will the evictee feel?'

'Well, how would you feel, Adam?' Dr Hicks asks him.

'Really embarrassed, to be honest. I'd want to crawl into a hole and die quietly,' he says, laughing.

'Well, yes, maybe. The housemate that leaves in the first eviction will feel a mix of emotions. At first, they will feel humiliated that they've been rejected. Then they'll experience a surge of delight as they think about being free to enter the outside world and reunite with their family and friends. Then, when they see the crowds that have gathered outside, they'll feel a rush of trepidation swiftly followed by excitement as they're cheered on.' He smiles. 'They went in as nobodies and they're leaving as household names. Their faces will be recognised by thousands around the country. They certainly won't be able to pop to the shops for a pint of milk in their slippers anymore.'

'But what if the crowd boos, not cheers?' asks Adam.

'Well, I suppose they might boo, yes,' says Dr Hicks.

'Oh no, oh no, oh no!' cries Hattie quietly.

'People who boo are probably just unhappy,' Jackie tells her.

'OK, thank you to all my guests!' cries Adam, with his finger on his earpiece. 'I'm being told we're just thirty seconds away from the big reveal and the final votes are being counted and verified as we speak. Who will the public decide to save? Who will be the first to leave *The Shelf* after almost a fortnight of making new friends, soul-searching with our star therapist, getting a celebrity makeover and so much more?'

A countdown timer appears on the big screen behind him

and he ushers his guests to stand up and hold hands like they're seeing in the new year.

5 . . .
4 . . .
3 . . .
2 . . .
1 . . .

The housemates scream and explosions go off everywhere, with so much glitter filling the screen that they can't see who has been voted off for several long and painful seconds.

'Who the fuck is it?' screams Gemma.

The glitter falls like a curtain.

Kathy.

They clasp their hands to their mouths and Amy shoots her head round to The Tracker. Dr Hicks was right. Hattie is still at the bottom, but Kathy got the fewest votes.

'I can't believe it! *Kathy*!' gasps Amy, grabbing her hand. 'No one's said a bad word about you!' she says.

'Kathy, you have five minutes to pack your bags and leave the house.'

The housemates all gather to console Kathy on the sofa, as she rubs her face with her hand.

'Don't cry, Kath, just think about it. You're free!' Lauren says, grabbing her in a bear hug and squeezing her tight.

After a few seconds in Lauren's arms, Kathy stands back to reveal a broad smile on her face.

'I know! I'm delighted to be getting out of here!' She beams as she stands up from her seat. 'I knew I'd never win this show at my age, and I never really cared about getting to the end. I just wanted the experience, and to start a new life. And I've got all of that in just twelve days!'

'I'm free!' she shouts as she walks to the bedroom. When she reappears with her suitcase, she's grinning. 'Sure, I won't be leaving with a million pounds, but ten thousand is enough of a leg-up.'

The housemates say their goodbyes as they watch her roll her suitcase towards the steel front door, with the GO button glowing green for the first time. She turns round as she reaches the exit and waves. And with a slam of the door, Kathy is gone.

Nineteen

'Zerz beeble nn ze gardol,' mumbles Hattie by the glass doors.

'You OK there, Hat?' Amy replies absent-mindedly from the sofa. She's engrossed in an argument on The Wall about who'd win in a fight, Gemma or Jackie, and whether women should have six-packs or not. All she can do to defend them is yell at the screen like a screaming banshee. She hasn't got used to life with no phone. She still reaches into her back pocket when she sits down. She still reaches over to feel for it on her side table every morning. She's coping better than Gemma, who's developed a nervous habit of scrolling her palm with her forefinger.

'Come again, love?' Lauren shouts from the sofa. 'Maybe without the cheese sarnie in your chops.'

There's a loud gulp.

'There are people in the garden,' Hattie repeats.

Amy and the others turn round on the sofas.

'What's going on in the garden?' Gemma asks, breathless after a session on the treadmill that nobody else touches.

'Is something happening?' asks Flick, entering from the bedroom in a face mask.

They line up along the window. Jackie taps the glass, but the runners continue to scurry without looking up, putting down old-fashioned wooden desks and chairs.

'It looks like they're setting up a classroom,' Amy comments.

'Well, well, well, whatever will they teach us next?' chirps Jackie, climbing over the back of the sofa and sliding down the other side. 'I do hope it's needlework. Knowing how to darn a pair of suit socks would really add to my repertoire.'

'Housemates. Please take a seat on the sofa.'

'Ugh, this tune will be the death of me!' Lauren moans when the music begins.

The screen cuts to Adam in his set chair.

'So, three months ago,' he says, 'we conducted a survey of sorts in partnership with *LAD* to seek out the answer to one of life's biggest questions. What do men want?' He strokes his chin. 'Well, here to tell us the answers and teach you girls the secret to holding down a man are *LAD* mag editor Danny Wells and Dr Howard Hicks!'

A cocky-looking twenty-something with a pencil moustache runs on stage. He races ahead of Dr Hicks and fist-bumps Adam before bouncing onto the sofa, chewing gum as he waves at the camera. Dr Hicks joins them a few seconds later.

'All right, mate, how are you?' Adam asks, laughing.

'Yeah, really good, mate, really good. Wicked to be here – this is the only show that matters to anyone right now, I can tell you. All right, ladies? How are you all doing in there? Lovely stuff.' He smiles and winks before turning to Dr Hicks, fist-bumping him and then mic-dropping. The whole exchange causes much confusion and awkwardness on camera.

'Ah, Danny's quite cute, isn't he?' says Gemma, playing with her hair.

'Raise your 'ands if you're gutted our girls aren't in school uniforms, eh! Who's with me?' Danny shouts up at the audience, his arm in the air.

Gemma drops the piece of hair she's been playing with and buries her hands in her lap. 'Oh my God, he's not cute, he's a creep!'

'You can blame Doctor Howard for that,' Adam replies. 'Spoilsport! So, Danny, tell the girls what you're going to be doing with them today.'

'OK, ladies, Adam, I'll go back to the start. Three months ago, we tweeted a really simple but profound message to our followers. It said . . .' He pauses for effect and draws a line in the air. '"The problem with women is . . ." And we just left it blank. The results have been awesome, Adam – thousands of blanks filled in. Tell you what, Jay-Z needs to rewrite that track.'

'"Ninety-nine problems and a bitch is most of them"?'

'Ha! Exactly, Adam, exactly.'

Amy hates that song. Jamie used to sing it to her all the time, thinking it was hilarious to switch 'a bitch ain't one' to 'a bitch is one' while pointing at her across the dance floor.

Dr Hicks chimes in.

'We spent six weeks analysing the responses, categorising them and ranking them in order of priority based on their emotional weight. Some responses felt deeper than others. A shallow response would be: "The problem with women is that they expect you to pay". A deep response would be: "The problem with women is that they expect you to provide".'

'Er, maybe twenty years ago, mate,' Jackie shouts, 'when we couldn't get jobs that paid us enough to be free.'

Adam nods vigorously. 'Fascinating. And how are you going to use that information to help our girls?'

'It's simple,' Danny replies. 'We're going to teach them what to do – and what not to do – when you're in a relationship with a man and you want it to last. It's not a test. It's not a challenge. Well, I suppose the challenge is staying quiet for longer than five minutes – am I right, lads? Ha, just kidding, girls!'

'Well, I don't know – what about our Gemma?' Adam cracks up and Danny joins him, slapping his knees. Dr Hicks scowls at them both.

'Oi!' Gemma shouts and looks at the others.

'Fuckwits,' Jackie says, under her breath.

*

Outside, the desks are lined up in two rows, facing a projector that's pointed at an outdoor cinema screen. Adam, Danny and Dr Hicks are on screen. Danny is kitted out in a fancy-dress teacher's uniform of corduroys, a knitted vest and fake glasses. He looks exactly like Dr Hicks, who hasn't dressed up.

'Hello, ladies, and welcome to . . . Keep 'Em Keen!' says Adam loudly. 'The class that will clue you up on everything that's in your power to do to make a man happy. Over the next hour, you'll learn what our pet peeves are. How to avoid henpecking, and how to boost your sex drive to stop us walking away with the life you're dreaming of. Goodbye wedding bells, and so long to the pitter-patter of tiny feet. Hello to a future of cats, takeaways and TV.'

'Sounds quite good,' says Hattie, quietly.

Amy looks around at the housemates. They're all staring at him in silent disbelief. She wants to burst out laughing when she sees that Gemma's giving a death stare and Lauren has her eyes shut. Meanwhile, Jackie's furiously scribbling a long list on a piece of paper in front of her. When Amy looks closer, she sees the title is 'The problem with men is . . .'

'We went through all the responses with a fine-tooth comb and managed to sort them into some clear categories,' Dr Hicks takes over. 'Those categories include appearance, behaviour, sex, communication, attitude and emotional stability. These are the key problem areas for thousands of men who are or have been in relationships with women.

What we're going to do now is go through each category, explain the problem and reveal some of the real responses we've received.'

Danny jumps in. 'Girls, this class is semi-interactive. We might ask some questions along the way. But what we'd really rather you do is stay quiet, listen and take notes on what we tell you. Don't just interrupt. If you need us to explain it a little more, just raise your hand. Do you understand?'

'Yeah, I think a dog would understand,' says Jackie, loudly.

'OK, we're good to go. Our first category is appearance,' Adam says as he clicks and a beautiful woman is displayed on the screen. Amy looks at Flick and wonders if she sees the resemblance, too.

Rule #1: Don't let yourself go

'This is Kelly. She's a computer-generated image of a perfect woman, created by us according to men's tastes from the data we've gathered. We're always asking men what their preferences are, and Kelly is all their answers in one perfect female form. Now, we aren't saying that you should look like this.'

'I should bloody hope not,' says Jackie, pointing at her face. 'I'm black, mate.'

Dr Hicks coughs and looks uncomfortable. 'We aren't saying all women should have blonde hair and blue eyes. It's more to do with grooming.'

Adam clicks the buzzer and Kelly morphs into a much older, grumpy-looking woman who's doubled in size and has unbrushed grey hair and no make-up. She's wearing a baggy tracksuit, dirty Ugg boots and has half a hamburger in her hand and the other half in her mouth.

Gemma bursts out laughing. 'Hey, that's me on Saturday mornings!'

Danny looks at her, deadpan. 'We'll get on to women being funny a bit later, Gemma. Now, ladies, this is Kelly if she quits caring. Over half of our responses said the problem with women is that they let themselves go. They stop caring about their style, shape and femininity. Some men complained their partners weren't as hygienic as they were before having babies. Men are visual creatures, and we hate it when you stop making an effort with your appearance. When you choose slippers over stilettos, it says you no longer care what we think about you, and that makes us feel like we don't matter.'

Danny clicks again to show a third version of Kelly. Older, but still slim and in a skirt and high heels. She's holding a green juice, smiling and has perfectly blow-dried hair.

'Meet Kelly the Cougar, who's still wearing her wedding ring! Kelly the Quitter doesn't have a wedding ring on, does she? That's because her husband didn't sign up for a dumpy, frumpy, grumpy wife. So the rule here, ladies, is really simple. Don't let yourself go.'

Amy raises her hand. 'How do you expect us to find the

time or energy to blow-dry our hair, do our nails, iron that skirt, make a green juice and smile about it every day? I'd find that impossible, and I don't even have kids. By the time I've finished work, I'm exhausted. I can think of a thousand better ways to relax.'

'You could wake up an hour earlier?' Danny replies. 'It's a small price to pay to make a loved one happy that he's with you and no one else. And it'll help with your confidence, too. There's nothing sexier than confidence. Well, confidence within reason, of course. We wouldn't want a woman with a big head.'

Amy would never admit this to anyone, but it took her three months to show Jamie her face without foundation. When she first started staying the night at his, she'd tiptoe into the bathroom and turn the tap on. Then she'd brush her teeth, smear on some foundation and spray the tiniest bit of perfume in the air to give Jamie the impression that jasmine was just her natural scent. Then she'd creep back under the covers, trying desperately to avoid putting smudges on his Harrods pillowcases, and quickly close her eyes before pretending to yawn. He did find a make-up smudge on the pillowcase once, and made her feel terrible about it. When she eventually stopped this tiring routine, he didn't seem to notice anyway.

Dr Hicks steps to the front of the class and takes the clicker from Adam. A stock photo of a model couple in bed appears on screen. They're both laughing while he big-spoons her.

Rule #2: Make an effort in bed

'Did she just fart on his leg?' stage-whispers Lauren, making the rest of the class laugh – apart from Flick, who turns round and tells her to shush.

'Ladies, it isn't only visual stimulation that men respond to,' Danny continues. 'It's sexual. The second biggest problem men complained about was their sex lives. Or lack of. Women are at their sexual peak in their early thirties. After that, hormonal changes can lead to a lower libido. I have a theory that it's linked to confidence, too. If you feel unattractive, you won't want to have sex. You're scared of rejection, so you reject us instead. It's a vicious cycle. Here's a tweet from one of our responders.'

The wife and I had sex five times a week before kids. Now she feels too tired, too full or too fat. Well, I'm tired of her rejecting me. If it doesn't change, I'm looking elsewhere. Why stay with someone who doesn't want me anymore?

'Being lazy at sex is a ticking time bomb,' says Adam. 'In a healthy relationship, you should be having sex at least three or four times a week. Listen, I get it. When you really aren't in the mood, it can be hard to overcome. But sometimes, you've got to put mind over matter and make the effort in bed.'

Amy and Jamie's sex life nosedived in the last six months. He'd be working late or at the gym, and would get back so late that Amy was asleep. If he was drunk, he'd wake her up in the middle of the night. And despite feeling annoyed, she'd often give in to fumbly sex in a cloud of alcohol fumes. It meant she could tick it off the list and he couldn't accuse her of never wanting to do it. It was either that or hangover sex, which he seemed into and which she found the worst, especially if she'd been out, too. When she felt at peak ugliness, smelliness and had a pounding head.

'Ladies,' Dr Hicks adds, 'if you love your partner, sex shouldn't feel like a chore. There are lots of ways you can inject more excitement into your sex life. Massage. Role-playing. Dressing up. Tickling. Feathers.'

'Oooh, Doctor, bet you like a sexy nurse outfit, don't you?' shouts Gemma, laughing.

'Yes, quite,' he says, almost dropping the clicker. 'Moving swiftly on to the third category.'

Rule #3: Don't nag, control or neglect

'This is all about your behaviour,' he continues. 'We received a wide range of responses on the subject matter, so I'm going to read out a few to show you what the problems are.'

The problem with women is all they do is complain. My girl-friend nags about the smallest things, like if I leave my clothes on the floor or don't rinse the sink. But she never appreciates the things I do do, like unpacking the dishwasher.

The problem with women is they turn into mothers. My wife treats me like I'm one of the kids. I'm forty-five years old, for Christ's sake, I can get my own f***ing Coco Pops. You'd think I'd like being waited on hand and foot, but I think it's just another way for her to control me.

The problem with women is they end up putting you second. I used to be the most important person in my wife's life. I disappeared when the kids came along. The other day I had to shout her name three times before she answered. It would be nice to be noticed once in a while.

Jamie always complained to Amy about her breaching the tidy rules around the house. He was obsessively neat, and she had to move around his flat like she was in the vault scene of *Mission: Impossible*, in case she left hair on the carpet, spilt her tea or dropped some crumbs.

'Oh my God, we can't win, can we?' shouts Gemma. 'If we do things for them, we get accused of smothering. If we don't do things for them, we don't care. And they say that *we* moan all the time. Talk about double standards.'

The women mutter in agreement.

'Relationships are all about balance, Gemma. Sometimes you have to give, sometimes you have to take,' Danny replies before Dr Hicks can. 'But complaining, controlling, neglecting – you can't get away with it, girls.'

'Now, ladies,' Dr Hicks continues, 'making men feel unloved when children appear is a huge problem. When you do have children, you have to make sure your attention is split evenly. Make time for each other. Arrange regular date nights. Give each other at least half an hour of one-on-one time together every night. When the kids are asleep, that isn't a green light to have a bath by yourself or watch Netflix. Turn the TV off. Let him join you in the bath. It might inject some passion into your sex life at the same time.'

'Ugh, I *hate* it when Jason gets in my bath,' says Gemma. 'It's not sexy, it's awkward and uncomfortable, and he takes up all the room. I lock the door now.'

The screen displays the fourth rule.

Rule #4: Tell us what's wrong

'Now, ladies, hands in the air – how many of you have said you're fine when you're far from it? Go on, be honest. No one? Ha, yeah right!' Danny laughs. 'I'm sure you've heard the saying that communication is the key to a happy relationship. Well, let me tell you, it's a cliché for a reason. Listen to this.'

The problem with women is they think we're psychic. Tell us when we do something wrong. Don't mutter that you're fine, punish us with the silent treatment and then let us know in a passive-aggressive text three days later that we didn't compliment you on your new haircut!

'It's always better to be open, honest and direct,' Dr Hicks interjects. 'Even if you're feeling nervous about confronting an issue. Keeping quiet and bottling it up just leads to tension that can boil over into an argument.'

Hattie puts her hand up.

'Yes, Hattie?'

'I understand that it's important to tell someone if they've done something wrong. But what if that person makes it impossible for you to complete the sentence before they're storming out? How do I communicate with them then?'

That was exactly Jamie's tactic in a fight. He could be like Dr Jekyll and Mr Hyde. One minute his face could screw up in hysterical laughter, the next it could twist into a purple fury if Amy said something that touched a raw nerve. He was impossible to criticise. So she just didn't.

'In that situation, Hattie, I'd have to say just let it go,' Adam replies, cutting off Dr Hicks. 'Tempers flare up and tempers fade. He won't stay angry forever. Keep trying, I'm sure you'll get through to him eventually.'

Hattie puts her hand down, still looking confused.

'Is everything clear so far, ladies? Want us to explain anything a bit more?' When no one bothers replying he carries on with, 'No? Let's move on to the next rule.'

Dr Hicks points the clicker at the screen to reveal the next rule.

Rule #5: Don't be bossy

'As I said before, men love a woman who's confident,' says Danny. 'But there's a fine line between being confident and bossy. We had loads of responses on this. Chipping away at your man's masculinity by ordering him around is a fast track to relationship failure. No one wants to marry a Little Miss Bossy Boots. It's important for men to feel like they're in charge. Raging feminists will try to deny it, but men are natural-born leaders, protectors, providers. It's genetics. Being in charge, physically and emotionally, is in their blood. Let him feel like a real man. Let him feel like a hero. Let him make some important decisions and feel like the head of the household.'

Adam nods to Dr Hicks to click, while the contestants collectively *pfffft* and *tsk* at the advice.

Rule #6: Learn to laugh more

'Now, here's an interesting response we had regarding your attitudes, which I think is a really common problem,' says Danny.

The problem with women is that they lose their sense of humour. My ex used to laugh at my jokes all the time. Now she says I'm stupid. My jokes haven't changed, so she must have. Either that or she pretended to find me funny, which I can't believe. My mates think I'm funny.

Sounds like Jamie.

'My theory? It's your lack of effort again. It's about how you don't make the effort to make him feel special anymore, just like with the letting yourself go and the lack of effort in bed. It's rude not to laugh at someone's jokes. Give your man a confidence boost, make him feel happy. Laughing is free and it'll pay off in the long run. If you can't laugh? At least smile, for God's sake.'

'But my ex only ever told jokes at my expense,' Amy interrupts. 'At first I thought it was like he was pulling my pigtails in the school playground, and he did it because he liked me. But then the more he did it, the more it felt like he was trying to chisel away at *my* confidence. Would you laugh if your girlfriend turned to her friends and said, "Let's not talk about the elephant in the room", and then nodded their head towards you?'

Jamie had made that joke early on in their relationship and Amy had laughed along. She didn't want his friends to think she was uptight. Had he made it six months later, she wouldn't have been so relaxed about it.

Danny snorts back. 'Come on, Amy – he's just teasing. It's a sign of affection.'

'But giving people complexes isn't funny,' says Lauren, staring at him. 'It's bullying.'

'Well, maybe women don't know what's funny,' he says under his breath. No one picks up on it.

'Shall we move on?' says Dr Hicks, clicking to show a picture of a man with his head in his hands at a restaurant table, an angry-looking woman sitting opposite him with her arms folded. In the background, a man is on one knee, proposing to his happy partner.

Rule #7: Stop the pressure

'Fuck me, how many rules are there?' Gemma sighs loudly, leaning her head back to stare at the sky. 'Do we get a toilet pass?'

'Just sit tight, Gemma,' Dr Hicks responds. 'We don't have long now.'

'Well.' She sits up. 'What if I told you that I just got my period?'

'Ha! Nice try. We know you don't,' Adam says. Then his eyes go wide, like he shouldn't have said that.

'You what, mate?' Lauren says, straightening up.

'Oh my God, did Jason tell you my time of the month? What a twat!'

'It was a tiny box on the form for the medical information we needed,' Dr Hicks interjects.

'Why the fuck would you need to know that?' Jackie starts. 'That's my private information, that's not legal.'

'We just needed to know so that we could be prepared for anything.'

'Were you lot scared of a really bad bout of PMS?'

'Prepared for your physical needs. That's all. Can we please get back to the challenge and forget this?'

Lauren folds her arms and sits back. 'Unfortunately for us, nothing about being here is forgettable, mate.'

The housemates sit in silence, stewing on the news that they're being tracked like farm animals, and Danny cracks on like it's fair game.

'Lots of our respondents said the problem with women is that they lay the pressure on. To provide, propose, have kids, do date nights, spend time with them, come home early, check in. The list goes on. Putting pressure on a man, particularly one with a high-pressure job, can be the nail in the coffin. Dr Hicks, anything to add?'

'In my book *Are You in a* Real*ationship?*' Dr Hicks replies, 'I advise limiting the amount of time spent talking about your relationship to once a month, and looking for telltale signs he's struggling under the weight of your wants. Is he snappier than usual, or staying away from home?'

Jackie snorts. 'Sounds like *he's* having some on the side.'

'It's important to make your partner feel you like to know when he's under pressure. That way you can work together to release that pressure and the strain it's putting on your relationship,' Dr Hicks concludes, and clicks again.

Rule #8: Chill out

A woman with tears in her eyes and mascara smears running down her cheeks appears on the screen.

'That's how you three are making me feel right now with this bullshit,' Jackie mutters.

'Jackie, if you aren't going to take this seriously, then I suggest you leave.' Danny looks hard at her.

She raises her eyebrows, stands up and walks to the front, before dropping her own list on the table.

'Fuck you.' She glares at him before turning and walking back inside the house.

'Perfect timing, ladies.' Danny grins. 'Let's talk about emotional stability. The problem with women, according to our readers, is that you're prone to flying off the handle. Now, we know you learnt a bit about this with our lad HuJo, so I'm hoping this will just be a reminder. Don't get your knickers in a twist over nothing. Don't overreact! Listen to this lad's story.'

> The problem with women is that they're fucking crazy. Simple. My GF got home from work last night and went mental because I hadn't taken the chicken out of the freezer and the kids weren't bathed yet. She didn't even care that I wasn't feeling well. Talk about an overreaction!

Amy's always thought of herself as the calm one. Jamie could blow up at a second's notice. Like the first time she met his friend Andy, and Jamie went wild when she touched his arm for two seconds, telling her she was giving him a signal. He ranted that it made her look easy and him look like a mug. Looking back, Amy doesn't think she ever overreacted to anything in their relationship. If anyone was a drama queen, it was Jamie.

Dr Hicks hands out a card with the rules, which is credit-card-sized to 'keep in their purses', while Danny clicks to reveal a digital wheel with their names on it.

'Ladies!' shouts Adam. 'Now that we've reached the end of the lesson, we have an amazing surprise for you. And for our viewers. Feast your eyes on our Wheel of Dates!' He taps the laptop in front of him and there's a beep. 'We've got one lucky viewer on the line. Are you there, Diane? Hello, Diane – can you hear me?'

'Oh my GOD!!' Diane screams down the phone, joined by a few other screams from people standing near her. 'Hi Danny!! Hi housemates!! I can't believe I'm on TV. Shut up, Mum, I can't hear!!! Hello?'

Adam smiles. 'Yes, hello Diane and hello Diane's mum!'

More screams.

'Now, we're about to spin the Wheel of Dates, and it's up to you to tell us when to click the buzzer and stop it. Are you ready?'

'Sorry, can you tell us what's going on?' Amy says, loudly. 'What happens to us if they stop on our name?' She looks around at the others. 'Is this an eviction?' she mouths.

'OK, Diane, one . . . two . . . three . . . go!' Adam clicks on the buzzer and the wheel starts spinning around.

'Hello, is this an eviction?' Amy shouts louder.

After a few seconds, Diane screams at him to stop. The arrow slows down until it's clicking and comes to a stop on Amy's name.

She looks at the rest of the housemates, who all turn to

her with worried faces. Is it over? Is she leaving? She exhales loudly, her hands on her hips.

'Thank you, Diane!' he shouts, before hanging up on her. 'Amy, Amy, Amy. Do we have a surprise for you!'

She feels sick.

'Tonight, Amy' – Adam wanders over to her with his hands in his pockets – 'you're cooking a special someone a Sorry Supper. A home-cooked meal to apologise for letting it go, for your lazy attitude to sex, for complaining, controlling, neglecting and pressurising. All the things you might not have realised you were doing, but I can guarantee that you were.'

'For who? Who am I saying sorry to?'

'Why, it's Jamie O'Connor of course.'

WEEK THREE

WEEK THREE

Twenty

Gemma clinks a tea down on the coffee table. 'I don't know, Ames. What about all that money?'

'Well, they say money doesn't make you happy,' adds Jackie. 'But that's just bollocks, isn't it? I was poor growing up, then rich for a few years. I know what I'd rather be.'

'If I win a million quid, I'm starting my own gym,' Gemma mutters, then gasps. 'I'm gonna call it Gymma!'

Amy's had her head shoved under a pillow in the corner of the sofa for the last twenty minutes. Making Jamie a Sorry Supper to apologise for doing nothing wrong in their relationship is taking it way too far. They're forcing her out. Ten thousand pounds is enough to get her to Asia, and there's no chance she's winning this thing. She's been sniffing around the middle of The Tracker since they started, so clearly no one is talking much about her. Sonia Cole was right: she is the human equivalent of drying paint. She can't compete with Flick or Gemma, so she might as well quit now and save herself the painful humiliation of a date with Jamie and anything else these evil puppeteers have in store for them.

She smiles, thinking about how she could be on her own sofa in a few hours, watching the rest of them rattle around in here without her. Maybe she could send a few messages to The Wall. Anonymously tell Jackie to take it easy on Flick. Or, not anonymously. Amy needs to be more self-assured and outspoken. She pledges to say something the next time Jackie has a dig at Flick.

On her way to see Dr Hicks, Amy stops as she passes The Tracker. She's slid up a place. It must be the Sorry Supper everyone's talking about. It doesn't change her mind. She can't cook for Jamie. She can't apologise to him. There's only so much she can take.

Gemma walks up behind her and squeezes her shoulder. 'Are you sure you want to do this, Ames? We love having you here – we're going to really miss you if you go. Besides, we're already half-way through the show. The next two weeks will fly by!'

'Yes, I—' Amy starts, but is interrupted.

'Oh my God, I'm at the top!' Gemma cries, looking at Amy with an open smile. 'I can't believe it – thanks, everyone!' She waves at the cameras. 'Sorry, babes, you were saying?'

Gemma's outburst brings home the reality of the situation. This is a competition, not a community. They've only known each other for two weeks. It might feel like they're close, but the cold truth is that every single one of them wants to win a million pounds, no matter what they say. They might be fond of each other, but in a month's time they'll have scattered back to their lives from before, and will probably never speak to each other again. She doesn't blame Gemma for the outburst – she didn't mean it insensitively. Amy would feel the same way if she was at the top, and Gemma is an open book. That's what Amy likes about her.

'Ames, everyone's behind you,' Jackie adds, joining them. 'On The Wall, everyone's saying how they've gone too far with this Sorry Supper. I really think if you leave, you'll regret it. If you can get through tonight, you can get through anything, and we'll be right behind you in the house.'

'You always regret the things you *don't* do,' adds Gemma. 'Not the things you do do.'

Amy gives them both a hug and turns to open the Therapy Room door. Perhaps her earlier thoughts were too harsh. Maybe this is more than a competition.

'Hello, Amy,' Dr Hicks says, walking into the Therapy Room. 'You've had a difficult few days, haven't you? Is that why you booked this session outside of our normal hours?'

'Yes, I suppose you could say that,' she says, trying to remain calm. 'This Sorry Supper you've organised. A bit much, isn't it?'

'Well, we were always going to test your strength on *The Shelf*, Amy. If you're feeling knocked to the ground, let's talk about how we can put you back on your feet.'

'I want to leave the house.'

He stops tapping his iPad and looks up, surprised. 'Isn't that a little dramatic?'

'I don't think so. If it is, I don't care. It's just how I feel.'

'Amy, you really shouldn't make important decisions when you have a hot head and you're feeling emotional. Consider your decision for a while longer – perhaps sleep on it before you choose what to do.'

'I can't sleep on it – the supper with Jamie is tonight!' she cries. 'And I'm sorry, but having to cook my arsehole of an ex-boyfriend an apology meal is ludicrous. I'm really not overreacting here – I think I'm reacting as any normal human being would. You're a therapist. Surely you can see that?'

'I'm sure you're stronger than you think, and your response to this challenge might surprise you. Seeing Jamie like this might help you let go. Cut the cord. Forgiving someone who has hurt you frees you from all the negative emotions that can hold you back, like anger or blame.'

His words hit a nerve. She stops herself in mid-response, sighs and sits back.

If she doesn't learn to forgive Jamie, she will always resent him. And why should she let him impact her life like that? Why should she let him have any sway over what she does or how she feels? She's in charge of her life now. She's already wasted two years too long worrying about his feelings towards her. Her decision to stay on the show should have nothing to do with him. Amy pictures his smug face when he hears that she's leaving because of him. She can't leave and let him have the satisfaction of thinking she still cares. What she really needs to do is embrace this Sorry Supper with total indifference. She needs to put mind over matter and be friendly, even if it's just for pretend. Because Jamie cannot leave here thinking he is the one in control.

His ego is big enough already.

Twenty-One

Hattie's panting as she paces up and down the corridor outside the Therapy Room, scratching and rubbing her arms. She looks like she's seen a ghost.

'I've made a terrible mistake, Amy. I shouldn't be here. What if they make me go on a date with Dylan? Did Dr Hicks say anything?'

'Woah, Hats, what's going on? Stop for a sec.' Amy takes her arm and guides her to the dining room. 'Take a seat. Breathe. Where is everyone else?'

Amy looks around. Jackie, Gemma and Lauren are outside tanning topless by the swimming pool. Roomba is rolling suspiciously close to them. Flick strolls carefree into the garden with a piece of toast and a cup of tea, takes one look at the topless trio and makes an instant U-turn back into the kitchen.

Amy looks at Hattie, who's struggling to catch her breath.

'I'm coming with you, Amy. I have to get out of here

too. I can't do this anymore, I can't go through with this.' She hides her face in her hands and sinks onto Amy's shoulder. 'They can't make me see Dylan.'

'Hattie,' Amy says calmly, 'no one has mentioned you having a date with Dylan – it might never happen. Besides, he's already been on the show. I'm sure he won't come on again. Gemma's probably made him run for the hills. Do you want to see Dr Hicks?' She eases her up off her shoulder and looks into her puffy brown eyes.

'No, I just . . . I just don't know where to go. I feel trapped. This is all too much. I can't breathe.'

'Hattie, you aren't trapped. You have a choice and you can be wherever you want to be, but I promise you're OK here with me. Now, I want you to do something for me.'

Amy guides her to a dining chair, sits her down and takes the seat opposite her.

Hattie nods, closes her eyes and carries on puffing.

'Name five things you can see right now,' says Amy. 'It can be anything. Like a chair.'

Hattie opens her eyes slowly, confused.

'Trust me,' Amy says.

Hattie looks around and says slowly, 'Dining room table.'

'Great. What else?'

'Fruit bowl, dirty mug, picture, door.'

Amy and Hattie continue to list things around them. It forces Hattie to focus on her senses. Four things she can touch, three things she can hear, two things she can smell and finally a positive affirmation. Sarah would be proud of her. She taught Amy this technique during their finals. Amy was overworked and sleep-deprived, and Sarah had found her crouched in a fetal position under her desk, repeating that she couldn't carry on. Since then she'd used the technique at least ten times when she felt work – and Jamie – start to overwhelm her.

'I am strong enough to get through this,' they say together. And for the first time since being here, Amy really believes it. In herself. She *is* strong enough to get through this. And if she can get through this, she can get through anything. Pressing the STAY button was the right choice.

Hattie's breathing is back to normal, and Amy's own racing heart has slowed.

'Thanks, Amy.' Hattie lowers her head. 'Sometimes I feel like I'm choking.'

'Do you want to talk, Hattie? Maybe somewhere a bit quieter?' Amy says.

They hear a splash outside, followed by a scream.

'Oh, you are dead, Lauren Hawk!' Jackie shouts, followed by the sound of someone jumping into the pool.

'Can't splash me if I'm already wet!' Lauren laughs.

Hattie nods her head. 'The bathroom.'

Amy locks the door of the bathroom and folds two towels on the floor. She takes a seat as Hattie leans against the shower door, closes her eyes and breathes out.

'Sorry, Amy,' Hattie breaks the silence after a few minutes. 'I was being silly back there.'

'Hattie, you don't need to apologise – there's nothing to

apologise for. Panic attacks are awful, but you managed to get through it just fine, and now it's over. You just talk when you want to, if you want to. I'm happy to sit here in silence. I love being in the bathroom – it's my escape. There aren't any mics in here, so if we're quiet we won't be heard. The ones in the bedroom can't pick us up if we whisper.'

'I wish I wasn't so scared of everything.' Hattie tilts her head back. 'I'm so stupid. I'm scared of things that might never happen. No one has ever mentioned me seeing Dylan, but I built it up in my head and made myself freak out. And then I freaked out even more, thinking it would be worse to go on a date with a stranger. I can't handle that – I've never been on a date. Ever. I wouldn't have a clue what to do or say. And with all the cameras watching me, it would be so embarrassing.'

'Didn't you and Dylan date?' Amy asks.

'Nope, we met at school and moved in together when we were eighteen. All our friends went off to do more exciting things. Some of them even went to London. But we stayed in Southampton, in the same street where we both grew up. After that we never made any new friends or went out. It was just the two of us, together the whole time. Always at home, because there was no money to do anything. No money to get married or have kids. It was sort of nice for a while. Safe, familiar. I got a job in the kitchen at the hotel down the road. Dylan was a labourer. But things started going pear-shaped when he got the sack last year, and he hasn't had another job since. He just sits around on the PlayStation. I tried to get him work at the hotel, but he told me he'd go nuts if he spent any more time with me. It was a fair point, I suppose. I felt the same way, but I was sick of worrying about bills. I've been paying them all on my little salary for over a year. We could barely afford heating last winter. When I tried to borrow money off my dad, Dylan went mad and said I was making him look like a loser. Luckily I picked up some extra shifts, which is probably what kicked this all off. He's really sorry now, crying and telling me he couldn't get a job because he isn't good at anything and that it doesn't help his confidence when I criticise him. But what am I supposed to do, Amy? If I don't say anything, he carries on wasting our lives away. If I do, I'm going to "push him over the edge one of these days". Anyway, it was better for a bit. Then he told me he'd got an interview at a construction site in London and that it would mean the world to him if I came with. Next thing I know, I'm in the Chat Room with him telling me what a big fat boring bitch I am and how he can't wait to be on his own without me telling him what to do.'

Amy remembers her mum's one piece of advice when it was getting serious with Jamie.

Always have your own bank account, even if he seems like a saint.

'But I am pleased to be here.' Hattie smiles. 'I couldn't press STAY quick enough when they asked me! I want to prove to everyone that I'm not just Hattie the Fatty. Hippo,

234

who'll never achieve anything in her life. Don't get me wrong, I have no idea what I'm doing and it scares the shit out of me. But the idea of going back to my old life is much scarier. Being here with you lot has really woken me up to what I could achieve on my own if I just took a chance. I just, you know, had a moment back there. I felt out of control. And the idea of seeing his greasy face again made me feel like running away.'

Amy squeezes her hand.

'Thanks, Ames. I'm going to remember that trick. It really helped. I'm going to go and join the others in the pool. Cool off a bit. Wanna come?' Hattie stands up.

Amy shakes her head. 'I think I'm going to enjoy the peace and quiet in here for a bit. Do some thinking. Figure out how I'm going to handle tonight.'

'I think you're going to handle it like an absolute boss.' Hattie smiles as she opens the door.

The idea of going back to my old life is much scarier. That comment in particular struck a chord. Being single isn't scary. What's scary is being stuck with someone who will make you miserable for the rest of your life. That's the real campfire horror story.

It isn't long before Amy is reminded that there is no escape in here.

'Hon, are you going to be long? I'm bursting!' shouts Jackie with a rap on the door.

'And that is why I like living alone,' Amy whispers, standing up.

Jackie doesn't wait for her to leave before she pulls her bikini bottoms down.

*

In the living room, Gemma's eating from a jar of pickles with her legs spread in a wide V on top of the coffee table. In between each bite, she sips the vinegar.

@**tomjef2** #Gemma has literally zero self-respect #theshelf

'Hey, Tommy J., I literally give zero fucks,' she shouts.

@**tomjef2** OMG #GEMMA JUST SPOKE TO ME #famousnow #theshelf

A tut comes from the dining room.

Gemma cranes her neck towards Flick, who's sitting at the table mending a button on Hattie's blouse. She looks up and shrugs one shoulder.

'Well, I'm sorry, Gemma, but they do have a point. I mean, aren't you supposed to care about how you come across if you're an influencer? Aren't you worried you might lose followers if you look like a slob?'

Gemma stares at her as she swallows another sip and exhales in satisfaction.

'I can't be picture-perfect all the time, Flick. It's exhausting. Jason must be loving seeing me without my phone, letting it all hang out. Trapped in here all day and all night, where he can watch everything I'm doing.'

Flick smiles. 'Jason and Simon should form a club.'

It's the first time she's mentioned Simon without a gushy follow-up about how brilliant he is.

Amy got trapped earlier talking to her by the pool about their relationship. It was a soliloquy about when they first locked eyes at the surgery and the electricity was palpable. How funny it was that he thought she was the receptionist! How he swept her off her feet, taking her to the most expensive restaurants in Cambridge, trips to the opera in London, cocktails in The Shard. How exciting it was that they kept their relationship under wraps at work, worried about accusations of nepotism. How brilliantly he had handled her leaving the surgery, how incredibly hard he works to support her and how much she appreciates being able to spend time at home, which she really does now prefer. When the one-sided conversation ended after fifteen minutes, Amy thought it might be because Flick had run out of superlatives.

'Well, he's certainly lucky to have found you, Flick.'

'No, Amy, I'm the lucky one.'

Twenty-Two

'Piglet!' Jamie shouts, with his arms wide open as he marches into The Secret Garden that evening. 'Are you cross with me?'

He looks different. His hair is shorter around the sides and he's grown his stubble out. And why does he look so brown? His tan is made even more pronounced by his clothes. All black everything. A jet-black shirt that's too tight, rolled up ripped jeans with his ankles showing and black velvet smoking slippers. Who the hell just walked in? He looks like he's trying to be Russell Brand.

'Of course I fucking am, you lying prick! Me, pressuring you into marriage, obsessing over kids? Who were you in a relationship with? Not me. Get over yourself – I hope your business fails and you have to move back in with your parents. And by the way, I never told you this but Sarah thinks you're going to end up looking like Tom Cruise. In *Tropic Thunder*.'

That's what she'd like to say.

Instead, she says, 'No, I'm not cross. I'm fine. How are you?' while standing up to endure a hug and a kiss on both cheeks without projectile-vomiting onto his chest.

The last thing she wants is to look upset. The aim here is to look like she doesn't give a shit, and never did. She stiffens as he squeezes her into his hard stomach. Amy tends to wear her emotions on her face and was worried it would show when he walked in. Not that he'd ever notice. He's as good at gauging her emotions as he is at giving her compliments. She's relieved that she feels detached. Perhaps the show does work. Perhaps ripping the plaster off is the most effective recovery method – not that she'll ever admit it.

'Woah, single suits you, Ames!' he says, looking her up and down.

She does look good. It isn't something she usually admits, but tonight she's taking it. It's all thanks to Gemma, who went to town on her make-up with some kind of magical contouring trick. She's wearing the strapless black and gold maxi dress she was saving for their first night on holiday, with oversized gold earrings.

'Go on, give us a twirl.'

She ignores him and sits down.

'So, what have *you* been up to these past two weeks?' she asks.

He takes a seat and reaches across the table, grabs the wine bottle and pours himself a glass.

'I hope you don't think I'm enjoying this,' he says, ignoring her question and suddenly looking serious. 'It's just part of the show, I didn't have a choice.'

'Oh, I know, Jamie. I'm fine. It's all a bit of fun, isn't it? Have you been watching?'

'Just the catch-ups at night. Headplace has kicked off a bit and I've had to do a few interviews for the show. I'm glad you think it's fun too – I thought you'd hate me for it!'

'Nooo, not at all – how could I hate you after everything we've been through together?'

How could you do it to me, Jamie, after everything we went through together?

'So, tell me all about these interviews. Sounds exciting. I hope you've been saying good things about me.' She smiles, pouring herself a glass of wine. 'It might help with my votes.'

He fake-laughs as he takes another sip and leans back.

✳

'Oh my God, tell us everything!' Gemma all but yells as Amy walks into the kitchen to fetch a bread selection for the table.

'It's not that bad. I think I'm managing to be as obnoxiously nonchalant as possible.' She smiles as she picks up the bread basket and balsamic-infused olive oil. 'But he did ask me to twirl for him. I blame you.'

'Ew,' says Gemma, scrunching up her nose. She picks up

one of the calamari that Amy helped Hattie to cook earlier. If helping means watching from a distance with a large glass of wine. 'Which one's Jamie's plate?'

When Amy points it out, Gemma licks the calamari piece and puts it back. Then she does the same to the rest of them.

✳

Jamie peers into the bread basket as Amy places it on the table outside.

'Anything gluten-free? I've gone gluten-free recently. Best thing I've ever done. I have so much energy now. Do you remember I used to be really heavy and sluggish all the time? It's amazing what a diet can do for you. You should try it.'

Amy grabs a white bread roll, takes a large bite and starts to butter the rest.

'So, Jamie,' she says with a loud swallow, 'business is booming, is it? Think you've picked up any new clients from this? Perhaps I'm owed a cut.'

'Amy.' Jamie sighs. 'Can we please stop being so nice and polite. Let's be real with each other. It's me. You can talk to me.' He grabs her wrist, pulling her towards him.

She wrenches it out of his grip, puts both hands back in her lap and glares at him.

Hold it together. You were doing so well.

'Chill out. Bit touchy, aren't you? Anyway, what I was trying to say is . . .' He lowers his head and looks at his feet. Is he about to cry? Amy isn't sure what to do. She's never seen him cry in her life.

'Isn't this whole experience incredible?' He lifts his head up, smiling broadly and shout-whispering, 'I mean, think about it, we're being watched by over a million viewers. Right now, Amy!' he cries. 'I'm famous! You're famous! Can you fucking believe it? Of course it's going to open up doors for Headplace! I mean, I've been dropping it into the conversation every chance I get when I'm asked to comment on the show, and in these interviews. Surely someone's going to pick that up, aren't they, Piglet?'

Amy can't believe she thought he was going to cry. When will she learn that he will never be the man she had hoped he would become?

'You don't get to call me Piglet anymore,' she says.

'Amy! For fuck's sake, if you aren't cross with me, why are you being so stand-offish?' He looks at her with that intense glare that would usually make her feel nervous, as if he's about to blow a fuse. 'Stop pretending to be someone else. This isn't you. What have you done with Piglet? And I'm still waiting for a thank you, by the way. It's the least I deserve. You're all over the Mail Online because of me. Let's face it, if you weren't in here, you'd be out there watching *The Shelf* happen for someone else, glued to the TV in your old tracksuit bottoms, eating fake cheese. I've put you on the map, Piglet. Sorry, *Amy*.' He downs the rest of his wine and reaches across the table for the bottle.

As she watches him, she quietly daydreams about

smashing him across the face with it like she's 'the Bride' from *Kill Bill.*

Amy can't hold it in anymore. She needs to know what the fuck he was thinking when he saw the ad for this show and thought it would be a good idea. She has to know why he's telling everyone lies about how she was in their relationship, and why he felt he couldn't talk to her about it. She wants to know how long he's been feeling like this, and when he decided to start making a fool out of her. Whether he's told his friends about it at the pub, and if they all cracked up. The ultimate joke at Amy's expense.

'Why did you do it, Jamie?' she asks him. 'Why didn't you just talk to me? Two years. Two years, and you didn't feel close enough to me to have a normal conversation. Why go to these lengths, just to break up with someone?'

He shifts in his seat, flicks his nose and brushes his hair back. 'How could I tell you to your face, Amy? There would have been screaming, crying, shouting, tears. I couldn't watch you be crushed. I'd have hated to see you like that.'

'Um, have you not seen the first episode?' she asks, frowning.

'God no, I couldn't bring myself to watch that. No, no, I've actively avoided that. It was really hard, too, because it was all over my Facebook feed.'

Amy could burst into hysterics at the absurdity of his response. But she manages to keep a calm face and a cool voice.

'OK, another question. Why are you going around telling everyone that I put pressure on you to marry me and have kids? We never had a single conversation about it. I remember talking about other people getting married and other people having kids. But it was never about us. The closest we ever came to talking about the future was when I suggested I move in, after you gave me the key to your flat. At the time I thought it was a sign that our relationship was moving forward. But maybe it was a sidestep for you. Were you just trying to put off the conversation? You knew that at some point we'd have to talk about where we were going – maybe you used the key to delay it, so we didn't have to. Is that what it was? You tell me, Jamie – I can only guess. I'm not angry, I just want to understand what this is all about so I can move on.'

Although Amy is angry. In fact, she's really fucking furious. But that isn't going to get her anywhere.

Jamie hangs his head before he speaks. 'I know we never talked about marriage and babies. That doesn't mean I didn't feel the pressure. I knew that's what you wanted. That's what you all want eventually, isn't it? And just knowing you wanted that made me feel like I was being forced into it myself. And I said loads of times that having a kid would be rubbish. So really, Amy, you should have got the hint. It wasn't even a hint – I couldn't have been clearer.'

'I thought you were joking.'

'Oh, Amy. There's a grain of truth in every joke. You know that.'

She does know that. And she did worry about it at the time. But she ignored it and hoped he would grow up and eventually want adult things. Amy remembers the first and only time he met Jane's twins. Her heart melted as he picked them both up at the same time and spun them around, their maniacal little laughs turning into screams of pure joy. He seemed like such a natural. Like the perfect fun dad. Not the man who turned to Amy as soon as they shut the front door behind them and said, 'Hey, Amy, what's more magical than having kids? Not having them.'

'So what do you want, Jamie?' she asks him across the table. 'In the future?'

'I don't know. I don't really think about it. I'm more of a live-in-the-moment guy. Maybe I will get married one day. Maybe I won't. What makes me happy right now is being single, free and selfish. What's wrong with that? I like to live my life knowing that I don't have to think of anyone else. I can come and go as I please. I don't have to check in with anyone, tell anyone what my evening plans are, text another person to keep them informed of my every movement. Now I can eat what I like, go out when I like, do yoga without someone staring at me.'

'Yes, OK, I get the idea, Jamie.' She's had enough of hearing how great life is in his post-Amy world. Besides, what he's just described is what he had before. He hardly ever thought of her. He did come and go as he pleased. He never checked in. She thought he did yoga in front of her to make her feel bad for not exercising.

The conversation continues for another half hour. There are no arguments, no raised tempers, no tears and no answers – and no apologies either. When it's time to say goodbye, there's a friendly hug with a pat on the back.

But not before Jamie finishes his whole plate of calamari.

Twenty-Three

'Welcome to *The Shelf*!' Adam Andrews shouts into the camera from the stage. 'It's time for the second eviction of the show, and what a week it's been! We've had humiliation . . .'

A boomerang clip of Gemma accidentally walking into the glass door and bouncing off it plays over, several times.

'Gawd,' mutters Gemma. 'Knew that would come up.'

'We've had confrontation . . .' Adam continues.

Grainy black-and-white footage of Gemma pointing her finger in Dylan's face appears on the screen. Dylan looks exactly like a garden gnome, with his arms folded. Identical scruffy beard and downturned mouth. Almost the same height. Fuzzy monobrow that seems fixed in a frown. Hattie must have completely dwarfed him. Amy wants to laugh when she pictures them walking down the street together, and even more when she turns to see Hattie death-staring him from the sofa like Brad Pitt in *Friends*.

'And we've had the stone-cold brutal truth!'

They show a clip of Amy and Jamie's date, with a close-up of him hanging his head. Amy's pleased his bald spot is showing. He'll hate that.

'What makes me happy right now is being single, free and selfish.'

'So, are the housemates beginning to crack? And who will be the second housemate to leave the show tonight? Stay tuned, Britain, we'll be back after the break!'

Amy gathers everyone's prosecco flutes and walks to the kitchen for top-ups, glancing at The Tracker as she passes. She's moved up to third place.

Day 16

1. Gemma
2. Flick
3. Amy
4. Jackie
5. Lauren
6. Hattie

The guests on tonight's eviction are Steve and Mike Barton, the twin brothers from *Double Diggers*, a show where they compete by renovating a different garden each. What they're doing here, and how they're qualified to comment on *The Shelf*, is a mystery. But they do have star appeal – both have identical good looks, but non-identical bad taste – Steve's T-shirt says *#teamgemma* and Mike's T-shirt says *#teamflick*.

'Go on, Steve, you first. Why Gemma?' asks Adam.

'Because she's me, Adam!' he cries. 'She's authentic, she's honest, she's hilarious. I want to say sod it and drink the pickle juice and let it all hang out. I think we're all Gemma.'

'I'm sorry,' interrupts Mike, 'but no one can beat Flick. She is The Keeper. Give her the crown and call it a night. Sure, we might not all agree with her life choices, but she's got a good heart. And at least she's holding it together. I don't know how she manages to look so immaculate every day. If Simon doesn't marry her, I bloody will!'

'Ohh, watch out, Simon, Mike's got dibs!' sqawks Adam.

'Flick? Yawn!' Steve looks disgusted. '"*Simon's incredible, Simon's amazing, Simon is the best. Simon, Simon, Simon.*" My God, I felt sorry for Amy yesterday, by the pool. I think everyone did. Did you see Jackie come outside and go straight back in again? Ha! What about that meme that did the rounds?'

'The one where Amy's been replaced by a skeleton?' Adam laughs.

'When Flick reaches the end of her story!'

'Classic! Sorry, Flick, time to get a new one. OK, so you both raise good points about Gemma and Flick, but who do you think will go tonight? Mike, you go first.'

'I'm torn between Lauren and Hattie. Lauren is basically MIA. I keep on forgetting she's even on the show. All she does is lie in bed or on a sun lounger in the garden like a rock lizard. And I'm afraid poor Hattie just won't hack it long-term.'

'And you, Stevo? Who'll be gone by bedtime?' Adam asks.

'Hattie, without a doubt. She's had her time. I think Lauren's time is coming, and she has way more to offer the show. I think the audience can't wait to see what she brings out!' He winks.

Amy gets up, moves across to Hattie and puts her arms around her. She's beginning to breathe heavily. 'Hattie, don't listen to a word. It's just for shock value.'

'Lauren, how are you doing?' says Amy, looking around.

Lauren isn't in the dining room where she was sitting a second ago. Amy cranes her neck but she isn't in the kitchen either.

'Where did she go? Is she OK?'

'She was right here a minute ago,' Jackie says. 'Maybe she's gone to pack her suitcase just in case. Lozza?' she shouts towards the bedroom, making Flick grimace.

There's no response.

'Lauren!' Amy shouts, standing up.

'Did anyone see her go into the bedroom?' asks Amy.

A collective shake of the head.

'Lauren!' Jackie yells again, walking into the garden.

'Check the pool!' Amy shouts through the glass. Jackie looks around and shakes her head.

All of a sudden, a siren starts wailing on the TV and Adam Andrews' face fills the screen. He's looking at the audience and reading from a card. The housemates gather back on the sofa.

'Where the fuck is she? She's missing the eviction,' Jackie whispers.

'Viewers, we have some breaking news coming in from behind the scenes,' he says, pressing his earpiece and staring to the side. He looks down before putting his finger to his lips and hushing the audience, nodding and mm-ing as he takes in whatever he's being told.

'OK, viewers, there's been a change of plan for tonight's show. I'd like to reiterate that this was not planned, and we will be refunding you all the cost of your votes.' He looks at the camera seriously. 'Is she there?' he whispers into his mic.

'Is who here?' Gemma says, starting to look panicked.

'Ladies and gents, what a shocker. Would you please welcome to the stage tonight's evicted housemate, Lauren!'

The housemates run up to the screen.

'Lauren, what have you done?' Hattie shouts at the TV.

Lauren takes a seat on the stage sofa, smiling and giving a peace sign to the audience as they start to calm down.

It's odd, seeing her on TV, Amy thinks. She looks like a celebrity with all those lights on her, almost like a stranger.

'Lauren!' Adam shouts. 'Welcome to the stage! What a completely unexpected but delightful surprise!'

'You all right?' Lauren says, a picture of perfect calm.

'Yeah, I'm all right,' he mimics her indifference, to the amusement of the audience.

'Lauren, can you explain what just happened?' asks Adam. 'Five minutes ago you were on the sofa in the house, and now you're here. How did you get here?'

Lauren looks at Adam, then at the Barton twins.

'Sorry, mate, which camera do I talk to?' she says.

'Don't worry about that, love, you can look at me,' Adam says.

'Nah, I don't want to look at you, I want to talk to Hattie,' Lauren says. A collective 'oooh' fades up from the audience and Adam looks taken aback as he points to one of the cameras. Lauren scans where he's pointing and fixes her face on the right camera, which zooms in. She smiles.

'Hattie, love, you don't deserve to leave the house now,' Lauren says. 'You've got plenty more to do. I want you to stay in there and prove all those haters wrong. I'm not interested in all this self-improvement bollocks and "better woman" bullshit. I've got what I came for – I've had the experience and I'm getting my ten grand. It's all good.'

'But Lauren, what about the million quid?' asks Adam.

'I don't need a million quid to be happy. I am desperate for a gin, though.'

The audience whoop and clap.

'Someone get this girl a drink! One final thing, Lozza – will you be following the girls on the telly?' Adam shrugs.

'Fook, no,' she laughs. 'I'll see the lads when they're out, in person. This show is festerin' garbage, and you're an absolute fookin' tit.' Then she stands up, removes her mic and walks off the stage.

For once, Adam has no response. The audience start up a slow handclap as he listens to his earpiece and the feed cuts out, fading the living room screen to black.

Twenty-Four

Gemma's screaming at Hattie and Flick in the garden. She's roped them into a fitness boot camp and has gone full SAS commando.

'Wish I had an excuse to scream at someone,' says Amy, sipping her coffee at the window. 'I think it would make me feel more relaxed.'

Jackie joins her. 'What about the Chat Room? I think it's soundproof.'

'True.' Amy nods, staring at the commotion outside as Gemma starts clapping at them to up the pace. Hattie's turned a bright shade of beetroot.

'I wonder what Lauren's up to?' Amy ponders. 'I can't believe it's already been two days since she left.'

'Signing a record deal with her fifteen minutes of fame, hopefully,' Jackie replies. 'So,' she turns to Amy, 'a million quid. Gemma says she'd open a gym called Gymma. Hattie was chatting about starting a food truck chain. What would you do with the money?'

Amy thinks about this all the time. If she did win, she'd get Sarah to help her decide what to do with it all. Amy's rubbish with money, and without advice would probably just let it sit in a bank, too scared to spend it.

'I don't know, really. Before now I'd have blown the whole lot on a house. But I'm not so sure that's what I need right now. I think the first thing I'd do is book a first-class flight to Asia. Settling down can wait.'

'Oooh, where in Asia?' Jackie asks, leaning over the kitchen counter.

'Probably Thailand – I love it. The sticky heat, the food markets, the people staring. Daytime drinking. Walk-in spas. The world's most beautiful beaches. What's not to love? It's like a perfect balance of buzz and bliss. I don't know – there's just something in the air. It's probably opium. What would you do?'

Jackie doesn't answer.

'Jackie?'

Amy looks up to see Jackie's cheeks crumple as tears start to fall. She holds her face in her hands.

'Jackie! What's wrong?' Amy puts her mug down and grabs Jackie's arm.

'I'm OK.' She sniffs. 'It's stupid. I'm being pathetic.' She sighs, rubbing her eyes. 'It's nothing, really. I'm probably just hung-over. But some dickhead was posting nasty comments about me on The Wall this morning.'

'Saying what? Who?'

'I think it's a bloke from my old law firm,' she says. 'He was the paralegal to a partner who had it in for me there. Well, they all had it in for me.' She shakes her head. 'I don't know why he's still after me – I left ages ago. Doesn't he have anything better to do?'

'Don't let them get to you – they just want you to take the bait,' says Amy. 'Yesterday a total stranger tweeted that she doesn't trust me as far as she can throw me. No idea what I've done to deserve that.'

'Amy, I've been dodging the bait for two years. But they make it fucking impossible not to bite sometimes, don't they?' she says quietly.

Amy looks at her sympathetically. 'What happened?'

'Oh, Ames,' Jackie turns her head back to the garden. 'It's such a long story. Don't want you turning into that skeleton meme again.'

She clears her throat and sits down.

'I was so happy when I started there. No other firms gave me a look-in, despite getting a first and a distinction on my legal practitioner diploma. They could only offer me a paralegal role, but I was still delighted. I worked really hard, then a few years later they offered me a training contract, saying they saw potential. Fast-forward lots of long hours, late nights and slow progress, and I qualified as an associate solicitor. Then became managing associate. But once I hit managing associate, progress wasn't just slow, it stopped. It seemed like everyone was being made a partner, apart from me. First in the office, last to leave, billing more hours than anyone and bringing in more business. The final straw was when a trainee I'd supervised – arrogant little tosser – overtook me. So, I started making a few noises and emailed the managing partner who hired me about it, hoping he'd have my back.'

She looks out of the window and exhales.

'Instead, he took me for a coffee and a little chat about what was in my best interests at the firm. How I didn't have the right managerial skills needed to take the next step. How partners have to be cool-headed, poker-faced negotiators who could leave their emotions at home. He said I would hate it, and that I should carry on building business at my level, with the kind of work I'd be comfortable with. And that it would be in the best interests of the firm, too.

'Then I bit the bullet and asked him if he thought it was strange how there were no female or black partners in my department. That I felt I was having to work twice as hard as everyone else to climb the ladder because of my gender and my race. That I was tired. Demotivated. I mean, it's hard to feel inspired in a room full of partners who are all old white men. Every single one of them. Can you believe it?

'Anyway, he went off at me. Told me I was ungrateful for all the opportunities he'd given me, and that it wasn't senior management's fault that no black women in the firm fitted the role. I was shaking. That day, I lodged a complaint to HR and said if the issue wasn't addressed, I'd be taking it to the Solicitors Regulation Authority.' She shakes her head.

'Did HR do anything?' Amy asks.

'HR did fuck all. They said they'd launch an inquiry, but I heard nothing for weeks. Then one morning I came into work and found them hovering around my desk, telling me I needed to come with them to an urgent meeting with senior management. When I arrived, they told me they were restructuring, and I was being offered voluntary redundancy. I took it. Left that day. At the time, it felt like my only option. The whole place was toxic after the falling-out with the managing partner. So I accepted, and then I never saw or heard from them again. Until now.'

'What did Aaron think about all this?'

'He was furious with me for losing the job, and didn't understand why I wanted more when being a senior associate was enough to pay the bills and live a good life. Especially because he thought I might come round to the idea of kids and that the maternity leave would help. Even though I've always said no kids. But he didn't understand me then and he doesn't understand me now. And because I haven't been able to get a job since, we've been under a lot of financial pressure.

'That's what eventually destroyed our relationship. It wasn't just me being close to my dad and Aaron feeling left out. That's why I decided to stay on here. Money. It's what it all usually boils down to, right?' She smiles and shrugs her shoulders. 'Although it wasn't just the money Aaron loved. He loved all the expensive company events we were invited to. Don't get me wrong, Aaron's the most antisocial person you'll ever meet. But he loved how everyone assumed he was the lawyer and I was the house-wife. He got to play make-believe, and he lapped it up.'

'Did you hear me say you could stop?' Gemma roars over Flick, who's lying panting on the floor.

A look of determination spreads across Jackie's face.

'But if I won a million quid,' she continues, 'I'd sue the shit out of them.'

'I think you should take Gemma into the courtroom if you do,' mutters Amy.

'She's loving that way too much, isn't she?'

Dooong.

Amy and Jackie look at each other. The class stops mid-plank and stares.

Twenty-Five

Dooong. Dooong. Dooong. Dooong.

'I'm coming, I'm coming! Jesus,' Jackie shouts as she walks down the corridor. Amy follows behind her through the dining room, when something catches her eye on The Tracker.

She's climbed to number two, after Flick. Overnight.

Her thoughts are disrupted by a heart-stopping screech at the door. She darts down the corridor to find Jackie holding a box with a beaming smile.

'What's that?' Amy asks as the other housemates rush up behind her.

'Civilisation!' she cries, showing them the box lid, which reads *Sponsored by Vibe Mobile*.

The housemates scurry behind Jackie like a flock of baby birds as she takes the box into the dining room, holding it carefully like it's made of glass.

'There's a note!' cries Gemma. 'What does it say?'

Dear housemates,
For two hours, you will have access to a brand-new
iPhone, courtesy of your fans at Vibe Mobile. Feel free
to explore, download, browse and send a message to
the world beyond your walls. Binge away!

Frothing with excitement, they each grab a phone and hurry
to find a comfortable corner. The house falls silent apart from
the occasional tap, ping and mutter of 'Oh my God . . .'

Amy hunkers down in the Tiki bar and logs into the
pre-installed Instagram app.

What the fuck.

She has 400,342 new notifications.

Too terrified to look at what might be an onslaught of
nasty comments, she bypasses the notifications and heads
straight to Sarah's profile. Her latest post is a cocktail at
Sticks 'n' Sushi, taken last night.

> Missing my fav **@amywrighty_88** Can't believe it's been 18
> days – not that I'm counting.

Amy's heart swells as she quickly types.

> Save one for me! Miss you x

She resists a fleeting temptation to look at Jamie's profile,
and opens Jane's instead. It's a photo of the twins watching
Peppa Pig. They're covered in jam.

Oh, for fuck's sake.

Then she spots an old photo of her and Jane from school on her feed.

So proud of my bestie **@amywright88**! Can't wait to celebrate with her when she WINS! #theshelf #amyontheshelf #bffs #tbt

Besties? Since when? The last time I saw you was months ago. And you made me feel like crap.

Amy moves on to Facebook.

Holy fucking shit.

Almost every post she scrolls past is about the show. There are photos of the housemates everywhere. Gifs. Memes. News articles. Cartoons. Songs. Even *This Morning* has run a segment on it. She feels sweaty.

When the actual fuck and how the actual fuck did this get so big?

OMG YOU WILL LEGIT DIE when you see what Amy used to look like!

The Shelf: Style Evolution on gossipyrabbit.com

Oh no. No no no no no no. Nooooo.

She stares at her sixteen-year-old self from 2004. She remembers the outfit vividly. A Von Dutch trucker hat, bell bottoms and blue lens sunglasses. And she was so much thinner.

'Where do they get this stuff from?' she asks in a trance, as she wanders into the living room. She's glued to her screen but wants to see if anyone else is on the verge of a heart attack.

'Old friends looking to make a quick buck?' answers Jackie, glancing over her shoulder. 'Oh my GOD, is that me?' she cries, grabbing Amy's phone.

In the same article, Jackie's towering over her dad in a shiny white pinstripe suit that's three sizes too small for her, with her ankles sticking out the bottom of the trousers.

'That was my first day of work experience,' she broods. 'Look at me! No wonder the boys ran a mile!' she laughs. 'Ah, miss you, Dad!' She looks up at the cameras.

The Shelf has occupied most of the Mail Online, and the housemates are freaking out about seeing their faces plastered everywhere. Amy's panic is a mixture of excitement about her newfound celebrity and horror that most of the pictures are taken at unflattering floor angles by Roomba. The little bastard has managed to capture every nail bitten, tooth picked, yawn and tummy slump. It's easy to forget the cameras are on you all the time, from every angle, in every room.

The Shelf Exclusive: Jamie and Amy – getting back together?

What?

Jamie's lying sideways on his sofa at the top of the article. One knee is raised and he's resting his head on his wrist. He couldn't look more obnoxious if he tried, holding the pillow Amy bought him for Christmas, embroidered with his initials. She also bought an *AW* pillow to put next to it, but he moved it to the guest bedroom, claiming the colours worked better. She couldn't be bothered to argue.

1. Why did you dump Amy?
It's simple. Amy's a lovely girl. We were just at different stages. She had marriage and kids on her mind, and I had Headplace on mine. That's my recruitment start-up. Headplace.

2. Why didn't you just talk to her?
You know what women of a certain age are like. Tears and drama. Amy's obsession with getting married put a lot of pressure on me, and I admit I buried my head in the sand. But I was trying to get Headplace up and running, and she knew that. It was all too much. Guys, I'm sure you can relate. But hey, that's in the past, and I can move on.

3. Will you meet up after the show?
We'll definitely be friends.

No we won't.

And who knows what the future holds?

Not you.

This experience has been amazing for us. We've both grown on the journey. We'll have to see what happens in four weeks. Never say never!

Never, you twat.

Amy looks up and opens her mouth to vent. But she stops when she sees that everyone's looking just as outraged. She'll save it for later, over a prosecco or few.

She turns back to the phone and googles '*Amy Wright The Shelf*'.

About 5,000,000 results.

And there she sees it, at the top of the images. A meme of her sobbing with that tissue stuck to her eye.

EVERY TIME A MAN SAYS ANYTHING #tissuefacegirl

She rolls her eyes, scrolls down the first page and clicks on a review.

Pick of the week: Gemma vs Flick: the battle of the same sexes continues

Are you *#teamgemma* or *#teamflick*? That's the question on everyone's lips this week as reality smash hit *The Shelf* continues to bring the nation to a screeching halt every night. We're halfway through the girls' four-week experience and we're hooked on the cringeworthy tension between Gemma Burns (Girl Power) and Flick Brimble (Girly Girl). It's brilliantly uncomfortable TV that's dividing the country in two and if you haven't already, it's time to join the conversation. One thing is for certain: the groundswell of support for Gemma

from the female half of the population is growing. And fast.
Watch out, lads! *The Shelf* continues on Real TV every night
at 9 p.m.

'My God, what drainpipe did he come crawling out of?'
mutters Jackie.

The rest of them look up.

'I went out with this moron years ago, and he's just given
an interview to *The Sun* claiming he regrets breaking up
with me and that I'm the one that got away! Believe me,
mate, you were draped in red flags from the moment I met
you. He tried to order my food for me on our first date.
Control freak alert!'

The comment stays with Amy as she moves back to the
garden, reading a post by a stay-at-home mum about the
discrimination she faces in the playground when other mums
find out she doesn't work.

Since when did staying at home become a crime? All I'm
trying to do is support my family, and it works for us.

Some of the comments she's had are awful, calling her
entitled, lazy, smug and spoilt.

Amy shuts Facebook down. She's sick of strangers
commenting on other people's lives. *Everyone needs to leave
each other alone and just let us be*, she thinks.

Jackie's comment about her ex has given Amy an idea
for a blog post. She opens up WordPress and logs into

Wandering Amy, the blog she was writing when she first met Jamie. The more time they spent together, which was a lot at the start, the less time she spent writing, and eventually she stopped completely. It was hard to post a listicle about '10 Things to Do in London This Weekend' if all you ever did was sit on a sofa at the local pub or at home watching *The X Factor*.

Her last entry was a month into their relationship: 'Why the Cotswolds is the Best Spot For Your First Couple Getaway'. She didn't think the Cotswolds *was* the best spot for your first couple getaway. She'd just always wanted to go. So she wrote it, published it and sent the link to Jamie with a wink emoji.

He never replied, and they never went.

The rest of her posts are clichéd London lifestyle features, about where to eat, date, drink, shop and explore. She remembers how much she'd loved it at the time, for giving her a reason to get up early and explore the city on a Saturday. She'd stroll the streets and eat happily by herself, knowing she was doing it for a purpose. Taking photos, jotting notes, making every weekend moment count. By herself. And, when she'd finally had the confidence to push the site live and start posting on social media, she'd felt a huge rush of personal achievement that she'd never felt before.

Well, maybe not about '21 Surprising Facts About Foxes'.

She had forgotten about *Wandering Amy*, but she hadn't forgotten how much she loved the process, which is why she'd started scribbling down ideas for a new blog last year. What Jackie just said has stirred something inside her, and she has thirty minutes to get it live.

Twenty-Six

All the Warning Signs He's Not the One

Hi. It's me, Amy Wright. Or perhaps you know me as one of those poor women who was dumped for entertainment in front of millions of people on hit show *The Shelf*.

Could you handle the humiliation of having your break-up broadcast for everyone to watch? Having every move filmed and every word analysed over a month? Having your worth valued on whether you can look after a baby, stay calm in the face of unfair criticism and keep your hair perfect at all times? I know I've struggled, but I'm still here, hanging on.

I've come this close *pinching my fingers* to leaving the house, but I'm so happy I've stayed. I've learnt more about myself in the last two weeks than I have in the last two years. But it isn't the tasks and challenges that have taught me. The lessons I've learnt have come from the unlikely friendships I've made with a group of incredible women who share much more than this ridiculous experience. With women who share the strength of character that it takes to stay, endure and come out the other side laughing.

I'm being soppy. I'll stop.

One of the biggest lessons I've learnt from the women around me is that listening to your gut is more important than obsessing over the size of it. To pay attention when that nagging feeling begins to scratch at the back of your mind. Almost every relationship story I've heard on here shares a similar beginning.

'I ignored the signs.'

'I heard alarm bells.'

'In hindsight, I should have ended it then.'

'It was a major red flag.'

I've come to realise the importance of listening to that quiet inner voice when it whispers that something's not right – not shutting it down in a desperate attempt to find love. To trust my instincts when they tell me he won't make me happy.

From this day forward I pledge to listen to my gut. And to help me remember, I've decided to list all the red flags I should watch out for, whether it's a first date or a fiftieth.

99 Red Flags to Watch Out For

1. If they call their ex 'crazy'.
2. If they never say sorry.
3. If they're rude to service staff.
4. If they accuse you of loving your family more.
5. If they only want to spend time with you, no one else.
6. If they only tell jokes at your expense.
7. If they hate dogs.
8. If they refuse to talk about the future after six months.
9. If you haven't met their friends after three months.
10. If they take credit for your achievements.
11. If they watch – or – worse, comment on, what you eat.
12. If they pour themselves a glass of wine and don't offer you one.
13. If they don't ask you any questions.
14. If they don't listen to your answer when they do.
15. If they play the victim when they're in the wrong.
16. If they can't have an argument without storming off.
17. If they're annoyed that you don't want sex at 1 a.m after a fourteen-hour day.
18. If they're annoyed that you don't want sex full stop.
19. If they answer the phone during sex when you do want it.

20. If they blame you for every little thing that goes wrong.
21. If they don't text you back, but they're always on their phone.
22. If they freak out if you don't reply to a message immediately.
23. If they tell you they love you after the first date.
24. If they don't like your friends.
25. If they text you constantly when you're out with your friends.
26. If their favourite show is *The Big Bang Theory*.
27. If they don't let you look at their phone.

Twenty-seven is a weird number, but sadly my time is up, readers. Women and men of the Internet, help me complete this list by tweeting your #99redflags and lets start taking better care of ourselves and each other out there.

Amy x

Twenty-Seven

'How many more days do we have left in here?' asks Gemma, picking the ham out of her sandwich and tossing the bread to one side of her plate. 'Who wants my bread?'

'You asked for a ham salad sandwich, you plonker,' Jackie says, sitting down with a liquid lunch of prosecco. 'Ten days if we make it to the final.'

'It's a breadless sandwich,' Gemma responds, picking up the ham, lettuce and tomato with both hands. 'I'm off carbs. But if I eat it like it's a sandwich, it tricks my body into thinking I'm fuller.' She takes a bite, with tomato juice running down her hands. 'Diet is all about mind control,' she says, placing her index finger on her forehead, leaving a smear of tomato juice.

'Maybe that's why I never diet,' says Jackie. 'I don't even think about it. When did everyone start hating carbs?'

'You don't diet because you never eat, you just drink. Prosecco is full of sugar, you know,' Flick says, disapprovingly.

Jackie pokes her tongue out at Flick and refills her glass.

'Housemates, please go to the living room.'

'Ugh, here we go,' grumbles Jackie, downing it.

'Oh hellooooo, ladies!' screeches Adam Andrews in an over-the-top posh voice. He's wearing a straw hat bedecked with flowers and a matching dress, holding a china teacup. 'How aaaaare we all?' he says, fluttering his eyelashes and pursing his lips.

He's in the garden of a stately home, having a cream tea. Two female guests are seated on a bench in front of him. They look as if they've stepped out of a Laura Ashley catalogue from 1994.

'Who are these curtains?' asks Jackie.

'Today we are graced with the presence of two princesses of elegance and etiquette' – he bows his head, flutters his fingers and clinks the teacup on the table – 'and they've been teaching me a thing or two about my table manners. It's Meredith Mercer and Jemima Soames from *Ms Prim and Ms Proper*!'

The camera pans to a clapping audience, dotted around the garden in front of their own cream tea spreads. They hold their cups up and cheer hooray.

'And a big welcome to our competition winners, who are lucky enough to join me and my two guests of honour at Kenwood House for this very fancy edition of *The Shelf*.'

The camera turns to Meredith and Jemima, who are sitting as though they have rods in their backs, smiling at the cameras.

'So, who's prim and who's proper?' Adam asks as he stands up, moves over and squeezes between them on their bench, making them visibly uncomfortable.

'Well, Adam,' responds the one on the left. 'We're both prim and both proper. That's what three years at an elite Swiss finishing school for young ladies teaches you.'

'How delightful. And isn't this just lovely,' Adam says as he grabs a brownie, takes a large bite and smiles with an open mouth to reveal chocolate-caked teeth. Meredith and Jemima audibly gasp.

Swallowing, and picking his teeth for the cameras, Adam continues.

'So, tell us what we have in store for our next challenge, ladies. It's a terribly exciting one, I know that much.'

'Well, Adam,' says Meredith, glancing occasionally at the camera. 'You may know that Jemima and I have a new show on Real TV called *Ms Prim and Ms Proper*—'

'It's on every Sunday at six p.m.,' interjects Jemima.

'Anyway, *Ms Prim and Ms Proper* is all about encouraging women to rediscover their femininity. Embrace their softer side. British culture has celebrated the ladette for too long, and we want to see a return to good old-fashioned values, where women are demure.'

'Glad to see I'm not the only one who thinks like that!' says Flick, smiling, looking around for support she won't get.

'Mates of yours?' asks Gemma. She's standing next to the TV screen scratching her bottom through her joggers.

'On *Ms Prim and Ms Proper*,' Jemima continues, 'we're on the hunt to find Britain's worst female offenders. The ill-mannered bottom-scratchers who are disgracing our gender.'

Gemma stops scratching and turns round to see who's looking.

'And where do you find these bottom-scratchers?' Adam asks.

'We trawl the darkest and dirtiest corners of Britain,' answers Meredith. 'Like kebab houses on a Friday night.'

The audience in the garden murmur at the offensiveness of Meredith's comment.

'Get a shag!' someone shouts out. Meredith looks outraged, craning her neck to find the source of the comment. The audience laugh and jeer, while Adam stifles his sniggers.

'It's true,' says Jemima, looking down her nose. 'If we aren't careful, we're going to reverse the evolutionary process.'

Meredith dives in. 'You should see the women we help. When we find them, they're complete animals. We teach them how to behave like the fairer sex by dressing properly, talking clearly and learning the importance of self-respect and refinement.'

Jemima continues, 'It's no wonder that more and more British women in their prime years find themselves single today. Their tomboyish behaviour is so off-putting to the good men they're so desperate to find.'

Another audience member interrupts. 'What if I don't want a man?'

Meredith and Jemima look at each other like they've heard this before.

'If a woman tells you she's happily single, she's lying,' Jemima replies.

The audience start jeering again and Jemima holds up her hands. 'We've done the research – it's true. Women don't talk about it openly because they're embarrassed they'll look desperate. But we aren't afraid to confront uncomfortable truths.'

Amy turns to the group. 'I can honestly say that I'm happily single right now. And I'm not lying.'

Hattie scoffs. 'Right now? Try forever.'

'Boo as much as you like, but when we're finished with these girls, they'll be beautiful inside and out,' says Meredith. 'We turn them into real ladies and give them a much better chance of finding a gentleman who isn't going to ditch them for some other floozy when they have a bun in the oven!'

'Meredith, please,' Jemima says, embarrassed.

Someone in the audience lobs a scone at Meredith's head, which knocks her hat off and leaves a blob of cream on her forehead. She gasps and marches off the set, dodging more cakes flying her way.

'Wait, come back, Meredith!' shouts Adam, laughing. 'Audience, please, if you throw things you'll be thrown out.'

'I'm not coming back until they calm down!' Meredith shouts as the camera zooms in on her face, peering out from behind a hedge.

'OK, well, we're on a schedule – this *is* live TV! So we'll have to carry on without you. Jemima, care to explain to the housemates what today's challenge is?'

'Certainly, Adam,' Jemima says. 'Today's challenge is called Isn't She Lovely? It's about proving they can leave a lovely lasting impression.'

'And how does it work?'

'It's simple, Adam. Five women, five men, five tea parties. Each housemate will host a ten-minute tea party during which their guest will ask a unique set of questions that puts their etiquette to the test. First, our housemates must choose an appropriate outfit. Second, they must choose an appropriate menu and execute it to perfection. Lastly, they must prove they know how to conduct themselves properly by taking a simple quiz during the tea party. The most exciting part is that we're gifting the ladies with a brand-new wardrobe, thanks to our friends at Cutie Pie! All the tea party supplies thanks to our friends at Waitrose of course. And we've thrown a few curveballs, too, on purpose!'

'And do you have any style tips for the girls before they start?' Adam asks.

'Of course. There are three basic rules I follow. One, wear a skirt or a dress. They're more elegant, and will accentuate the feminine form men love. Two, less flesh is best – revealing clothing will leave a guest thinking he's not the only man you want to impress. And thirdly, wear a smile. The international symbol for loveliness, and it's free!'

'Are you buying all this, Flick?' Jackie turns to her.

'I know it's hard to hear, but it is true. Men won't think you're wife material if you're running around with your cleavage on parade like you want people to look.' She sighs. 'And now here come the insults and death threats . . .'

'OK, housemates, you know what you've got to do,' says Adam. 'Your tea party ingredients and clobber will arrive at the front door at three p.m. No bun fights, ladies – I know what you're like!'

Twenty-Eight

Dooooong.

At the front door is a carpet of Cutie Pie boxes with notes attached, addressed personally to each contestant.

Dear Amy,

We hope you love your new Cutie Pie collection! Inside this gift box, you'll find a selection from the new summer season, never seen before by the public. Your task is to choose the perfect outfit to wear on a date to a traditional English garden tea party. And before you panic, our style experts have been watching you since the start of the show and are confident that size 12 will fit you perfectly.

We can't wait to see what you choose!

Your fans at Cutie Pie xxx

Amy runs into the bedroom, ecstatic. She's been itching for something new to wear. She listens to the others around her ripping the cardboard with mixed reactions. She opens her box and spots what she wants to wear in two seconds flat.

'Gem, that's stunning!' says Amy, when she returns to the living room and sees Gemma spinning around, looking in the mirror, examining every inch of her look. It's a maroon dress with a high-necked lace bodice and a pleated skirt that reaches down to her calves, just showing her ankles. The look on her face says she hates it.

'I look so boring and frumpy,' she grumbles. 'I don't care what Ms Prissy Pants said – it's not sexy if you don't show skin!'

'The last thing a husband wants is for his wife to look sexy at a tea party, Gemma. They want classy, understated and elegant.' Flick sighs, ignoring Gemma's glare as she turns to look at herself in the mirror. She's wearing a high-necked red tea dress with a white butterfly print. 'I'm not sure this is right. Red is a bit too . . . bold, I think. Bold isn't lovely.'

'Is *this* lovely?' Jackie struts into the living room with mile-long legs stretching out from under a bright green playsuit with gold heels that make her five inches taller.

'Oh my God, you look *amazing*, babes!' Gemma cries.

'Oh, come on.' Flick stares at her. 'What's the point of these challenges if you lot don't take them seriously? You can't wear that to a tea party, that's absurd.'

'But what's the point of taking these challenges seriously when they *are* so absurd?' Jackie rolls onto the couch and lifts one leg in the air like Victoria Beckham.

'I bet this is the option I'm supposed to pick,' Flick says, holding up a long-sleeved white midi-length wrap dress with ruffles at the front. 'It looks like a wedding dress!' She smiles and daydreams in the mirror.

Gemma starts rifling through more of her pieces, bringing out bits of lace and velvet. Exhaling sharply, she stomps off to the kitchen.

'Is this appropriate for a tea party?' Hattie asks, walking down the corridor stairs and pausing at the bottom, looking hopefully at the housemates for approval. 'I've never been to one.'

She's wearing a perfectly fitted sky-blue shirt dress with a bright pink belt and matching low wedges.

'Oh Hat, you look awesome!' Amy shouts.

Hattie's cheeks turn as pink as the belt on her dress. 'It has pockets!' She shows them, delighted.

'Hot damn, Hattie!' Gemma shouts, coming back from the kitchen with a pair of scissors in her hand. 'Or should we call you Hottie?'

'Gemma, don't!' cries Flick.

Too late. Gemma slices into the fabric at the tops of her thighs and turns a midi into a mini in less than a minute.

'Ah, that's more me!' she says, beaming and twisting her tanned legs in the mirror.

Back in the bedroom, Amy tries on her chosen piece. It's

a white maxi wrap dress with tiny coral flowers and long chiffon sleeves to hide her arms. It's the perfect fit. Amy's hoping she can keep this wardrobe when she leaves, because this would also be the perfect dress to wear on a night out in Phuket.

Hattie suddenly appears by her side, looking out of sorts.

'You OK, Hats?'

'We're all so distracted by these new clothes that we haven't talked about what's really happening. Who are we dressing up for, Amy?'

*

The housemates are sitting at each of their tables, waiting for their guests to arrive.

'They've done the whole exes thing. It can't be them again,' says Jackie. 'I'm pinning my hopes on the cast of *Magic Mike*.'

'Oooh, maybe some single celebs! Get the ratings up!' cries Gemma, excited.

'Sadly, I don't think they have a ratings problem, my love. But you could be right.' Jackie glances over at Flick. 'Jesus Christ, would you look at her go? I'm surprised they haven't had to change her batteries yet.'

'Jacks,' Amy whispers, and holds her finger to her mouth.

Flick's tea party is miles ahead of everyone else's, which surprises no one. Earlier on, as she was laying out her cucumber sandwiches under a refrigerated damp cloth to keep them fresh, she told them that she hosts a tea party every month in the summer. Coming last in the catering stakes is Jackie, without a doubt. On her menu, which took her under five minutes to prepare, is white sliced bread with butter and sugar, a plate of hard-boiled eggs and a bowl of oven chips.

'What?' she asks Flick, who's staring at her tea. 'It represents my childhood, and I want my guests to know where I come from.'

Amy's menu is OK. She knows what to serve at a tea party, but she's no Flick. She picked her menu based on what she fancied eating, which was mini cheese quiches, cheese scones and mini cheesecakes. She was tempted to pick a third savoury cheese option, but reluctantly accepted she needed a sweet.

Hattie doesn't seem to care about the sweets, and she's a chef. On her menu are honey-glazed cocktail sausages, sausage rolls and pork pies. 'They're men. They like meat, don't they?' was her logic. There seem to be fewer cocktail sausages than there were earlier. When Amy sees Jackie distract her and Gemma steal a few, she understands why.

KNOCK!

'All right, girls?' shouts a buff man in a tight v-neck T-shirt and blazer as he steps into the garden, followed by a small squad of fellow meatheads.

'Jason!' Gemma shouts. 'What the fuck are you doing here? I don't wanna see ya!' She folds her arms and looks down at her lap, hiding a smile.

'Oi, babes, that ain't how you greet a guest, is it?' He grins, chewing gum with his mouth open. 'Hug?'

'Oh, sod off, you silly prat,' she mumbles. 'Hold on, isn't that . . . ?' Her words get stuck as she peers behind Jason.

It is. It's Ricky from *Single Dads*. He broke hearts on the show last year by attending lessons on how to do his daughter's hair for school.

'How you doin', Gemma? I'm Ricky. I think I'm with you today.'

'Aw, bless you, Ricky!' She reaches her arms around his enormous torso and gives him a squeeze. Jason coughs and looks down.

'Calm down, Jase, it's just a hug!'

'I didn't do nothing!' he protests. 'Besides, I'm with the lovely Amy this afternoon.' He grins at Amy with teeth the colour of fresh snow.

Ricky isn't the only familiar face here. Hattie's hosting health and fitness influencer @bicepsnberries. Amy only recognises him because Jamie's obsessed with his mushroom tea. Hattie won't have a clue who he is. Or that he's vegan. He greets her with a forced smile and a friendly tap on the shoulder. She reciprocates. That date is doomed.

'All right, Jackie, I'm Deano. Nice to meet you,' says a short but ripped redhead, taking two steps forward and holding out a hand that's too small for his beefy arm.

Jackie, who towers over him, takes it with caution.

'Well, I dunno about you,' he adds, 'but I'm glad we're

gonna be sitting down. Not sure our necks could take the strain.' She immediately relaxes into a smile.

'You're that bloke from *Stand Up Britain*, aren't you?'

'I certainly am. Runner-up last year. So, I'm funny but not *that* funny. Sorry.' He shrugs.

'Love, I need all the laughs I can get,' she replies, nodding towards their table.

The producers have to be joking with Flick's date. It's Garth from *Serial Offenders*. Amy's surprised he's even allowed on TV, after that police chase last year. All of his crimes were minor. Petty thefts here and there. But still.

'Hello, I'm Flick,' she says with a shaky voice. 'I guess you're with me.'

He smiles to reveal his four front teeth, which are gold. Flick gasps.

Garth's famous skull tattoo makes him look more intimidating than he probably is. It takes up the entire back of his shaved head, like a second face. When they sit down at the table opposite, Amy feels like it's watching her.

'How do you do?' Jason says, distracting her.

'Fine, thank you. And how are you?'

'Oh dear.' He scribbles something on a card.

'What?' she asks.

'When someone says, "How do you do?", the correct response is—'

'"How do you do?".' She sighs. 'I know that. But no one says that nowadays.'

'I've never said that in my life,' he whispers. 'In fact, I

didn't know the answers to any of these questions, so good luck, darlin'!' He smiles and looks back at Gemma.

'How come you're the only ex here?' she asks.

'I told them at the start that I'd never go on a date with another lass unless Gemma was there. Those were my rules. Got it in the contract 'n' all. Not just a pretty face, am I?' He grins.

Jason is still head over heels. And Amy guesses the feeling is mutual, as she watches them play a tennis match of glancing in each other's direction and missing each other by a few seconds each time.

They haven't even begun properly talking when Jason marks something else on his notepad. When he sees she's confused, he whispers again. 'You didn't put your napkin on your lap immediately. Sorry! And another thing,' he says as he looks under the table. 'Uncross your legs. You're supposed to sit with your legs together and your feet on the floor! Bloody upper class. Bunch of stuffy old bores. But they are the rules, Amy, sorry.'

Amy uncrosses her legs, puts her napkin on her lap and looks around to see if there's anything else she's forgotten. When she looks over to Flick for some pointers, she hears Flick schooling her guest on proper etiquette, as she tells him politely how he shouldn't reach over the table for the egg and cress sandwiches but ask her politely to pass them.

'But they're hot! If I don't blow on it, it'll burn my mouth!' Hattie says loudly to her guest, who's making notes.

'Well, I didn't know you weren't allowed to blow on hot food. What a stupid rule.'

When Amy looks back at Jason, waiting for the next question, he's noting something again.

'What now?'

'It's your fork. The prongs are facing down, not up, while it's on the plate.'

'Oh, for God's sake.' She tuts as she turns her fork over and then looks at Jason.

'You still love Gemma, don't you?'

He puts the card down and starts playing with his fork. Then he looks up at her and raises his eyebrows. 'Is it that obvious?' he asks quietly. 'I do. I really miss her. Thank God I can see her on telly every day, so I know she's OK. I feel terrible for doing this to her, you know. I honestly thought it would be good for her. To have a break. Not from me, but from that bloody phone of hers. Someone told me about doing a digital detox the other day, and I kind of felt this would be the same thing. Plus, I really wanted her to have some proper thinking time about what she's been like these last few months, with her following taking off. I love her so much, I think she's amazing and I couldn't be prouder of all her hard work. But I just think she needs balance. And I'm not the only one. I talked to her ma and pa about it, too. They were all for me putting her on the show. It's like . . . what do you call those things? An intervention. I just hope she can forgive me.'

As he says this, looking at his plate, Amy sees Gemma glance over in his direction again.

'I think she probably can, Jason.'

'Has she said anything? You know, off camera?' he asks, with a look of desperation.

'Yeah, she talks about you all the time,' Amy fibs.

His face lights up with a broad smile and he blushes.

The moment is interrupted by a burst of laughter from Jackie's table. Deano has one of those infectious laughs that spread like wildfire. Both of their faces are crumpled in giggles and tears are streaming from their eyes, and Jackie actually folds out of her chair and onto her knees, holding her stomach.

'I'm sorry, this is just so stupid!' she manages to get out in between breaths. 'He just told me that I have to store my caviar in a champagne flute!' She cracks up again.

Their hysterics start to reach across the garden, and, in a few seconds, everyone else is crying with laughter, shoulders shaking all round. It's impossible not to catch it in such a formal setting. When Amy turns her head towards Flick, she's happy to see she's caught the bug, too. Even the skull is having a jolly old time, bouncing up and down with its mouth hanging open.

*

The housemates are sitting in a row on the sofa, watching stony-faced Ms Prim and Ms Proper staring at Adam with arms folded and mouths turned down.

'Good evening, girls! I'm hoping everyone has recovered from this afternoon's tea party hysteria? Did anyone learn anything? Does anyone feel more polite or refined? Ms Prim, Ms Proper, what's your verdict?'

'Adam, no one really took this challenge seriously at all, so it's going to be extremely difficult for us to judge. But we made a commitment, and we're here.'

'And what a delight it is to have you with us,' he says with a hint of sarcasm. 'Shall we recap what happened today?'

The screen cuts to a montage that includes slow-motion footage of the scone hitting Meredith in the face; the housemates parading around in their outfits; Gemma cutting her dress in half; Hattie sitting in silence opposite @bicepsandberries and Jackie falling on the floor, laughing. It ends on Jason and Amy's conversation.

'I love her so much, I think she's amazing and I couldn't be prouder of all her hard work.'

'Ah, Gem, that's lovely,' says Hattie. 'Reckon you two will make up?'

'I don't know. Maybe. We'll see.' Gemma smiles, shrugs and rubs her lips with balm.

'Jason, stop, you're making us well up!' Adam winks. 'Now, moving swiftly on to our judging panel. Prim, Proper, what have you got to say about it all?'

'Well, even though she let us down by laughing at The Jackie Show,' Jemima replies, 'the award for exquisite elegance, excellent hosting skills and knowledge of etiquette is Flick. Congratulations, Flick! She is the loveliest by far. For her efforts, she wins a three-course meal for two tomorrow evening, prepared by a Michelin-starred chef.'

The audience cheer.

'We haven't finished yet,' shouts Meredith. 'There's still the booby prize to be awarded. And that prize, for worst contestant, has to go to Jackie, who has shown nothing but contempt for this challenge. From her ghastly outfit to her revolting menu, to her outlandish behaviour that would see her get thrown out of any decent establishment. Really, I think there's no hope for Jackie. I don't know how she's still on the show.'

The audience start booing the more offensive Meredith becomes, and she looks nervous that she might become a target again, with her hands resting in mid-air.

Unexpectedly, Flick stands up.

'I have a question,' she states. Not loudly enough, as Adam continues talking. 'Hello, I have a question! Hello!' she shouts, and waves her arms.

Adam finally notices her and hushes his guests. 'Let her speak, ladies and gentlemen! Our winner has something she'd like to say, I think. Flick, what's your question?'

'Can I take anyone to the three-course dinner by the Michelin-starred chef?'

'Yes, of course! We'll see if Simon is free.'

'I don't want to tame Simon, I want to take Jackie.'

'Ah, isn't that lovely, audience?' Adam interrupts the moment. 'I feel like releasing a flock of doves. But sadly, folks, it's not a flock of doves that I'll be releasing tonight.'

The audience *ooh* as Adam walks up to the camera and the housemates look at each other nervously.

'No, ladies and gentlemen. Because tonight, I'm releasing a housemate.'

Twenty-Nine

Adam is standing at the back of the stage. Behind him is a giant screen with their five names on a bar chart: Flick, Hattie, Amy, Jackie, Gemma. The bars are level at the bottom of the chart.

'That's right, everybody, tonight it's up to our studio audience to buzz in their votes from the buttons in front of their seats. So, who will it be? She might be the hostess with the mostest, but is Flick the *housemate* with the mostest? Or will it be Chatty Hattie with her pork meat patties? Gemma the Gym Queen? Or Jack Attack? Finally, who could forget our girl-next-door Amy? Some say she's too boring, but maybe Miss Wright will be Miss All Right in this round. Wait, is it Miss or Ms? Ms sounds a bit *mis*erable now, doesn't it? But you know what they say, folks, if the cap fits . . . Studio audience, only you have the power to save your fave. It's time to get those fingers on the five buttons in front of you. You have thirty seconds to decide which housemate you want to remain in the house. ARE. YOU. READY?'

The housemates inch towards each other on the sofa and hold hands. This has all happened so quickly, they've barely had time to gather their thoughts, or stress about who will be the next to leave. The Tracker is all they have to go on, and Hattie is coming last. But Amy's seen that turn at the last minute, so there's nothing stopping it from turning now.

'Voting starts . . . *now*!'

A countdown clock starts as the bars begin to grow.

Flick, Gemma and Amy's bars start rocketing up the graph. Amy's slows after five seconds. Followed by Gemma's. Followed by Flick's, which eventually reaches the top. Hattie and Jackie's are moving, but crawling compared to the rest.

'Oooh, audience, it looks like it's going to be a very close call between our Jackie and Hattie!' shouts Adam. 'Come on, ladles and jellyspoons, who's it gonna be? Just one vote could make all the difference to one of our girls!'

Five seconds to go, and they're both still head to head.

'Ladies,' says Jackie. 'It's been a pleasure. Well, some of it. That dinner would have been nice.'

Three seconds left.

Ping!

Jackie overtakes with a second to spare and an explosion of on-screen graphics spell out *Hattie*.

'What a nail-biter, audience! You certainly know how to keep these housemates on their toes!'

The housemates wipe tears from their eyes as they gather round Hattie.

'Don't cry, ladies,' smiles Hattie. 'I'm ready to go. You've been the best thing that's ever happened to me. Besides, it's only . . .' she counts on her fingers '. . . ten days until I see you on the other side!'

*

'Flick and Jackie. Please take your seats at the table in The Secret Garden in fifteen minutes.'

'Jacks, you could have made a bit of an effort.' Gemma scuttles over to the sofa in her towel. It's the night after Hattie's eviction and Flick and Jackie are getting ready for their mate date. 'Flick's wearing a new dress and has blow-dried her hair 'n' all. No disrespect, but that's what I'd wear if it was my first day on the blob. Not to a fancy dinner.'

Jackie stands up and laughs, looking down at her baggy brown tracksuit bottoms and oversized T-shirt.

'Uh, firstly . . . elastic waist means extra food. And secondly, it's not a fancy dinner. It's a fake dinner. Fake restaurant, fake friend. Fake Flick didn't invite me to this dinner out of the goodness of her heart, ladies. She did it to score points with the public. Can't you see that? Everything she does is a game, it's . . .'

'Jackie,' Amy murmurs and shoots her eyes over to the door.

'. . . so fucking obvious. She doesn't give a shit about me, or you . . .'

'*Jackie*,' Amy murmurs louder. 'Stop.'

Flick is standing in the bedroom doorway, staring at the three of them.

Jackie coughs and sits down, as Flick clicks across the living room floor on her way to the kitchen in a floaty pink floral dress and pale pink heels, her hair swishing as she goes. She looks like a walking advert. She turns around at the kitchen door.

'Jackie, would you like me to wait for you?'

Jackie doesn't look at her. 'Nah, you're all right, mate. See you in there. I'm gonna pre-drink.'

Amy follows Flick into the kitchen.

'Jackie, that really wasn't very nice,' Gemma says, in the distance.

Flick turns round. Amy had expected to see tears, but she looks utterly composed.

'Look, I'm sure Jackie didn't mean it. I think she has a hard time trusting people.'

'No, I'm sure she did mean it. But I'm OK with it. She doesn't know me and she hasn't once tried to get to know me. She walks away when we're alone together and she pretends not to hear me when I ask her about her life. That's the whole point of this dinner, Amy. It's not to score points with the public. It's to force Jackie to be alone with me and have our first proper conversation. If someone knows me and dislikes me, that's fair. If someone doesn't know me and dislikes me, that's unfair.'

'Well, that's big of you, Flick.'

'It's called being an adult, Ames. And that wasn't a dig at you, promise.' Flick smiles and puts her hand on her shoulder. 'Thank you for checking up on me. Wish me luck!'

Somehow, Amy doesn't think she'll need it.

∗

'Oh my God, I want a miniature lobster roll!' Gemma whines, dropping her dry pizza crust on the plate and wiping her hand on her leggings.

'This pizza has to be frozen,' Amy adds, snapping her crust in two and watching the dough dust fly into the air. 'Is this even real ham?'

'Probably not. That gave me instant stomach cramps, babes. Yuck.'

The two of them are sitting on the sofa, watching the Flick and Jackie show unfold on the TV. So far, the dinner has been uneventful. No shouting, no wine in the face, no choking each other from across the table. It helped that Jackie apologised for her earlier rant at the start of the meal, and that Flick accepted it. Right now, they're discussing Jackie's controversial departure from the firm. Flick is shaking her head repeatedly, a look of genuine anguish in her eyes.

'I'm knackered, Ames,' Gemma says through a loud yawn.

'Me too. Do we have to watch this? I thought it would be a bit more dramatic. And that we might need to stay up to deal with any emergencies. Don't get me wrong, I'm glad we don't. I'm happy they've found something in common with this whole equal pay conversation. I wonder if Jackie would ever start her own firm? What do you think?'

There's no response. When Amy turns her head, Gemma is asleep with her mouth open.

'God, maybe I am boring,' Amy whispers, sitting up and stretching. 'Gemma. *Gemma*. Wake up. Time for bed.'

Like a zombie, Gemma rises and drags herself into the bedroom.

As she brushes her teeth, Amy wonders how the mood will have changed tomorrow. With just four of them left in the house, any tension might appear magnified. Will Flick have turned Jackie around?

She stops mid-brush.

What was that?

She carries on, albeit a bit slower. And stops again.

That was definitely shouting.

'Gemma, can you hear that?' she shout-whispers from the bathroom door. Gemma stirs, but does nothing more.

There it is again. Definitely shouting, and it's getting louder. The dinner has been a disaster. Amy hurries through to the living room and switches on the TV. The Secret

Garden is empty and the table has been cleared away.

'Flick? Jackie?' she shouts, moving into the kitchen. 'Hello?'

Her heart thumps when she hears the sound of shouting again. It's coming from the garden. She slowly slides the door open and peers out.

It is Jackie and Flick. They're sitting at the Tiki bar, Jackie with a glass full of champagne in her hand, swinging it around. Flick is folded over, but when she sits up, she's smiling. More than smiling. Laughing. They are both in hysterics.

Amy slides the door shut and tiptoes back to the bedroom with a smile on her face and her heart feeling full. That should make the next nine days easier.

Assuming she survives for that long.

FINAL WEEK

FINAL WEEK

Thirty

'I can't believe there are only seven days left,' mutters Flick, breathlessly. She's lying on the grass motionless as Roomba scuttles around her taking photographs like she's a crime scene.

'Gonna join me, Ames?' Flick shouts. 'With Hattie gone, it's a bit boring with just me.'

'What gives you the impression I want to exercise?' Amy replies, as she strokes the new Cutie Pie! Activewear set she has on. 'Besides, I'm seeing Dr Hicks in ten minutes. There's no time. Where's Gemma?'

'She isn't feeling her best today,' Flick replies, sitting up.

Amy slowly paces up and down the dining room with her arms folded, waiting for the little hand to hit the hour so she can open the Therapy Room door. She glances up at The Tracker and pauses. She's in first place. *How?* She looks around the room to see if she can locate anyone, but they're all outside. She walks to the corner of the dining room and squints at The Wall for a clue. A few messages are coming in and she can see her name, but she can't read what it's about. As she leans forward, frowning, she hears Dr Hicks shout for her to enter.

'Hello, Amy. Please come in.' Dr Hicks smiles and shuffles his papers. 'Are you all right?' he asks when she sits down.

'I'm feeling really good. Like, the happiest I've been in ages.'

'Glad to hear it. Tell me more.'

'I'm sleeping like a baby, waking up early to watch the sun rise, which has always been my favourite thing in the world. I'm just really enjoying my own company, as much as I can with three housemates. The air feels different, and I'm feeling positive about what I'm going to do next. I'm not scared of being single anymore, I'm excited. I keep on smiling inside when I remember that I'm completely free to do what I like, go where I want, say how I feel and be who I want to be. Once I get out of here, obviously. It's like a huge weight has been lifted and all that pressure has gone. I don't know why I was so afraid of being single before.'

'What kind of pressure?'

'Lots of kinds. The pressure of caring about someone else's happiness. I don't have to worry if Jamie is OK anymore – all I have to worry about is whether I'm OK. And the pressure that comes when you're in a long-term relationship. I don't have to worry what people think or make excuses about why we aren't engaged yet. The pressure of having to share your time with someone, so you have less of your own. Now my time is all mine. I'm going to do anything and everything. Find out what makes me really happy. Who I am and who I want to be. Maybe the love of my life isn't a man – maybe it's a secret beach in Asia somewhere. Or maybe it's my writing. Or maybe it's me, as self-centred as that sounds.'

'I think it sounds empowered.'

She smiles at this.

'Amy, I'm delighted you no longer fear being single, but you also shouldn't fear being in a relationship. Or think that you have to be single to achieve your goals. The right person should help you fulfil those dreams, not cause you to abandon them.'

'I think I need to figure out what those are first. If there is a "Mr Right", maybe our paths will cross one day, but if they don't, well, there's always . . . Netflix. Or travel. Or cheese. I'm not scared of being in a relationship, I'm just focusing my energy on myself for a while. I haven't done that in a long time.'

'Sounds sensible. I read your post. It's been a bit of a hit on the outside, you'll be pleased to know. Do you want to talk about it?'

'My post?'

'"Ninety-nine Red Flags to Watch Out For". The one with the long list. Well, I assume it's the only one you've been able to post in here.'

'How did you hear about it?'

'It's all over the Internet, Amy. I'm surprised you haven't seen anything on The Wall yet. You've sparked a bit of a movement. Seems like everyone's sharing their red flags on social media with the red flag emoji. It was even on *The 10 O'Clock Show*. Think it featured in their top trending hashtag segment.'

'I didn't even realise there was a red flag emoji,' Amy says quietly, as her heart starts pounding against her chest. She can't believe her stupid little blog is being read by anyone beyond her mum and Sarah. 'What does it all mean?'

'Well, I imagine it means that people can relate. They're starting to take more notice of the problems in their relationship, and realising that even if they seem small, they could be symbolic of deeper issues. I suppose that in itself is a positive thing. We shouldn't ignore problems in relationships. But there was one thing that made me worry when I read it.' He puts his papers down and crosses his legs. 'I worry that it will lead to a lot of overthinking. Analysing every word we utter, watching every movement we make in case we should put a foot wrong. I don't think that's healthy either.'

Amy raises her eyebrows. 'It sounds like you just described *The Shelf*!'

He stares at her for a few seconds. 'Well, yes. I suppose you're right.'

✳

When Amy leaves the room, she hurries straight to The Wall and finds the rest of the housemates watching the tweets pour in. Every one of them has *#99redflags* at the end.

@elliemnelly If he brings you 10 bunches of roses on the first date and sends you 10 more the next day to say thank you #99redflags #theshelf

@wicheyt If she spends the whole night looking at her phone taking pictures of the food, the place, a selfie, a photo with you, her cab ride on the way home – alone #99redflags #theshelf

@janeyben20 If he makes too many jokes and never wants to take anything seriously – including us #99redflags #theshelf

@aliheming3 If he tells you his name is Dave and when you find his passport his name is actually Brian #99redflags #theshelf

@angels00s Once went to the loo on a first date and came back to him reading my text messages. Made worse when they were replies to messages I sent my friends asking to be rescued! #99redflags #theshelf

@simeondoc If she texts you at the end of the first month with an itemised list of what she's paid for and asking for you to split it #99redflags #theshelf

@emmawats75 If he has a bath and lets his mum come into the bathroom to chat #99redflags #theshelf

Amy feels a sense of pride washing over her when she realises that she's created something meaningful. Something important. Something that could help people. It's probably the first time she's ever done something like that.

Thirty-One

Gemma's in bed, moaning.

Amy sits on the edge. 'Gem, it's 11.30 a.m. Shouldn't you be doing laps?'

'She's been vomiting,' says Flick, coming in with a cup of ginger tea. 'Quite violently, too. Ginger should help, but if it persists, we'll have to tell the producers.'

'I'm feeling a bit better,' Gemma says, taking the tea. 'I'm telling you, it was that fucking frozen pizza last night. That's when it started.'

'Gemma, I know we have had our differences,' says Flick, sitting down on the other side of the bed and putting her arm on Gemma's leg. 'But I *am* a doctor. Let me have a proper look at you. I might be able to spot something. Or at least help you rehydrate.'

'OK,' Gemma says, a little reluctantly. 'Thanks.'

'Amy, can you give us ten minutes?'

Flick marches over to her bed, reaches under it and pulls

out a large medical kit like she's Mary Poppins. She opens the kit and looks through her equipment feverishly. This isn't the Flick they know. This is a completely different person. An assertive, powerful and determined one. Probably the one she was up until a few years ago. Probably the one she is now, behind that happy housewife facade.

Amy leaves her in her element.

Jackie's on her hands and knees, scrubbing sick out of the kitchen floor.

'My God, this reeks,' Jackie says, through a pinched nose. 'Where's Wifey gone off to?'

Amy turns her head to see Flick entering the Chat Room, looking agitated.

'I thought you two were friends now?' Amy turns to Jackie.

'We are. Mates can tease mates.'

'*Housemates. Please go to the living room.*'

There's a new message on The Wall.

Amy,
Please join me in The Secret Garden for a sundowner at 6 p.m.
Regards,
Dr Simon Ash

Uuuuuugh.

'Ha ha, what FUN!' Jackie claps her hands and laughs. 'I'm sure you're going to get on like a house on fire!'

'Simon's coming here – tonight?' Flick says nervously, as she joins them at the screen.

'Yup,' Jackie replies. 'And Amy's really looking forward to it!'

*

Later that afternoon, Amy's staring at herself in the mirror in a black spandex mini she's borrowed from Gemma. It's far too tight for her but she's wearing it anyway. Three weeks ago, Amy wouldn't be seen dead in a spandex minidress, but tonight she couldn't give a shit about whether she's 'beach-body ready'. This scrap of plastic she's squeezed and squeaked into is the perfect outfit for her mission. To shock.

Amy has contoured her cheeks following Katie's instructions, lining her lips to double their size, applying red lipstick and styling her hair in beachy waves. She's also wearing heels for the first time in over a year. The Secret Garden is close enough for her to risk it. She's feeling her look as she power-walks over to the table in The Secret Garden with 'Crazy in Love' stuck in her head.

Amy's pre-drink prosecco has given her a taste for it, but as she reaches for the bottle of white on the table, a voice calls from the door for her stop.

'Please, allow me,' says a smooth voice.

She looks up to see a tall, tanned and silver-haired man striding towards the table with his arm outstretched. He takes the bottle from her hands and pours her a glass.

'Chivalry isn't dead,' he says, sitting down opposite her and pouring a glass for himself.

'You sound just like Flick,' Amy replies. 'Funny, that.'

Parts of Simon Ash are exactly what Amy has expected. Early fifties, suit, pompous. Parts of him aren't what she has expected at all. He's handsome in a Mr Big type of way, and that's probably why he's so cocky, which Amy can see immediately. Like Flick, everything about him is shiny. His eyes, his teeth, his perfectly coiffed hair. He looks like an old-school movie star.

'I suppose you disagree with all that, don't you? Pouring wine, opening doors, being a gentleman. I suppose you think I handcuff Flick to the oven in a pinafore?' He smiles and stares at her so hard that she has to look away. The sexual undertones of the statement and the intensity of his eyes make her feel deeply uncomfortable. She feels a nervous heat rash start to spread across her chest. Thank God this minidress has long sleeves and a high neck, and she's wearing enough foundation to ice a cake. She'd hate him to think he was making her blush.

'I don't think men need to protect women or treat us like we're precious. I think people should look after people.'

He sits up and stretches his hand towards her. 'I'm so sorry, I haven't introduced myself yet. Dr Simon Ash.'

She hesitates before taking it and answering, '*Ms* Amy Wright.'

He reciprocates her firm grip and holds the shake for a

few seconds too long, continuing to stare at her before letting go and smiling widely.

'So, how is my little wifelet? I hope you're looking after her. Tell her I *am* proud of her, in response to her message. She's kept her dignity intact and she hasn't let her values go. And tell her she gets more beautiful every day. I love watching her.'

'I'm sure you do. What she's wearing, what she's saying, what she's revealing, where she isn't going.'

'Exactly. When she isn't on the show, she wears a collar with a tracking chip in it. I gave it to her on her birthday.'

Amy glares at him.

'I'm joking, I don't need to know where she is. Like I said, she's handcuffed to the oven.' He smiles, raising his eyebrows in the same way Jamie used to. My God, he *is* Jamie! He's Jamie in twenty years. Although Jamie wouldn't have said that cheesy line about getting more beautiful every day. The best Amy got was a wolf whistle. Never words.

Amy shifts her chair back and goes to stand up. She can't do this anymore.

'Sit down, Amy. Give me a chance. Don't you want to hear my side? I was only joking. Can't you take a joke? Flick thinks I'm funny. I do miss her, you know. You might not understand our relationship, but we are very happy together. It works for us, having Flick at home and me at the surgery. You've spoken to her about it – you know she's happy. So why do I get the impression I'm in the doghouse with you? Why are you sitting there staring at me with such animosity? I don't understand what I've done that's making you so uncomfortable.' He tilts his head and trails his eyes from the top of her forehead to the tip of her chin. Like Jamie used to.

Amy avoids his eyes and looks down at her glass. 'I just feel sorry for Flick. All those years spent in training, just to give up? She says she's happy, but if she is, why is she here trying to improve herself? For you, of course. Why don't you just ask her to marry you? You know that's all she wants. She's desperate to get married and have children. If you love her so much, why are you denying her her happiness and forcing her to jump through these ridiculous hoops?'

'Amy, I've been married before and I have two children already. I don't want to do it again. What Flick and I have is perfect. It's so much better than when I was married. Why would she want to change what's working?'

'Maybe because the truth is she doesn't think it's working. How can it be working when you want entirely different things? Have you been clear with her about all this, or are you just leading her on until she's too old to have kids?'

'The marriage and kids thing is a phase. She never used to want marriage and kids. It's just because she's getting older and she's worried she's going to have regrets. I've assured her she won't. Kids put a huge strain on relation-ships. It did with my ex-wife, and we never recovered from it. There were other reasons, too. She worked full-time and wouldn't compromise. She was jealous of my friendship with Flick when I started at the surgery. And that turned into paranoia. She was crazy. Flick's not crazy. Flick is perfect, just the way she is.'

'Well, Simon, half the population must be mad. All ex-girlfriends are crazy, according to you lot. I'm sure Jamie's telling people I'm crazy, too.'

Amy thinks of Jamie's interview. Just like Simon, he was too spineless to admit that she was normal. He had to say she was crazy to avoid any blame and admit he was at fault.

'Amy, the truth is that I'm too old to have more children. That stage in my life has passed, and I'm delighted it has. I'm fifty-five, and I just want to enjoy our lives together, without anyone getting in the way. And yes, let's be honest, Flick is no spring chicken either.'

'Oh my God, she's only thirty-four!' cries Amy.

He snorts and looks confused. 'Flick isn't thirty-four.'

'What do you mean?'

'Flick's forty-two. Good God, is the Botox I give her that good? Anyway, men her age might say she's past her sell-by date. But not me. I adore her. See, Amy, we're actually the perfect match. She's too old to have children and I'm too old to want them. We're lucky that we found each other at this stage of our lives.'

Amy's heart bleeds when she flashes back to all the times Flick's mentioned marriage, babies, children and the daughter she wouldn't allow out wearing a short, tight dress.

The daughter she might never have.

Thirty-Two

Dawn is Amy's favourite time of day in here. It's the only time she has to think in peace and quiet, as she watches the stillness outside through the steam of a fresh hot tea.

Finding solitude has been one of Amy's biggest struggles in the house. Sometimes she finds it lying on the bathroom floor, staring up at the ceiling with no cameras or housemates in sight. But it's never lasted longer than five minutes. Someone always needs the loo in here. Her love for alone time is one of the reasons she's been getting up earlier these past few days. No one's watching. Or at least, that's what she thinks as she leans against the counter blowing across the top of her mug.

A shadow moves in her peripheral vision, but when she looks up there's no one there. It's only 5.15 a.m.; she'd be surprised if another housemate was up already.

'Hello?' she says quietly as she switches on the kettle for a refill. There's no response as the water starts to boil loudly.

She tiptoes to the kitchen door and bumps into Flick on the other side.

'God, you gave me a fright!' Amy whispers, and laughs.

'Sorry.' Flick smiles. 'I did reply, but I don't think you heard me over the kettle.'

'That's OK,' Amy says. 'Tea?'

Flick nods as she takes a seat on an island stool.

Amy wants to talk about last night. She wants to find out why Flick is wasting her time in a hopeless relationship, as handsome as Simon may be. She also wants to find out why Flick felt the need to lie about her age, but she needs to use tact. Flick is going to feel humiliated when she realises that Simon's exposed her real age on TV and that she's been fibbing.

'So, how was Simon? I was desperate to ask you last night, but knew you'd be feeling tired. I couldn't sleep.'

'Simon was . . .'

Arrogant, chauvinistic, never going to give you children.

'Chatty.'

'Sounds like him.' Flick smiles and sips her tea, adulation in her eyes.

Come ON, Flick.

'Remind me how you two met?'

'At the surgery. Typical office scandal, dating the boss.'

Amy smiles. 'Did you get a promotion out of it at least?'

'You mean, did *he* get a promotion out of it at least.'

Flick gives a wry smile. 'I hired him. I was the boss, not the other way around.'

Amy is floored. How did she miss that? Neither Simon nor Flick had mentioned it. And how could their relationship have gone through such a U-turn?

'Don't worry, I won't tell the others you assumed the man was the boss. I'm sure you only thought that because of our age difference, didn't you?'

'Thirteen years is quite a lot,' Amy says, hoping she'll pick it up. She does.

'Twenty.'

'Flick.' Amy leans over and lowers her voice. 'Simon told me you're forty-two, not thirty-four. Is that true? It's nothing to be ashamed of. You didn't need to hide your age from us – we weren't going to judge you.'

Flick turns red. 'Please don't tell the others,' she says under her breath. 'They'll think I'm awful.'

'I won't tell them. But I can't guarantee the millions who are watching can keep a secret. It's on TV, Flick. Lots of people probably know by now. It might be better for you to tell them yourself, or it will look worse. Besides, who cares? So what if you're eight years older? Women feel pressured to lie about their age all the time. I'm sure half the population will completely relate.'

'I only said I was thirty-four because I didn't want you all to feel sorry for me. Unmarried and childless at forty-two! I get enough pressure about it out there.' She sighs, nodding her head at the garden wall. 'At least in here I can pretend

I have more time. And let's face it, forty-two-year-olds aren't exactly keepers, are they? There's no chance of me winning the show now.'

'Of course they are! Flick, we're all in the same boat. If we felt sorry for you, we'd also have to feel sorry for ourselves. And that sounds miserable. We should all support each other. When I came on here, I was terrified about being single and running out of time. If I'd known you were feeling the same way, we could have vented our frustrations together. Misery loves company, and all that. You talk about Simon so much, I just assumed you were happy and everything was fine.'

'Amy, you're only thirty-two. I wasn't like this when I was thirty-two. I thought I had loads of time then, because I did. When Simon and I got together, I was thirty-eight. I was so busy running the practice I never had time to meet anyone. And then he came along and promised me the world. He promised me he was getting a divorce so that we could get married. He got the divorce, but he stopped talking about us getting married. Two years went by and still no sign of progress. I stopped asking about it. I was sick of sounding desperate and needy. But when I reached forty, I really started to worry. Then I began to feel like there must be something wrong with me. Why wouldn't he want to marry me? I've been willing to sacrifice so much for him. I gave up work, I handed him the keys to the practice. I'm a stay-at-home wife and mum in everything but name. But doubt got the better of me, and I thought perhaps coming on here would make me irresistible.'

'Flick, you *are* irresistible. You're already perfect. Why him?'

'Well, I'm not perfect, am I? Simon sees past my age. He doesn't think I'm washed up like other men would if I were single. They hear forty-two and it's alarm bells in their head. It's either alarm bells because there must be something wrong with me to be single at this age, or because I must be desperate to have kids because of my age. Truth is, they're right. I'm not going to pretend I don't anymore, just so men think I'm easy-going; I want to get married, I want to have children. But I've made poor life choices, and I've let time pass me by. I came on here to change that. I really believe Simon will realise how great our relationship is and will agree to marry me and have more children. I am happy with Simon. I don't want to find anyone else. Besides, it's too late for me to start again, anyway.'

I know the feeling.

'Flick, men would be lining up if you were single. Especially after the show.'

'It's nice of you to say, Amy, but we both know that's not true. My dating days are over. Single women over forty like me just disappear. Men my age want a younger model. Younger men want to laugh about dating a cougar with their friends. And older men have already done the marriage and kids thing. They can't be bothered. What choice do I have?'

'Flick, you want marriage and kids, don't you? Simon doesn't. He told me that. So why stay? You've got a better shot at those things with someone else.'

'But this show is going to help me persuade him. And the alternative is much worse. If it weren't for Simon, I'd be single at forty-two and alone. Forever. I wasted my thirties focusing on my career, without thinking of my personal life. Then one day I blinked and realised that if I didn't start thinking about it now, it might never happen for me. Simon rescued me.'

Rescued, or trapped? Amy wonders.

Thirty-Three

Dooong.

The four of them pause mid-chew and look at each other across the dining room table. There's been no warning of visitors, challenges or tasks this morning. And the only comments on The Wall have been men and women telling Flick that she's in 'great nick' for her age and telling her to leave Simon.

Amy puts her spoon down and gets up to answer the door. A postman is standing on the other side with a handful of letters.

'Housemates, please go to the living room with your letters from home.'

The rest of them scream, abandon their breakfasts and take their teas to the sofa where the screen switches on.

'Good morning, housemates! Have we got a treat in store for you, and for us! Now that we're in the last week of the show, we thought it was high time you heard from home. We've asked your nearest and dearest to touch base, and we can't wait to hear what they have to say. Will it be words of encouragement? Will it be good news from beyond the walls? Take your letters, take your seats, take a box of tissues and clear those throats, ladies. I have a feeling we're about to get teary.'

The audience *ooh* as Adam takes his seat.

Amy can feel her hands go clammy around her envelope as she clutches it tightly, wondering who it's from. She's relieved it isn't too thick because she doubts she'll last one minute. She feels like she could cry now. Flick passes round the box of tissues as they all look apprehensively at each other.

'I don't know if this is a good thing or a bad thing,' says Jackie, laughing nervously. 'If this is a letter from Dad, I might be tempted to walk out that door right now.'

'I've been trying not to think about my family while I'm in here,' says Gemma, quietly. 'It makes me feel too sad. I mean, it's only been a few weeks, it's not like a lifetime. But I just feel like I'm so far away from everyone.'

'Ladies, what's with the sad faces?' Adam shouts. 'This is a celebration! A reminder of who's waiting for you on the other side! I want to see smiles and tears of joy! Right, who wants to go first? No volunteers? Well, I guess I'll just pick one myself. Amy! Gemma, would you do the honours, please?'

Amy hands Gemma the envelope and takes a seat. The moment Gemma opens it, she knows it's from Sarah. She knows that handwriting as well as she knows her own.

During uni holidays, they used to write each other letters, despite being just an hour away. It's a good thing. Sarah's message won't be gushy, it'll be funny and uplifting, which is exactly what she needs right now. Had it been from her mum, she might have collapsed on the floor at the first word.

Gemma coughs and starts to read out in a serious voice that doesn't quite match the content. Amy sits still with her eyes closed and her hands shaking.

AMY!
HOLY MOTHER OF GOD.

Amy smiles. It's definitely her.

I can't believe you're doing this, it is totally bananas. I didn't think it was possible to love you more, but I really do now that you're a celebrity. When can you introduce me to Daniel Craig?

So, Jamie's a complete dickhead, isn't he? He was on the front page of Metro *this morning, so I stole all the copies I walked past and put them in the recycling bin at work. I told your parents to do the same. I've got chronic backache now, but it was worth it.*

The lump in Amy's throat is hard, but so is her laugh.

Revenge and kidding aside, I am so proud of you, Ames. I can't imagine how hard this has all been for you, but you are handling it like the legend you are. Brave, honest and just fucking real. It's like you're shedding all those long-term relationship layers you've built up over the last two years, and we're finally starting to see the true you again. Stop crying.

The laugh has gone and her lip starts to wobble. Flick moves closer and puts her arm around her. It's sweet, but if she squeezes, Amy will lose it.

Squeeze.

Amy grabs a tissue to stop a tear streaming down her cheek and puts it against her mouth, exhaling hard into the paper while she tries to blink away her tears. A few seconds pass and she manages to compose herself.

This might be the sappiest thing I've ever said, but I love you and I miss you! Screaming, talking, pointing and laughing at you on the telly isn't the same as doing it across the table. My neighbours must think I've got an imaginary friend or a passionate secret lover.

Amy, I am so happy that you're finally doing something for yourself and putting your happiness first. You've put them on pause for too long. I know you're going to achieve amazing things, and this is just the beginning of your incredible, unique, daring and exciting journey. Keep on being you. It's got you this far, and I know it'll take you to the final. And at the end, I'll be watching from the other side with your mum and dad, cheering you on so loudly you'll be too embarrassed to admit you know me.

Sarah xox

PS Is Dr Hicks single? Can you put in a good word?
PPS Be brave and breathe. You only have a week to go.

Amy laughs and wipes her eyes as she takes the letter from Gemma and thinks of Sarah watching her now. She looks up at the camera and blows her a kiss.

'Oh deary me, I'm not crying, you're crying!' Adam pretends to wail, ruining the mood. 'Flick, are you ready to read Jackie's letter?'

Flick takes Jackie's letter and sits up straight.

My dearest Jackie,
I am so proud of you, my brilliant girl. I have always been proud of you. I raised you to fear nothing and to stand up for what is fair and you have never let me down. I don't know what I did to deserve such a strong, smart and beautiful daughter.

Jackie's eyes don't shift from her feet. 'God, *strong*? More like pathetic. Come on, Jackie, have a cup of concrete.' She laughs nervously, her voice wobbling.

'You OK for me to carry on?' Flick asks.

Jackie nods, looking down at her feet again.

I miss your visits, but I am so happy that I can see you on the television every day. I'm so happy you are spending time looking after yourself for once, instead of always looking after me. I love your visits, but I want you to have a life for yourself, too.

My friends at church have put up a poster of you in the hall and sometimes we watch the show together on the community projector. They want to have a Welcome Home party for when you come back. It has been a difficult year for us, my girl, but good things come to good people and God has exciting plans for you. Remember, I will support every path you choose to take.

My heart was singing when I saw you laugh with your friends at the tea party. It made me laugh, too. I have not seen you laugh like that since you were at school. No matter how big you get, you will always be my little girl, laughing until the tears fall from her eyes. All I want from life is for my little girl to be happy. And also maybe for you to not drink or swear too much, because that is not very Christian.

I love you, my star girl. I am watching you every day and wishing you luck in this exciting time of your life. I will be waiting for you with open arms when you return in six days.

God bless you,
Your Papa xxx

Flick folds up the letter as Jackie stands and goes over to the glass doors. The reflection in the window gives away her glistening cheeks. Amy wonders if Jackie has thought of her mother since being in here. Could she be watching her, wherever she is? Would she know that Jackie is her daughter?

'Papa Adu, what a legend! I want him to be my papa!' Adam interrupts. 'Don't get jealous, Dad, I love you too. Now, Flick or Gemma, Flick or Gemma, Flick or Gemma . . . Gemma! Amy, you choose!'

Amy sighs loudly.

'Gemma, are you happy for me to read out your letter?' Amy asks.

'Sure. I know what this is going to be about, I've heard it enough times.' Gemma rolls her eyes.

Darling Gem Squash,
We couldn't be prouder of you. For having the guts to stay on the show and for everything you've achieved in the last year with your Instagram business.

So far, Gemma's showing little emotion.

We miss you so much, Gemma, and it's not just since being on the show. We miss the old you, too.

She sighs again. 'Here we go.'

The Gemma you used to be. The Gemma who looked at us when we talked to her, the Gemma who left her phone in her bag at Sunday lunch, the Gemma who would join in the conversation like you used to. Family time was so important to you, Gem, and I know it still is. I think you've got caught in a trap and you're struggling to find balance. But we can help you. We just want what's best for you, all of us, including Jason.

Gemma's lip is starting to shake.

Do you know he told us he was putting you on the show? He wanted to know if we thought it was a good idea. We were behind him all the way. He's such a good lad, Gemma. Please don't be hard on him. He pushed you away to get you back, not because he doesn't love you anymore. You are still the same Gemma we have always loved. An amazing friend. Strong, kind and supportive. But also the life and soul of everything. It's wonderful to see the real you shine again. Instead of the top of your head as you stare into your hands.

Jason loves you. We all love you. We can't wait to welcome you home. Maureen's organised a street party!

Love Mum xxx

'That's lovely, Gem,' Amy says, as she hands her the letter.

Gemma folds it in half and smooths the paper seam she's created as she looks into her lap, deep in thought.

'I know they have a point,' she says softly. 'But they don't understand the pressure I'm under. I know it's easy to take the piss out of people like me, but you try posting something new three fucking times a day. Or replying to every single comment, when there are hundreds and hundreds. And God help me if I ever miss one.'

What was a wobbly voice is starting to get defensive.

'You OK, Gem Squash?' Jackie asks, smiling and moving back to the sofa.

'Ha ha. And yeah, I'm fine. I'll figure it out.'

'Now, last but not least,' shouts Adam. 'Jackie, can you open Flick's letter and tell us who it's from, please!'

'I'm sure it's from Simon,' Flick says as Jackie opens the letter. 'He always writes me little love letters and leaves them on my dressing table.'

Jackie skims to the bottom of the letter.

'Nope, sorry, love. It's from someone called Emma.'

'Oh. My old surgery partner. We went to uni together. That's very . . . sweet,' she says, staring at the letter. 'Perhaps Simon's busy.'

'Oooooh, Simon's in for a tongue-lashing later, isn't he, audience?' Adam shouts. 'OK, Jackie. Crack on.'

Dear Flick,

We were so shocked to see you on the show when the first episode aired. Simon had warned us, but we still couldn't believe our eyes. You look incredible, but then I wouldn't expect anything less. Everyone at the surgery is supporting you fully and we'll be voting you into the final and out as The Keeper. All the kids miss you, too!

Flick, you are the hardest worker I know, and are nothing less than exceptional at everything you put your mind to. I'm not surprised you've won almost every task. You've always been top of the class. You deserve this, Flick. You deserve to be recognised and rewarded for your hard work. It's time you were truly appreciated for your commitment, and I'm not just talking about the show. Sometimes I think Simon doesn't know how lucky he is. I'm going to get in trouble for saying that!

We're all thinking of you, and everyone sends their love.

Emma x

Flick, who has remained calm and composed throughout the reading, takes her letter from Jackie and walks into the garden, leaving the others in silence on the sofa.

'Hope she's all right,' mumbles Gemma.

'Yeah.' Jackie sighs. 'I thought those letters would make us feel better.'

'Well. Not long to go now, guys,' Amy says.

Sarah's words have given Amy a kick. She wants to see this through. She wants to be the brave, honest and fucking real person she described in her letter.

'Thanks for watching, everyone!' Adam shouts, waving at the screen. 'And don't forget to tune in tomorrow, for what will be our housemates' hardest challenge yet! I guarantee there will be shouting, tears and shards of broken hearts scattered all over the floor.'

All three of them sigh at once.

Thirty-Four

'Ugh, I'm too tired for this,' mutters Jackie, the next morning. She's lying on the carpet in her pyjamas, looking half asleep. 'I had such a terrible night's sleep. I couldn't stop thinking of my dad and wondering if he's really OK.'

'I couldn't stop thinking of bits of my bleeding heart all over the floor,' Amy replies. 'I mean, this show is horrific, but it isn't an actual horror show. At least, I hope not.'

The housemates are eating their breakfast on the sofa. On the coffee table are four pieces of card each with a name on, and four felt tip pens. The screen flickers on and the show's intro starts.

'HOUSEMATES!' shouts Adam Andrews.

Jackie puts a cushion over her head and groans.

'How are we all today? Jackie – looking tip-top, I see!'

She puts a middle finger up at the cameras, without moving the pillow.

'OK, ladies, so today you'll be facing one of your hardest

challenges yet. Well, I would struggle, wouldn't you, Doctor?' he says, turning to Dr Hicks on the sofa.

'Certainly, Adam. This challenge is all about having the courage to be direct. I'm afraid it's going to be deeply uncomfortable, and I doubt the housemates are going to like it.'

'This sounds mysterious!' says Gemma, sitting down.

'How are you feeling this morning, Gemma?' asks Flick.

'Yeah, I'm OK. Still feel a bit iffy.' She sighs and leans back on the sofa. Amy notices Flick staring at her.

They turn back to the TV to carry on listening to Dr Hicks.

'Is he still talking?' mutters Flick.

'. . . And that's why I think this challenge could reap some very surprising results indeed,' Dr Hicks concludes.

Adam and the audience stay silent.

'I'm finished,' he says, looking around, confused.

'Oh, right, sorry,' Adam says, standing up for the audience. 'Let's hear it for the Doc! A man of many shades of brown and even more long words,' he says, turning his back on him and pretending to snore, making the audience laugh.

'Oi, leave Dr Hicks alone!' Gemma raises her voice.

'If it weren't for him, I'd have walked in the first week,' Amy adds.

The rest nod in agreement.

'All right, housemates and viewers. We have a big surprise for you all today. It's called Truth Hurts.' Adam walks into the audience and signals to someone seated to get off their chair. He steals the seat, as members of the audience behind him wave and make crude hand signals.

'So, who wants to know what the surprise is?' he shouts. 'Do you want to know what the surprise is?' he asks the teenage girl sitting next to him, who nods excitedly. 'And do *you* want to know what the surprise is?' he asks the young man in front of her, who gives a thumbs up. 'And do *you* want to know what the surprise is?' He points at the cameras.

'Get on with it, you moron!' shouts Jackie.

'Well, everyone, the surprise is . . .' There's a drum roll, and a hush falls on the crowd.

'. . . that it's time for the housemates to vote each other out!' Adam yells over the audience's screams, as he covers his hand with his mouth.

'That's right, housemates. Today is all about being honest with each other. No more pretending to like someone when you hate them. No more hiding behind sweetness and smiles. No more Ms Nice Girls.'

'But I don't hate anyone.' Gemma looks around. 'Believe me, if I did hate any of you, you'd know.'

'So, ladies, I'm sure you're dying to find out how it works. Here's the deal. You have one hour to decide who you want to vote off the show. Mark your choice on the card in front of you and pop it in the Chat Room postbox when you're done. When your name is called, stand up and explain yourself! And remember, no discussing the votes!'

The housemates turn and look at each other in horror.

Adam shakes his head and puts his hand on his hip. 'We're just awful, aren't we?'

*

In the shower, Amy tries to keep her thoughts rational as she decides who to vote for and why.

Flick.

Jackie.

Gemma.

She can't bear the thought of Flick going back to that selfish bastard, Simon. And her story has touched a nerve with Amy, who's desperate to convince her to leave him and be happily single like she is now. But is Flick's happiness really any of her business, or responsibility? She didn't sign up to be Amy's project. Perhaps only Flick can rescue herself.

Then there's Gemma, the resident ray of sunshine. Without her, the house would be much gloomier. If Amy were ruthless, she'd vote for her. Gemma's her biggest competition on The Tracker, after all. But Gemma has only been lovely to Amy since they first arrived. She couldn't do that to her.

Last is Jackie, the housemates' biggest champion. The housemate who is desperate for money to help her dad, to sue her firm and to right the wrongs of the world. She's also the housemate who hates it here the most. And she does seem to seriously miss her dad. Would Amy be doing her a favour by voting her out? She'll earn money from the publicity when she leaves, like she said, and she could still achieve all the things she's set out to do. It might not be a million pounds, but it might be enough.

'Housemates, you have five minutes before you have to cast your vote. Please return to the living room.'

Shit shit shit shit shit shit shit. This is it, she thinks, as she jumps out of the shower in a panic. *You're going to lose a friend, no matter what you decide.*

Back in the living room and waiting for the show to start again, the housemates stare at some of the tweets pinging up on The Wall.

@wandawoman I'd vote Jackie! All she brings is a big batch of angry #theshelf

@bustaboy Gemma, you need to get your ass back to the gym girl! #justhavinalaugh #theshelf

'Ha! That's my mate, Buster! Cheeky sod.' Gemma laughs as she stands up, looks down at her stomach and blows out.

The TV flickers on and the show begins.

'Welcome back, everyone!' shouts Adam into a handheld mic, facing the camera on stage wearing a T-shirt that says TEAM GEMMA on the front.

'Yay!' yells Gemma at the screen with her hands in the air.

'Is he allowed to do that?' asks Flick.

Adam drops the mic onto the sofa and takes off his T-shirt off to reveal another shirt underneath that says TEAM JACKIE. The audience laugh.

'So, as I was saying,' Adam says before he pauses and does the same thing again. This time it's a TEAM FLICK shirt.

'For fuck's sake,' says Jackie. 'Why does he have to draw it out every single time?'

'Sorry, this one's rubbing me up the wrong way, actually,' he says, and the audience laugh. The final shirt is a TEAM AMY.

'I just can't decide, viewers, I'm stumped. But luckily it's not up to me. So, let's hand over to the housemates! First up to explain who they'd vote off *The Shelf* is Jackie!'

He takes Jackie's card from a producer, opens it and raises his eyebrows.

'Well, ladies and gents, no real surprise here. Jackie wants Flick out! Jackie, tell us why.'

Jackie stands up confidently. 'I'm really sorry, Flick. I loved our dinner together and I was so glad we had that time to get to know each other and work out our differences. I made this choice simply because we are so different and we always will be. I know that you're The Keeper, based on the show's ideals, but I'm against these ideals in the first place. I'd rather The Keeper wasn't someone like you. I want to prove the producers wrong, and I want to show everyone watching. I want The Keeper to be someone they never expected it to be. I hope you can understand.'

Flick nods, reaches over and squeezes Jackie's hand.

The audience erupt in a frenzy, some cheering, some booing.

'Aaaaah, how touching!' Adam laughs. 'Thank you, Jackie, we've heard you loud and clear. That's one vote for Flick! Speak of the devil . . . Flick! Please stand up and tell us why you want to see . . .'

He reads the card with raised eyebrows.

'. . . Amy out of the house!'

Amy doesn't move an inch as she carries on staring at the screen in shock, watching from the corner of her eye as Flick stands up, smooths out her skirt out and coughs. How could Flick vote for her after their heart-to-heart this morning? Amy feels sick, realising she's made a terrible mistake with her vote.

'It isn't personal, it's strategic. I'm sorry, Amy, but you are at the top of The Tracker. What choice do I have but to pick you? Of course I want to win the competition. We should all want to win this competition, otherwise what are we doing here?'

'Oooh, that's cold! Amy, it's your turn. Let's hope you've chosen Flick, or this could be super awkward!'

He opens the card and his face drops.

'You chose . . .'

Amy buries her face in her knees. She needs to find the nearest hole.

'Jackie?' He looks up, confused.

Gemma gasps. 'Amy!'

Amy can't bear to look at Jackie as she straightens up, but she knows she deserves a proper explanation. She turns round and looks Jackie in the eye. And when she does, she sees Jackie has welled up.

'I'm so sorry, Jackie. You know I love you so much,' she says, her voice breaking. 'And that's exactly why I chose you. I want you to be happy, and you aren't happy here. You hate every task, you object to every challenge and you don't participate properly. And that's fine because it's your choice, but I genuinely thought you might be delighted to leave. To be reunited with your dad. Can you see where I'm coming from? Even just a little bit?'

'The girl has got a point,' Adam interrupts.

'Aren't you forgetting about our pact?' Jackie speaks quietly, staring at her. 'I mean, I know this is a competition, but I thought we were in this together.'

Jackie and Amy, the first two housemates. A new and improved #Jamy, as they'd laughed about the other day. There's bile in Amy's throat and beads of sweat on her hairline. Ten minutes ago, this speech made complete sense in her head. She was even stupid enough to think Jackie would be grateful.

It should have been Flick. It should have been Flick. It should have been Flick.

'We *are* in this together, Jackie. Please don't think I don't support you. I genuinely chose you thinking you wouldn't

338

mind leaving. You can carry on the good work out there. Gemma and I can carry on the good work in here. I promise we can do that for you.'

'Well, lucky me,' Jackie says, staring at the screen.

'Uh, no, you can't,' says Adam, looking at the next card.

'What?' Amy replies.

'In five minutes, there will be no more Amy and Gemma.'

She turns to Gemma, frowning. Gemma must have voted for her. She sits back down on the sofa and folds herself into her lap.

Amy's show is over.

Thirty-Five

Gemma stands up and moves in front of the screen. 'You can carry on the good cause, Amy. It's me who can't.'

'What's going on?' asks Jackie.

'I'm the one who's leaving. And because I'm choosing to leave, your votes are invalid. They mean nothing. You're all staying.'

'Gemma, why? You don't have to do this!' Jackie stands up and grabs her arm. 'We've only got a few days left – I need you in here. Don't leave me alone with them!'

Harsh, but fair in the circumstances.

Gemma smiles. 'Jacks, I'm afraid there is someone who needs me more out there.'

'Jason? He's a grown man, he'll be fine! It's a week, for fuck's sake, what's he crying about?'

'There'll be a lot more tears in eight months, I can tell you.'

'Oh my God, you're pregnant,' Amy whispers. 'Aren't you? Gemma, are you pregnant?'

Gemma looks at the three of them and nods, clutching her stomach.

Amy and Jackie shoot off the sofa and smother Gemma in hugs and kisses. Congratulations fill the air and the tension of a few minutes ago is forgotten for now, as well as the millions of viewers who are probably going mad.

'Have you told Jason?' Amy asks, when the excitement subsides.

'I told him on the phone in the Chat Room an hour ago. Flick helped me figure it all out.' Gemma reaches out and rubs Flick's arm. 'Even though I'm sure she's shocked I'm having a baby out of wedlock. Jason is going to be a great dad. I think it'll make him grow up. And I think I'm going to be making a few other changes in my life. Maybe give my family a bit more attention than I have done in the last year.'

Flick is smiling, but Gemma being pregnant is probably a painful reminder that she isn't and might never be.

'So, you guys are getting back together?' Jackie asks, holding her hand.

'We were always going to get back together.' Gemma smiles and strokes her stomach. 'And now that this little bub is here, I've never loved him more.'

*

Water. I need water.

Amy sits up, immediately regrets it and drops her head back onto her pillow with her fingers pressed against her

HELLY ACTON

temples. Her brain is throbbing against her skull and her mouth tastes of sour milk.

Where am I?

She lifts her neck and blinks a few times. She's on the floor next to Jackie's bed. And desperately hoping she was sensible enough to leave some water and two painkillers next to her makeshift bed last night. Fat chance.

She hasn't eaten since lunchtime yesterday and her hands are shaking. That's what nine glasses of prosecco will do. Or was it ten?

Can I make it to the bathroom by using my feet to slide myself forward on my stomach? she wonders, considering how to reach the tap with minimal effort and energy.

'Jackie?' she whispers.

There's no response.

'Flick?' she whispers again.

Still nothing.

She finds enough energy to pull herself up. Why do her legs hurt so much?

'Mmmy.' She hears a mumble next to her.

'Jackie?' Amy croaks.

'Mmmy,' Jackie says.

Amy looks up at the side of the bed and sees Jackie's little red eye poking over the edge.

'What am I doing down here?' Amy asks.

'Don't you remember?' Jackie groans, shifting under her duvet. 'You wanted to prove your love by sleeping next to me.'

There's silence for a while before they both burst out laughing, quickly followed by moans when they realise that laughing is the worst thing they could do right now.

'How much did we drink?' Amy asks.

'I think we finally drank the tap dry,' Jackie replies. 'Why do you have a massive bruise on your knee?'

'Housemates, please go to the living room.'

Amy and Jackie grab their heads and whine.

'Tut, tut, tut, ladies,' says Adam Andrews, shaking his head to the camera and rolling his eyes.

'Jackie and Amy, what the devil were you two up to last night?' he asks, as the screen switches the feed to house footage from the night before.

Amy sinks into the sofa, mortified.

It's the living room. Flick's sitting on the sofa with a cup of tea, watching The Wall. There's a movement behind her and suddenly Amy and Jackie enter the picture.

Oh, God.

They're shouting at each other.

Then they're hugging each other.

Then they're weeping.

Then they're slut-dropping on the coffee table, and Flick's leaving the room.

Then they're falling off the coffee table and onto the floor, collapsed in hysterics.

The camera feed switches back to Adam's face on the screen and he lifts one eyebrow.

'Very mature, ladies,' he says. 'Flick, enjoy your lap dance?'

She smiles. 'Not as much as the others, I'm sure.'

'OK then, mooooooving swiftly on!' shouts Adam. 'Please welcome Dr Howard Hicks to the stage! So, Doc, you've got something really exciting in store for our three girls this evening, haven't you?'

Dr Hicks takes his usual seat. 'I do, Adam. Tonight, we're treating them to a night on the tiles in the Tiki bar with twenty eligible bachelors! This is no challenge. It's some well-deserved time off from all the tasks they've undertaken so far.'

The thought of having another drink makes Amy turn green.

✳

A few hours later, and they're in the Tiki bar, surrounded by strange men who know everything about them. Amy's been talking to a guy called Ed for almost an hour without interruption, slowly sipping on an Aperol spritz and managing to hold it down.

Amy doesn't really fancy Ed. What she fancies is his life. He had her at 'I'm a digital nomad' when she asked him what he did and he went on to explain how he's a technology writer who spends half the year in Singapore and half the year in the UK writing for different publications remotely. She wants to know everything, and how she can be one too.

He isn't unattractive. If Amy was in a different headspace,

she'd be into his scruffy brown hair, woven cardigan, John Mayer vibe. He seems laid-back and he laughs easily, looking down at his feet each time.

'Ed, it's been so lovely talking to you.' She smiles. 'Thanks for letting me in on your nomad secret. Perhaps I'll see you on the beach in Thailand next year.'

'Sure. Perhaps we could carry on chatting when you're released.' He writes his number down on a card.

Amy looks around as she walks away. Jackie's shouting and gesticulating about politics to a surprisingly captivated audience of three men. Flick is smiling and talking to a handsome older man, tucking her hair behind her ear and acting bashful.

Suck on that, Simon, Amy thinks as she wanders past, listening to her talk about how she's an old-fashioned home-body, with him hanging onto every word.

'Amy?' A soft voice distracts her. When she turns round she comes face to face with a short, stocky blond guy. He has kind eyes and an Aperol spritz.

'Hi, I'm Charlie. I noticed you like Aperol spritz!' He whispers, 'My favourite, too, but don't tell my mates. They think I like ale! Grrr.' His dimples are so distractingly cute that she stumbles over her words.

'Hi Amy. I mean Charlie. I'm Amy, *duh*!' She laughs, embarrassed. 'Thanks,' she says as she takes the Aperol spritz and has a long sip, hoping to God he'll say something next because she can't think of anything apart from how beautiful those dimples are.

Charlie starts with small talk and Amy feels relieved she can listen instead of chat about herself. He's a city type turned country bumpkin, raising dairy cows with his mum on his family's farm near the Devon coast. It seems idyllic.

'This is all so surreal.' He laughs. 'I never thought I'd get picked for this. And I'm such a massive fan of the show. Mainly of you.' He quickly looks down. 'Sorry, that was a slip. I probably just made you feel really awkward. I promise I'm not a stalker. This is so unfair for you all. I feel like I know you so well, and you know nothing about me.'

'Well, tell me more about yourself, then. Like how come you're such a huge fan of the show? You don't seem like the type. I didn't think we'd have too many dairy farmer groupies on here.'

'It is a bit odd, isn't it? My mates rip the piss out of me, the bastards. It's actually because of my mum. Dad died a few years ago and she's been amazing on the farm by herself, but she is getting on a bit and finding the physical stuff a struggle. She's going to hate me for saying that. She broke her hip last year. So, I decided to quit the city and go down and help her. I couldn't be happier. Cut a long story short, Mum didn't have a TV. Long hours, the radio and books were enough to keep her happy in the evenings. But being trapped indoors all day with her cast, she was climbing the walls, so I bought her a telly. *The Shelf* is the first show we've watched together, and she's completely hooked. We watch the catch-up every night after supper. It's like the best thing that's happened to her. We used to bond over milking the cows – now we bond over who's going to be The Keeper around here.' He points his beer around the garden and then leans across and whispers, 'It's you,' in her ear, sending shivers down her spine.

'Would it make you uncomfortable if I burst into tears and gave you a big hug?' Amy says, her eyes feeling misty and her fingers wanting to squeeze his cheeks.

'Nah, 'course not. It's classic Amy, right?' He laughs, clinking her glass.

She grins. 'Oi!'

'Anyway, so that's the reason. I'm a complete mummy's boy and proud of it, too. I hated the city. I hate money, so I was pretty awful at my job. I should have been a teacher, that's what I always wanted to do. All my mates were going into finance, so I thought I'd better go into it too. Stupid, really.'

Kind.

Funny.

Handsome.

Lives on a dairy farm in Devon.

Loves his mum.

Will support and supply my cheese addiction.

So far, it feels like Charlie could be Amy's dream man. Perfect fling, boyfriend, husband and father material.

*

Later, The Wall is flooded with Charlie fangirls and someone's already set up a Charlie the Farmer page. Amy doesn't
blame them. He's a total catch.

She feels a bit sad knowing she has absolutely no interest
in taking this further, but at the same time she's hopeful,
knowing there are Charlies in this world who will make
her happy whenever she's ready for it.

If she's ever ready for it.

Thirty-Six

Amy's eyelids are sticky. The telltale sign that she's had far too many late nights. She hasn't done two nights in a row since the first days of Jamie, and her dusty head and slug-gishness is a painful reminder that she isn't twenty-five anymore. She forces her eyes open and shuffles up the pillow until she's half sitting to stare at the others across the room. Jackie is snoring; Flick's bed is already made. The room feels so empty with just the three of them left.

Would she have predicted this would be the final three? Flick, yes. Her and Jackie, not so much. Her tactic from the start has been to keep her head down and not make a fuss. Jackie's tactic has been to put her head up and cause as much fuss as possible. Both seem to have worked, although she can't help feeling that Gemma should be here.

Amy kicks the duvet off and swings her legs over the side of the bed. She knows exactly what she needs today.

Absolutely nothing.

She starts with a face mask: *Beach Bomb: a blast of rehydration after a day in the sun.* It's a bittersweet reminder. Next on the list is a hot shower, scrubbing her scalp and exfoliating all over with the mini loofah she bought to remove dead skin for a deeper tan. Another pointless purchase, but she is enjoying the tingling sensation on her skin and the idea of all those toxins from the last two days being washed away. She finishes with an inch-thick layer of moisturiser all over her body and a mug of whitening Listerine that she lets sit in her mouth until her tongue stings and her eyes water.

Today is not a hair and make-up day. Instead, Amy scrapes her hair back into a bun and a headband to make sure not a single strand can irritate her forehead as she puts on stretchy leggings, a huge hoodie and slipper socks. Outfit complete, for the rest of the day. She realises she's swapped pyjamas for more pyjamas. She doesn't care.

It had taken her a long time to start dressing this way in front of Jamie. The first time she had, he'd teased her for getting a bit too comfortable, with his great big manic laugh that she loved back then and loathes now. After he'd said it, she'd gone back to dressing up every morning in case he really did think she was letting herself go. Then one day they both had a hangover from hell and he seemed to accept her like that.

She wipes the steam off the mirror and stares at her blank, barefaced reflection. It's going to be the first day she hasn't worn foundation since being here.

Well, world, this is me. Fucking real.

She's relieved to see Jackie's still fast asleep and Flick is getting into the swimming pool. She doesn't have to talk to anyone for at least another half an hour.

In the kitchen, she makes herself a tea with two sugars – what a treat – and puts four pieces of white bread in the toaster. Yes, four. Lashings of peanut butter, lots of jam and cut into long triangles, because for some reason it tastes better that way. With her sweet tea and her toast mountain, she takes a seat on the sofa and curls her legs up. She's never missed Netflix – or her phone – more. The comments on The Wall will have to do.

@mrgrumpypants Bit hungry are we, Amy? #theshelf

Oh, fuck off.

She takes one big bite of her toast before the worst thing that could possibly happen, happens.

'Amy, please go to the Therapy Room. Dr Hicks would like to see you.'

*

'Amy! It's good to see you. I feel like it's been a while.' Dr Hicks smiles from his armchair. 'How have you been? Just three days to go, now!'

Amy doesn't answer immediately as she takes a slow seat on the sofa and leans back.

'I'm actually feeling pretty drained today, Dr Hicks. I really don't feel like I have a lot of conversation in me.' She fake-yawns to make a point.

'That's OK, we don't have to use up the full hour. Let's just see how far we go. But before we start, I want to show you something funny that I thought you might enjoy.'

He passes the iPad over to her. On the screen is a picture of a woman wearing sunglasses in the shape of red flags.

He chuckles. 'Isn't that funny?'

Amy sighs. 'This whole red flag thing is getting ridiculous, Doctor. It's embarrassing. It's not like I came up with the phrase "red flags", and there are probably a thousand similar articles out there. I don't deserve any credit for it, let alone some viral trending hashtag and sunglasses.'

Wow, she's in such a bad mood.

'Why did the blue and gold dress catch on, or that shark song? Enjoy it, Amy. Own your moment. Anyway, we don't have to dwell on it if it makes you feel uncomfortable. A lot has happened since we last spoke to each other. I want to start with the Sorry Supper. In our previous session, you wanted to leave over it. I'm so pleased you didn't. So tell me, how did it go?'

'I felt nervous before, and nothing much afterwards. He looks different, but he's exactly the same Jamie as before. Anyway, I got a few answers out of him, but I still don't buy his *you put me under silent pressure, I'm the real victim here* story, and I think he's a coward for not having the guts to break up with me in person.'

'Are you pleased that you went through with it?'

Siiiiigh.

'Sure. It wasn't such a big deal after all, and it hasn't changed how I feel about him. But I suppose it was good in the sense that I didn't feel upset when I saw him – I just felt detached. Maybe that's a sign I'm moving on. At least I don't have to dread bumping into him anymore. Not that I ever would, but you know, if we're ever in the same bar or on the same tube.'

'Good, Amy. I think that sounds like a solid result there. And let's talk about your other date this week, with Simon Ash. How was that?'

'It was awful! It scared the life out of me, thinking how it could have been me in five years' time with Jamie. It almost made me feel relieved to be here, which is a first. I didn't think I had anything in common with Flick until I met Simon and had a deep and meaningful conversation with her the next day. I just think the whole thing is so tragic. How she's waited so long for him, how he's wasted her time with false promises and blatant lies. And how the one thing she wants to happen in life might never happen for her now. I just can't believe Flick, who's so together, so clever, so perfect, still thinks he's the good guy.'

'So, how did it make you feel when she voted you out in Truth Hurts, the day after your chat?'

'Yeah, I was a bit shocked at the time. I mean, yes, I thought she would choose Gemma or Jackie because of how much friction they've had in the past. Not me. Not when I'm the one she's closest to in the house. But, you know, whatever, it's fine.'

That was convincing.

'You didn't want to confront her about it, like Jackie confronted you about your choice?'

'Not really.' She sighs. 'What would that achieve? She made a rational decision, and I can't take it personally. We can all just . . . move on. Do a HuJo and let it go.'

'But you and Jackie talked it out and it looks like you're fine with that, too. Maybe even more fine with Jackie than with Flick.'

'OK.'

'Amy, it's good to get our feelings out. If it's on your mind and you want to know why Flick chose you over Gemma and Jackie, you should talk to her about it. Take a deep breath. Have the conversation. The art of confrontation can be tricky to master, but it's worth investing the effort in doing so. What are you afraid of?'

'I'm not afraid. The truth is, I just can't be arsed. What would I achieve from asking Flick why she chose me? It's not like we're going to be lifelong friends when we leave here in a few days. We'll just go back to our same old lives, like we never knew each other at all. Besides, she already said why she chose me, and it was a perfectly valid response. I was the closest contestant to her on The Tracker. She's a doctor. It's science.'

'Amy, I'm using your situation with Flick as an example

of your continuing fear of confrontation, which is something I think we need to work on.'

Yes, I know that, Doctor, but not today.

'It's especially important in relationships. You need to have the courage to confront someone without feeling worried they're going to shout back, storm off or break up with you. The courage to confront your partner will be crucial in your next relationship, and it's something you need to build. And I think one of the ways that you can overcome this fear is through practising on people like Flick. The earlier you confront someone in a relationship over a matter that makes you profoundly unhappy, the sooner you can find out whether they're right for you. If they break up with you over it, they weren't right for you and you can feel happy you don't have to waste any more time on them. Now, I don't mean you should confront every little issue. I mean the important stuff. The big conversations. Like Flick. You thought you were close. And like Jamie. You thought he was The One.'

Amy stares at him for a few seconds.

'So, you're saying I should confront people if they're doing something that makes me feel deeply unhappy?'

'Yes, exactly.'

'Well, Dr Hicks, I feel deeply unhappy about having this conversation with you right now. I'm really not in the mood.'

'I can see you aren't in the mood for talking, Amy. Thank you for coming in anyway.' He smiles as he picks up his iPad and stands up. 'There's just one more thing we need you to do.'

A familiar face enters the Therapy Room with a piece of paper in his hand.

Thirty-Seven

'What is all this?' Amy asks Sam the producer as he lets Dr Hicks out of the Therapy Room through a side door.

Sam smiles as he gestures for her to sit down again and hands her the paper and a pen.

'A test?' Amy asks, looking down at the front cover.

Amy Wright: Progress Assessment

'We want to try and establish what you've learnt since you've been on the show,' Sam says. 'It's a chance for us to find out if we can fairly crown you The Keeper in two days if the votes swing that way. If you've made no progress since being here, we're going to struggle to hand over a million pounds. That's a lot of money for doing nothing.'

'Isn't that up to the public?' she asks, flicking through the pages.

'Ultimately, yes. But as we approach the end of the show,

we need to start filtering. We can't have three girls in the final. So, all three of you are taking this exam and the house-mate with the lowest score will be evicted.'

'Wait, what? Why didn't you tell us about this before?' Amy cries. 'You could have at least given us a chance to . . . I don't know . . . revise, or something.' Her voice fades as she turns the page and sees how short the test is.

'You've got fifteen minutes to answer all the questions in front of you, and you'll see why you didn't need to revise.' He's already walking towards the door. 'Some of the multiple choice options are . . . absurd.'

As he opens the door to leave the Therapy Room, he turns back to Amy.

'Amy, I just want to say that we aren't all like the men you see on The Wall. Or your exes. And I think you're all doing great, given the circumstances. I really hope you don't leave here thinking that all men are trash and there's no hope. That wasn't our intention. Our intention was to help get you out of bad relationships, get you thinking about what would make you happy and send you off with a positive outlook. I think some of that's been lost in trans-lation. And I'm personally sorry about that. There may have been questionable choices made along the way.'

Amy stares at him. 'We're fine, Sam. We can handle it. We don't need you to worry about us.'

He returns her stare for a few seconds before closing the door behind him and leaving Amy running her eyes over the front page.

PART I: PRACTICAL ASSESSMENT
Multiple choice

1. Oh, Baby!

Your baby isn't going to sleep and you're exhausted. What do you do?

    a. Turn up the TV to drown out their cries.

    b. Leave the house to get some peace and quiet.

    c. Continue with your chosen routine and sleep when they sleep.

Oh, come on.

2. Keep CALM

Your boyfriend is out with friends. He says he'll be home at 7 p.m. to eat the supper you've made specially, but he still isn't home at 11 p.m. What do you do?

    a. Throw his supper in the bin and leave an angry note on the fridge.

    b. Sleep on your response, ask him for an apology in the morning and move on.

    c. Eat his supper and wait in the dark for him to return, then unleash hell.

I'd love to see what responses Jackie's choosing.

3. Beauty School Soldiers
What does make-up have the power to do?
- a. Stop your husband from leaving you for a younger woman.
- b. Highlight your natural features and make you feel confident.
- c. Hide your real face so you can pretend to be someone else.

Lol.

4. Keep 'Em Keen
There are eight rules for holding onto a man. Which of the below is *not* one of them?
- a. Chill out.
- b. Make more effort in bed.
- c. Say I love you more often.

The last point was one of Amy's pet peeves with Jamie. She always said 'I love you' first. He never said it back. If he did respond, it would be with a robotic 'yeah, me too'. She teased him about it once and he told her that saying 'I love you' didn't mean anything when you said it all the time. She wanted to reply: *But you never say it, so surely once in a while would mean something.* But she didn't bother.

5. Keep 'Em Keen

According to our survey, what is the most important rule to follow?

    a. Don't let yourself go.

    b. Don't complain. Don't control. Don't neglect.

    c. Make more effort in bed.

6. Isn't She Lovely?

You've found a man with husband potential. How do you dress for your first date?

    a. A revealing minidress that shows a lot of flesh.

    b. A loose T-shirt, baggy jeans and trainers.

    c. A slim-fitting knee-length white dress that doesn't show too much cleavage.

7. Isn't She Lovely?

Where should you position your knife and fork when you have finished eating your food?

    a. 6.30.

    b. Off the plate.

    c. I don't care.

8. Isn't She Lovely?

What is the correct way to eat peas?

    a. With a spoon.

    b. Individually with your fork.

    c. Crush them with the back of your fork or stick them together with mashed potato.

While the questions are ridiculous, Amy has learnt a surprising amount since she's been here. Nothing to do with this exam paper. She's learnt that she can be happy alone. And that she has so much to look forward to when she leaves, whether that's tonight or on Friday. Her stomach cramps with excitement when she realises just how close she is to reaching the final, and being set free to get on that plane.

Thirty-Eight

'Credit where credit's due, Flick,' Jackie says, putting her knife and fork on her plate at 5.15. 'Your views might stink, but that tagine was the best I've ever had. I'd say if only you talked less and cooked more, but then I'd sound just like Simon, I suppose.'

'Why did you have to ruin a lovely compliment with that last part?'

'So, how do you think we all did yesterday?' asks Amy, changing the subject. 'In the exam, I mean.'

'The questions were ridiculously easy,' Flick answers. 'A two-year-old could have passed.'

Jackie swirls her prosecco. 'Well, how could you have learnt anything in here when you're already a keeper?'

'Actually, I think I have learnt something. But it's nothing to do with being a keeper – because, of course, you're right, I already am one.' She smiles. 'I've learnt something about myself. And that is, you'll be shocked to hear, that I miss the surgery. I miss my patients.'

'You miss working?' Amy asks.

'Yes, I do. Helping Gemma is what brought it on. And that note from Emma. I miss looking after people other than Simon. So, I'm considering going back when I leave. Not full-time – probably a couple of days a week. I think it'll be enough of a balance. I'll need to talk to Simon about it, obviously. About that, and maybe a few other things.' She sips her coffee and glances at Amy.

'Next thing you know you'll be marching with placards in Parliament Square,' says Jackie.

'Well, I've learnt a lot more than stupid rules on how to keep a man or dress for a tea party since being on here,' says Amy. 'Mainly, that it's OK to be me. In my next relationship, if that ever happens, I'm not going to pretend to be someone different at the start just to make them like me. Or worse, just in case they dump me. I'm going to speak up when I'm unhappy about something and trust that if he's right for me, he won't be scared away. Because he'll like me for me and everything I come with.'

'Quite right too,' adds Jackie. 'I've learnt that my dad can probably survive without seeing me every day and that I don't need to feel guilty about him the whole time. You heard him, living it up with his church mates. And when it does come to meeting someone, if that ever happens . . .' She pauses and looks at Amy. 'They're going to have to be confident enough to let Dad and I have our time together, instead of feeling threatened by it.'

'Actually, wanting to start at the surgery again isn't the only thing I've learnt on here. I've learnt that no matter how much you do for someone, no matter how much you sacrifice,' Flick's voice cracks to a whisper, 'you can't force them to do what they don't want to do. You can't force someone to love you.' She closes her eyes to plug her tears, taking a few seconds to compose herself. 'You can lavish them with attention, you can attend to their every need, you can make every effort not to let yourself go – but it doesn't mean they won't break their promises to you.'

'Flick, you've tried your best. That's all you can do.' Amy takes her hand.

'Housemates. Will you please come to the living room.'

Adam's in a graduation gown and cap, standing behind a podium on stage.

'Welcome, audience, and class of 2020. Please do take your seats for what will be a night full of glory for some, and shame for others. It gives me great pleasure to announce that this year's top student is – you probably guessed it – Miss Felicity Brimble! Felicity, if you could stand up, please.'

She sighs as she does.

'Well done, Miss Brimble – you got an A. And you know what that means, don't you? You've made it through to the final tomorrow!'

Confetti falls down onto the stage from above and the audience cheer.

'That's right – you can rest easy knowing all that hard work has paid off. Now, ladies and gentlemen, that leaves us with two housemates. But only one of them can go through. Everything rests on their tests, the results of which I can reveal now. Amy, your performance in this assessment was average. I mean, everyone knows that you eat peas by squashing them or eating them with mash!'

Really?

'And now for our last contestant, Jackie.'

Adam takes his fake spectacles off and puts them on the podium.

'Jackie, you made up all your answers. You don't fling your knife and fork behind you. You don't lean over your plate and suck your peas into your mouth like a Hoover. And you don't hold onto a man by his balls. That leaves you with no points and last in the class. And that, ladies and gentlemen, is how we've reached our decision tonight. It was an easy choice, I can tell you.'

He walks to the front of the stage and looks into the camera. 'The housemate leaving us tonight is the contestant who challenged the challenges, the firecracker who took us to task over the tasks. Tonight we're saying a final farewell to the formidable and the frankly infuriating *Jackie Adu*!' He raises his hands and claps.

The audience are surprisingly loud for the show's most divisive contestant. And when the cameras turn to the crowds, Amy is thrilled to see a crowd of hundreds of women holding signs in support of Jackie and her message.

SAVE JACKIE

WE'RE WITH JACKIE

THE CONVERSATION DOESN'T END HERE

'Well, ladies, I might be leaving,' Jackie turns to face them, her hands resting on her suitcase, which she packed the night before, 'but it looks like I have some work to do out there.' She sighs and smiles. 'Ames.' Jackie turns to her as she opens the door to the house. 'This show was never going to work on me because I'll never change. I love being me. This is who I am, and this is who I want to be.'

Amy thinks of the moment they first met. The bright red lips, the smile that could be seen from space and the laugh that could be heard from even further.

She never expected to survive this long. Last month she was Plain Old Amy, living her life, moving steadily forward on the escalator of normal life. Now she's Celebrity Amy Wright, *The Shelf* Finalist. And although she's feeling proud of how far she's come, and bursting with excitement to be leaving soon, seeing Jackie make her exit has filled her with dread. She has got used to the safety of these four walls. Tomorrow, she'll be leaving too. And whether she's a winner or loser, she has no idea what kind of storm she'll walk into.

The door slams shut.

And then there were two.

Thirty-Nine

'I can't believe we've made it to the finals,' Flick says to Amy, poking at her cereal on the sofa. Amy's lost her appetite from nerves too.

'Well, we still have a few hours. Who knows what could happen?' Amy stares out through the glass doors in the living room. She might sound calm, but the truth is she's been counting everything she can see in the garden, Sarah-style, for the last fifteen minutes.

'Amy and Flick, please take a seat on the living room sofa for your final challenge.'

The screen flickers on to show Adam Andrews walking down a stage that snakes through an empty car park outside the studio, with a cameraperson following closely behind him. The stage is buzzing with producers, camera equipment and people setting up screens and speakers at various points, which he dodges as he talks into a microphone. As he passes a runner, a sparkler bursts out of the floor and almost knocks him over.

'Woah, careful there, Johnny!' he shouts into his mic. 'Cameraperson, stay safe, stay close!'

'Can you hear something?' Amy says, looking at Flick. There's a low-level hum coming from outside.

Flick gets up, walks over to the glass doors and slides them open. The sound of a huge crowd screaming, shouting and whistling floods the living room.

Adam reaches the end of the stage and turns around.

'It's behind me, isn't it?' he says to the camera.

The camera zooms out to reveal an enormous crowd gathering by the car park gates. When the crowd see they're being filmed, they erupt into cheers and hold signs up in the air.

WE'RE ALL WRIGHT!

FLICK ME!

'I think that's where the sound is coming from,' Flick adds, looking nervous.

The camera pulls back onto Adam's face as he inches towards the screen.

'WOAH!' he screams into the camera, before turning round and running back down the stage, giving Amy and Flick a better glimpse of the size of the crowd. Thousands of people are queuing up for entry, all holding signs in support of either *#teamamy* or *#teamflick*.

'Oh my God,' Amy whispers.

'Are those tents? Have people camped overnight to be here?' asks Flick.

The TV cuts to Adam running onto the studio stage, where he turns round and catches his breath.

'Hello, everybody!' he shouts. 'So, is it just me, or does it feel like something massive is about to happen?' He puts a finger to his lips and pretends to think for a few seconds as the audience dies down. 'Oh yes, that's it, I remember, it's only the flipping live final of *The Shelf* 2020!'

The theme tune bursts through the speakers and the crowd dances in their seats, with Adam egging them on from the stage, waving his hands in the air.

When the tune abruptly cuts out, Adam takes his seat, looking into the camera.

'Now, the show still isn't over yet, folks. Today is the housemates' final chance to state their case to win before the live voting begins. Like a presidential election, but better, cleverer and way more fun, the girls will deliver a speech in the garden that tells the world why they deserve your vote tonight. Girls, grab your notepads and pens from the front door and start pouring your hearts out. We'll be back in two hours to hear it all, along with a few special guests.'

Doooong.

'Congratulations, girls!' screams a familiar and friendly

voice. 'I can't believe you two have reached the final! Well, I suppose I can because you're both gorgeous human beings who deserve every happiness.'

'Katie!'

She gives Amy and Flick dramatic air kisses on both cheeks.

Amy obliges with a loud lip smack. 'What are you doing here?'

'What do you mean, what am I doing here? I wouldn't miss your Armageddon for the world. It's time to brush this, blush that and fix you both up for the biggest night of your lives. Haven't you heard? They're expecting the highest ratings in the history of Real TV.'

Amy turns to The Wall. The tweets are flying in so quickly they can't be read.

That afternoon, two rows of chairs with VIP labels and an enormous outdoor screen dash Amy's hopes that she'll be speaking just to Flick and the gnomes. The four walls of the garden can't muffle the sporadic cheers from beyond. Each roar is louder than before and makes Amy break out into a sweat.

Katie styles Amy in a black tuxedo with a crisp white shirt and pointed stilettos, which just peek out under her fashionably oversized trousers. Her lips are scarlet and her hair is slicked back in a high bun, which looks like the chocolate doughnut she can't wait to eat when she gets out of there.

'It's very Kourtney Kardashian,' Katie insists.

Flick is wearing a halterneck sky-blue dress with matching heeled sandals.

'I feel like we're getting married. Look, it's Gemma and Jason!' Amy shouts, knocking on the glass door and waving. Gemma looks up and waves back, beaming from ear to ear, and then elbows Jason to do the same.

'Amy, please go to the Therapy Room. Dr Hicks is waiting for you.'

'Amy!' says Dr Hicks, looking smarter than usual in a tweed suit. 'Please come in, this will only take five minutes.'

Amy absorbs the bittersweet feel of the room as she looks around it one last time.

'I have something for you.' Dr Hicks turns round, holding a certificate.

'What's this?' Amy asks as she takes it.

'It's a certificate to say that you've passed. It doesn't mean you're The Keeper, but to have got this far means that you've done something right. It's an official acknowledgement and celebration of your participation and development on the show.'

'Will Flick get one?' she asks.

'Of course,' he says, smiling. 'I think she's on a good path, too.'

'Thank you, Doctor.' She wonders what they've spoken about in their sessions, and what he's advised Flick to do about her relationship. 'If it hadn't been for you, I'm not sure I would have survived. I'm sure – in fact, I know – that we all feel the same way.'

'Nonsense. You were the one who figured out the path on your own. I knew you would. Remember, we're all stronger than we think we are. Are you still planning your Thailand adventure?'

'Absolutely.' She smiles, staring at her certificate.

'Who knows, maybe you'll meet someone like-minded there.'

'I hope not.' She looks up. 'I've got far too much me time to enjoy.'

Forty

Amy stands at the side of the podium, beaming at her mum and dad, who are sitting at the back of the VIP section in the garden. She wants to laugh when she sees her mum giving Jamie an exaggerated side-eye from across the garden as he hands out business cards to the audience.

'What the bloody hell is that complete arse doing here?' her mum said earlier, when Jamie approached her. When he realised who she was, he'd made a last-minute dash behind a garden gnome.

Joining them in the audience are some familiar faces, who Amy's greeted like long-lost friends. Amy's only known Jackie, Gemma and Hattie for a few weeks, but it feels like forever. Lauren is playing a set in Ibiza, and Kathy can't make it. She's taken herself on holiday to an over-fifties singles club in Greece to celebrate – she and Jeremy have finally agreed to sell the house and split the proceeds.

'Amy!' Jackie runs up to speak to her. She can't get her

words out fast enough. 'You cannot believe how much support we have out there. How much support *you* have. We've started something important, I think. Something we can be really proud of. Apparently, young female viewers have begun to see being single as a positive, something to strive for. They're calling being single *#shelflife*, ha! It's exactly what we were hoping for. I'm so excited, I really want to do something with this. Maybe some kind of online community. You're a writer. Are you in?'

'One hundred per cent,' Amy replies.

As they take their seats at the front, the three ex-housemates start whispering and laughing like schoolgirls.

'Stop it, you three! You're making me feel nervous!' Amy shout-whispers to them.

'Imagine how they're making me feel,' Flick mutters, standing next to her. 'I'm assuming they aren't crossing their fingers for me to win. They're probably laughing at me.'

'No, they aren't. I promise. I don't think they know who they want to win. I actually think they're laughing because Jackie just pretended to blow her nose on Jamie's business card and wipe it on Gemma's dress.'

Simon is sitting in the corner at the back of the garden, away from everyone else. When Amy caught his eye earlier, he looked the other way. It annoyed her, because she wanted to stare him out. She'd seen Flick greet him as he took his seat, with an unfeeling kiss and an uncomfortable silence. Whether their relationship will survive this experience looks suddenly questionable. Hopefully not, if Flick meant what she said a few moments ago.

'Look at him, Amy. Sitting there like he hasn't a care in the world. Like he expects me to stop being silly, come home and put the supper on,' she whispers.

'Flick, please step up to the podium and tell us why you should be The Keeper.'

Amy breathes out, relieved she doesn't have to go first.

Flick steps up onto the stage, places her notepad in front of her and looks around the walled garden. She seems ice-cool, but when she speaks it's not with the confidence she had when she first arrived. There's a humility to her that Amy hasn't noticed before.

'I came on *The Shelf* to prove that I'm a keeper. And I believe that I've accomplished that goal. I've committed to every challenge. I've come top in almost every task. I have shown that I am willing and able to give my all to a relationship, while putting aside the things I care about. If that was the purpose of *The Shelf*, I feel it's only fair that I win. But even if I don't win the public vote, I know in my heart that I entered the house a keeper and I will be leaving a keeper.

'Not once did I compromise my ideals. When I walked through the front door a few weeks ago, it felt like I was entering a lion's den. I knew I wouldn't be the most popular person among my new housemates, but I took the risk and I didn't cave under pressure. I was here to prove I was marriage material, and I wouldn't let anything or anyone change me.

'Amy is a good person, who I've come to love in the few weeks I have known her. Despite our differences, she has shown understanding, kindness and compassion where others have not. But she isn't a keeper by the show's standards. If you crown her The Keeper, you'll be sending the wrong message to me and to the millions of housewives around the world who, just like me, work tirelessly to support their families. The millions of housewives who are often made to feel like lesser females because of their choices, and in spite of the sacrifices they have made.

'To deny me the crown would be wrong.'

She pauses, and then looks up at Simon.

'As wrong as it would be for you, Simon, to deny me what you promised four years ago. Marriage. A family. My name on our mortgage. A home that's filled with more than just you, me and your vintage red wine collection. I proved to you years ago that I would make the perfect wife and mother. I have waited on you hand and foot. I have attended to your every need while ignoring my own. All I ask is that you show some appreciation for what I left behind.

'And all I ask of you right now, right this second, Simon, is that you tell me, with everyone watching: are you going to marry me? Are you going to give me children, like you promised you would? It's a yes or no answer.'

YESSS! Flick!

Amy eyeballs a red-faced Simon, sitting at the back of the garden, glaring at Flick with steely eyes.

'Felicity, we will talk about this later.'

377

'Yes or no, Simon,' she says, remaining cool. 'You've had four years to think about it. You are not going to steal any more of my time.'

He becomes flustered as he looks at everyone staring at him.

'For God's sake, stop being so hysterical. This isn't like you. What are you doing?'

Flick smiles at him and then looks down at her notes. She drops one of the notes on the floor, where Amy can see the title.

If He Says Yes

'Ladies, gentlemen and viewers, I proved years ago that I was marriage material to one person. But now the whole world can see that I am, even if the one person I wanted to see, can't. As I said at the start of this speech, I entered the house a keeper, and I will be leaving a keeper. I know that I could be a good wife and a great mother one day. And I'm delighted to say that applications are open for the position of potential partner, for those who are kind, fair and keep their promises.'

The crowd laugh and clap. Simon looks furious as Flick takes a seat at the front of the studio audience, next to Jackie, not at the back in the seat he's kept free.

'Congratulations, Flick,' shouts Adam. 'What a statement! You'll need a PA to handle all those applications! Give it up for Flick, everyone. Simon, mate, what can we say? You had your chance!'

The audience laugh again, as Simon stands up and leaves the garden, glaring behind him as he goes.

Amy's heart is thumping as she steps up to the podium, looking at the floor.

She takes a deep breath, looks at her first line and begins.

'This is a letter to my sixteen-year-old self. And it goes something a little like this.'

Dear Amy,

I have bad news. When you're thirty-two, you won't be married to Leonardo DiCaprio and living in his mansion in LA. In fact, you won't be married at all. But there's no need to panic. You will be in a loving and committed relationship with someone who will never leave your side. Someone who has your best interests at heart.

You.

You alone are enough. If or when you are ready, you will open your heart and let someone inside who's the perfect fit.

You don't need a man to complete you.

You are whole already.

You are enough.

Be kind to yourself. Some of the hardest conversations you have will take place in your own head. Be kind to other people, even the ones who aren't kind back. You don't know what they've been through. Choose your words carefully. Words can be weapons of mass destruction and leave lifelong scars. Don't let yourself down.

Amy, I have more bad news. Your girl band Take Two will never perform at Wembley, despite all that practice. But you will be famous one day. You will have your own stage to spread important messages to the sixteen-year-olds who are watching. Like I said, choose your words carefully.

You are going to make some terrible choices in men. I mean, really awful. But you have to go through them all to get to where you need to be. Although I do wish I could stop you from grabbing that drink with Steve. That's eight months of pretending to like Mexican food and heavy metal you'll never get back.

Be grateful for every opportunity you've had. Remember to thank your mum and dad for everything they've done to get you to where you're going. Aspire to be like them, but in your own unique way. Your identity is yours. Protect it.

Lastly, stop it. I can see what you're doing, pinching your hip fat in the hallway mirror after school and sucking your cheeks in to look like Kate Moss. Stop comparing yourself to supermodels. They were born their way; you were born yours. Be happy in your beautiful skin. Worry about the size of your heart, not the size of your slice. Eat the bloody cake.

With love,
You

'Ladies and gentlemen,' she says, shuffling her papers. 'Flick is right. She's The Keeper, not me, according to the show's definition of the word. I didn't follow all the rules in every challenge, and I'm not top of the class. I'm delighted to be single, and I'm looking forward to spending more time on my own. *The Shelf* hasn't made me ready for someone else – *The Shelf* has made me ready for me. Right now, I'm not capable of giving my all to someone else. Right now, I'm not prepared to sacrifice what makes me happy.

'Crown or no crown, I pledge to be kind to myself, look after myself and protect my own interests. I'll never forget about those interests or cast them aside again. And this letter will be a ready reminder that, from this day forward, I am my own keeper. And to all the young girls who are watching the show, you will have your hearts broken one day. There's no avoiding it. But, like me, you are strong and you are worthy of everything in life you want to have. Be your own keeper. Each and every one of you.'

Amy jumps off the stage as the show breaks for the ads. She rushes to her parents, hugging them for a solid three minutes while the audience look on.

'Babes, that was amazing!' Gemma calls from the front row.

She needs to talk to someone.

When Jamie sees Amy making a beeline for him, he opens his arms.

'Piglet! Great tux. Gone totally off men, have you?' He laughs. 'Only kidding.'

'Jamie, why are you here?'

'I wouldn't miss this for the world. I got a pass in the mail. Thought it would be another good opportunity to plug the business. Why? You don't have a problem with me being here, do you? I thought we were friends?'

'I don't have a problem with you being here. In fact, I'm glad you're here, as I have a few things I want to say, and now I don't have to contact you out there.'

'Well, I'm glad you've decided to take some time to figure things out for yourself. Although I'm a little disappointed I didn't get a mention in the speech. Where's my thanks for helping you find your happiness?'

'I'm not here to thank you. I'm here to forgive you.'

'For what?'

'For everything. How you've treated me for the last eighteen months. How you've made me feel like a visitor in your home. How you've made me feel fat when I was fine. How you made me feel needy when it was only because your mixed messages were confusing me. They would have confused anyone. How you made me look and feel like I was the crazy ex-girlfriend, putting pressure on you to tie the knot when that wasn't the case at all.

'How you played the victim, when I was the one getting hurt. How you spoke to me like we had a future, then shut me down when I tried to talk about it seriously that one time. I'm forgiving you not because I'm weak, but because I'm strong. By forgiving you, I can cut our ties, let you go and move on. From you, our relationship and this entire experience. So no, I'm not here to thank you, Jamie. I'm here to forgive you. So. I forgive you.'

He stares at her for a few seconds with his mouth hanging open.

'I . . .' He pauses to run his fingers through his hair and clear his throat. 'Cool. OK. Nice one. So, should we, like, catch up after . . . ?'

'No, I don't think so, Jamie. Let's just leave it at this, shall we?' She smiles. 'Good luck with everything.'

'Yeah, you too Pi— I mean, Amy. You too, Amy.'

'Amy and Flick, please return to the stage. Audience, please take your seats.'

This is it, thinks Amy, taking a deep breath in as she walks towards the front. She hugs her mum and dad again and steps up to the stage.

The garden lights switch off and they're left in the glow of the TV screen. All of a sudden, the crowd on the screen go wild when they see Adam Andrews walk on stage in rhinestone-covered cowboy boots. He waves to the crowd as he walks up and down the runway, occasionally bending over to high-five them as he passes. The theme tune has never been louder, but Amy can hear her heart beating in her chest and her breath getting shorter with each inhale.

Just breathe. It's over.

Reaching the end of the stage, Adam turns.

'Hello, everyone! And welcome to *The Shelf*'s Grand Finale, where we get to find out who you've crowned The Keeper!'

383

The crowd roar.

'My goodness, it's been an eventful month, hasn't it, everyone? We've had ups, downs, U-turns and some pretty massive car crashes along the way. How about we take a look at some of the best bits?'

The screen in the garden starts to play footage from the last month.

They watch the housemates meeting each other for the first time. The slow-motion footage is set to a sad violin soundtrack, which triggers an instant lump in Amy's throat. They show Jackie hosing down her baby doll, while pulling a middle finger at the camera. Gemma screaming at Hattie working out in the garden. Hattie and Amy taking deep breaths in the dining room. Amy and Jackie falling off the coffee table; Lauren quitting the show; Kathy crying with her baby; Gemma announcing her pregnancy; Jackie's contagious giggle sparking ten minutes of hysterical laugher at the tea party.

And then her farewell, followed by a poignant moment between Flick and Amy when it hits them that they're the last to leave. Their embrace at the front door, tears streaming down their cheeks.

The footage is cut and the audience are left in silence.

'Ladies and gentlemen,' says Adam with a slowed, lowered voice. 'The time has come.

'The public have decided and the votes have been counted and verified,' Adam shouts.

A countdown appears on the screen, which lights up the chairs.

5 . . .

'I can confirm that I have been given the green light to go ahead and tell you what we've all been dying to know.'

3 . . .

'The Keeper from *The Shelf*, for the first time ever, is . . .'

1 . . .

Fireworks explode across the screen and light up the sky.

The crowd on screen look like they're moving in slow motion. Signs fly into the air above them like mortarboards at a graduation ceremony. Amy lowers her head to look at the audience in front of her and braces herself for the rush of people racing towards the stage.

Epilogue

The only way this view could be more perfect is if Leonardo DiCaprio was sitting in front of me, thinks Amy, as she sinks her toes deeper into the hot, silky sand.

But then again, he would be blocking the sunset over the sparkling water of Buffalo Bay. And she'd have to shave her legs.

Everything in Koh Phayam makes Amy feel like she's permanently drifting in a flotation tank. The still air is the perfect temperature, not too hot and never too cold. It wraps around her like soft cotton wool from the moment she wakes up, and follows her as she glides from day to night.

She has settled into a routine that satisfies her needs for both peace and purpose. She starts every day with a slow wander through the buzzing atmosphere of the morning market, where she buys her breakfast smoothie. With banana, honey, almond milk and lashings of peanut butter, it's really just a milkshake in disguise. But she gets them to throw in a sprinkling of kale to make herself feel as virtuous as the health bloggers and Instagram influencers that she's met here, who have made the island their home. The market was recommended to her by Jane, of all people. Jane now messages Amy weekly, wondering when she's getting back so she can throw her a Welcome Home party with some eligible bachelors from Pete's work. But Amy doesn't have the answer to that. Her ticket was one-way, and she has no intention of returning any time soon.

After winding her way through the bustling food stalls to kick-start her mind, senses and soul, she's ready for her morning writing session at her favourite café on the beach. Her desk is stacked driftwood and her seat is a wicker armchair that's covered in soft crochet cushions she can sink into. After two flat whites and two hours of researching new topics, she'll close her laptop, remove her sarong and swim once up and down the length of the bay, thinking about her topics and refining them in her head. And afterwards, she'll write down everything that came to her in the gentle waves. By the end of the morning, she's ready to return to her villa to dry off, clean up and answer more emails.

Today's routine is no different. Although when she opens her inbox after lunch, she's surprised to see an email from someone familiar.

Hi Piglet,
I hope you're enjoying the sun in Thailand. I'm so pleased for you. That's exactly what I wanted for you when I put

you on the show, for you to be happy. I know you've forgiven me, but don't forget me now that you're rich and famous! Maybe I could even get a cut! ;) Only joking.

I'm emailing you because I thought you might be interested to hear about me. I've decided to put Headplace on a back burner. Seems like the market isn't ready for what I have to offer.

Anyway, you might like to know that I have a new venture, and I think it could be a really amazing investment opportunity for you. After my moment in the spotlight on *The Shelf*, I've identified a gap in the male matchmaking market. I want to set up a service where men are groomed to be a better catch and taught how to tackle the dating scene.

It's a growing industry, with more and more people meeting online, like you and I did, I suppose. I'm at seed-funding stage and I need £50,000 to build my website, get premises and for marketing. If you're interested, it would be great to chat. I'll send you the full business plan and then perhaps we could talk on Skype on Friday? Or you could fly me out there to chat face to face! ;) Lol.

Jamie

Amy responds immediately.

Dear Jamie,
Thanks for your email.
Now that I'm living my best life in Thailand, I'm used to

translating things into English every day. Luckily, I also speak
fluent Jamie, so here's my attempt at translating your email:

1. Headplace was a complete failure
2. Everyone thinks I'm an arse
3. I need money

Sound about right?
Thanks, but no thanks.

Amy

Three months ago, Amy won *The Shelf* and one million
pounds. She was also offered ongoing therapy sessions, a
makeover, a holiday and a year's subscription to Love
Market, the latest dating site. She rejected them all.

After a month of media commitments, interviews, TV
show appearances and fan meets, she was finally able to
sit down and start working out what to do with the money
and the time it bought her. The truth is, Amy was more
excited about her freedom than her fortune. But she accepted
that she could buy more freedom if she invested wisely.

She kept the promise she'd made to herself to buy a first-
class flight to Thailand. She also booked her parents and
Sarah on a flight out to join her after a few months, and
they'll be arriving next week.

Her first investment was a two-bedroom flat in Putney,
which she bought in cash and with Sarah's expert advice.

It was already tenanted, so Amy is living on the rental income and saving her winnings.

Her second investment was in an exciting all-female fitness industry start-up in Cheltenham called Gymma. Her investment was helping to kit it out with brand-new equipment, and Gemma promised to send her daily updates, like the one she received this morning.

Subject: Power racks have arrived!

The image attached to the email shows a pregnant Gemma hanging from a jungle gym, with her thighs wrapped around Jason's neck.

Amy smiles at the ridiculous scene and then jumps when she feels her phone vibrate in her pocket. It's a WhatsApp from Jackie, which is a close-up of red lips wrapped around a chocolate doughnut.

> All right, love? Ate this,
> thought of you 🍩

Amy replies.

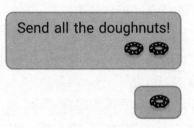

> PS Actually do not, I'll be an outcast in the land of the influencers

> Do not. Donut.

> Now I can't stop thinking of doughnuts 🍩

Jackie sends another picture, this time of her smiling with doughnut in all her front teeth.

Amy replies with 😆 , then puts her phone on the table.

In two months' time, Jackie's lawsuit – Amy's final invest-ment – will be over (fingers crossed) and their platform will be launched.

Shelfish.org.

Where women come first.

The tag line probably needs some work. But they have time. Jackie is preparing conversations with partners, and Amy is working on the content they'll launch with.

Gemma's their Fitness columnist.

Hattie's on Food.

Lauren is on Sex.

Kathy's an over-fifties agony aunt.

And Flick is on Home.

They form the perfect team.

She hasn't felt this whole in years, and she hasn't needed her 'other half' to do it. Her being is completed by the love and support of her family, her friends and the comfort she takes in knowing that she can accomplish anything she wants to on her own. She looks up at her new painting on the wall. It's a quote she came across recently on her social media travels. It spoke so loud and clear to her that she decided to have it painted and framed.

The secret to having it all is knowing that you do

Perhaps she'll have someone to share the painting with one day. But only when she's ready. She isn't ready yet. The quote also reminded her of something Sarah told her over a bottle of prosecco at Amuse Bouche, the night before she flew to Bangkok.

'Amy, we're all so busy trying to find the right person, we aren't trying to *be* the right person.'

Amy turns to her screen and the clean Google doc in front of her, and starts to type.

How I Finally Found The One

Acknowledgements

Two years ago, I was pretty clueless about the world of book publishing. And let's face it, I still am. But one thing I do know is that I didn't write this book alone. It took a small, highly-skilled army of brilliant people to shape this book into its best self.

Thank you, on repeat at full volume, to my agent Hayley Steed for changing my life. Without Hayley's wisdom I wouldn't be writing this. Thank you, into a megaphone in front of a mic, to my editors Sarah Bauer and Katie Lumsden, and the team at Bonnier, whose belief, enthusiasm and energy have made me fall in love with *The Shelf* even more, over and over again.

To my family who waded through the earliest, crudest and cringe-worthiest drafts, thank you for giving me the encouragement I needed to continue. To my friends, who continue to lift me up and make me laugh, thank you for the inspiration. And to Milo, who keeps my feet warm under my desk and brings me endless joy, woof.

Lastly, thank you to Chris, who has been my cheerleader from the second the lightbulb flickered on a balcony in Corsica three years ago, who read every single chapter as I wrote (and multiple drafts of), and who never complained about the four a.m. alarm. Chris, you're an absolute keeper.

What's the worst thing that could happen to you on TV?

Hello, my name is Helly Acton and I'm a reality show fan.

We live in a world that's captivated by romance and fame. Where reality shows, like *Too Hot to Handle*, eclipse social media feeds and water cooler conversations across the country for weeks and weeks on end. The idea for *The Shelf* was sparked after I stumbled across *Naked Attraction*. Surprised by the lengths (*titter*) that people will go to, to find love or get their face on-screen, I asked myself: 'What's the worst thing that could happen to you on TV?' At the time, my answer was getting dumped.

Reality TV isn't for everyone, but for me it's a way for my brain to unwind after a long day at my desk. In saying that, I also think shows like *Love Island* offer us far more than an escape from the daily grind. Reality TV is full of life lessons about relationships – romantic or not. I love how it shows what relationship red flags to watch out for (something Amy *desperately* needs to learn!) and puts the spotlight on important topics like gaslighting. I love how it (mostly) shows the strength of female friendships. I love how it (mostly) shows men being open with their emotions. And I love how it (mostly) encourages us to talk about how we feel. As a writer, I also love that reality TV is full of unique characters who represent the diversity of human behaviour and personalities. Characters who are often stranger than fiction, but also completely *real*.

In *The Shelf*, I wanted to capture and replicate what I love about this type of TV. The excitement us fans feel when these shows are on and the fun we have when discussing them with our friends. But, I also wanted to send a message that makes women from all walks of life feel empowered, whatever their relationship history or status. I wanted to highlight what it feels like to be under constant surveillance, pushing ourselves to be perfect as a result. It was also important to me to point a finger at those viewers online, watching with their thumbs at the ready, who forget that they're talking about real people when they post. Many of the comments you will read in *The Shelf* were inspired by actual comments I have seen. I hope they will serve as a reminder for us all to always be kind.

I'd like to think that today, my answer as to what would be the most humiliating thing to happen on TV would be *very* different, having completed Amy's journey.

I wrote *The Shelf* as a pep talk to an early-thirties me, and to every woman who has felt the pressure to find the partner, get the mortgage, have the kids and buy the five-door family estate with the stick figure family on the boot. My fear of being left behind saw me bounce between relationships in my twenties, until I landed at the altar with Mr Wrong. With *The Shelf*, I hope to empower readers by reminding them that having a partner isn't pivotal to happiness, to never settle for the sake of fitting in and to always feel confident that they alone are enough.

THANK YOU for spending time on *The Shelf*. I hope you loved reading it as much as I loved writing it.

Helly Acton
Currently over the moon
xxx

Loved *The Shelf*? Hated Jamie? Have a burning
question to ask? Or just desperate to discuss?

Follow Helly Acton on Instagram at
@hellyactonauthor or on Twitter at @hellyacton,
and join in the conversation using #TheShelf2020.

For all the latest news and updates,
follow @theshelfuk on Instagram.

Hello there, wonderful human!

A big thank you from the bottom of my fluttering heart for picking up *The Shelf*. Every show of support helps keep me in a steady supply of Yorkshire Tea, cheese and ramen noodles, which has fuelled my writing for the last few years and will probably fuel the next few too. You'll just have to imagine me giving you an awkwardly long hug and whispering my undying appreciation into your ear. Or, on second thoughts, perhaps you'd prefer not to. #Creepy.

I first had the idea for *The Shelf* in August 2017, sitting on an apartment balcony in Corsica and staring at the bright pink sunset. The next morning, I woke up early and work began. I mapped out all of my original chapters in one day, writing at the speed of Popeye on spinach, on a notepad the size of a smartphone. A fact about me – I only write in black ink. I'm superstitious about other colours! I opened that little notepad the other day, and let's just say, I'm sure I heard the pages laugh at me for some of my original ideas. I'll let you in on a secret: one of my first characters was a vegan who gets dumped for a beef farmer. I mean . . . I'm pretty sure I wrote her well after wine o'clock. Interestingly, the first line of *The Shelf* is still the original. And while Amy Wright is not based on me, I currently have a chocolate doughnut bun on my head as I type this letter to you.

Since then, the last two years have been a whirlwind, a dream come true and a lot of hard work. Not just on my part, but on the part of the whole team behind it. I'm eternally grateful for everyone who has helped make *The Shelf* a reality, and to the readers – like you – who give me the encouragement to continue doing what I love – telling light-hearted, uplifting and ultimately empowering stories about women and relationships.

If you would like to hear more about *The Shelf* and my other books, you can visit **www.theshelf-uk.com** where you can become part of the **Helly Acton Reader's Club**. It only takes a few moments to sign up, and there are no hidden catches or costs.

Bonnier Books UK will keep your data private and confidential, and it will never be passed on to a third party. Nor will we spam you with loads of emails. We'll just keep in touch now and again with news about my books, and you can unsubscribe any time you want.

If you would like to get involved in a wider conversation about my books, please do review *The Shelf* on Amazon, on Goodreads, on any other e-store, on your own blog and social media accounts, or talk about it with friends, family or reading groups! Sharing your thoughts helps other readers, and I always enjoy hearing about what people experience from my writing.

Thank you again for reading *The Shelf*.

All the best,
Helly xxx

If you enjoyed *The Shelf*, you'll love the
brilliant new novel from Helly Acton:

The

COUPLE

Would you risk everything for love?

Coming 2021

20